Firsthand

Firsthand

A'Dreana Anderson

Joyfully Unbound
PUBLISHING

Joyfully Unbound Publishing

This book is a work of fiction. Any references to historical events, real people, or real places are used fictitiously. Other names, characters, places, and events are products of the author's imagination, and any resemblance to actual events or places or persons, living or dead, is entirely coincidental.

Copyright © 2024 A'Dreana Anderson

All rights reserved. No part of this book may be reproduced, distributed, or transmitted in any form or by any means, including photocopying, recording, or other electronic or mechanical methods, without the prior written permission of the copyright owner. To request permission, or for any other inquiries, contact the publisher at contact@adreanaanderson.com.

Joyfully Unbound Publishing and the Joyfully Unbound Publishing logos are the sole property of A'Dreana Anderson.

ISBN: 979-8-9900085-0-2 (Paperback)
ISBN: 979-8-9900085-2-6 (Hardcover)
ISBN: 979-8-9900085-1-9 (ebook)

Library of Congress Number: 2024905834

First edition: July 2024.

Edited by Annie Jenkinson and Paige Lawson
Jacket and interior design by Predrag Markovic (Smashed-Grid Studio)
Author headshot photo by David Herbert
Character sketches by A'Dreana Anderson

Excerpt from the public domain work *Lay This Body Down*.

Printed in the United States of America.

www.adreanaanderson.com

*To my second mother, Kiki, for wanting
to read this story before it was even written.*

AUTHOR'S NOTE

Before you read this book, please note that certain parts may be unsettling for some readers. *Firsthand* combines nineteenth-century history with elements of magical realism, including depictions of violence, enslavement, and sexual assault. Please read with care.

"As you sow, so shall you reap."

— Bible, Galatians 6:7

CHAPTER ONE

Richard leaned against the trunk of the old willow tree that stood tall at the end of his long winding driveway. He found shade from the hot Georgia sun under its vast, sturdy branches. Summer had never been his favorite season, filled with too much sweat, too many bugs, and a hellish amount of sunburn. But that afternoon, his distaste for the heat dwindled as he watched his young neighbor pruning her garden through the drooping leaves of the tree as though peering through softly hanging curtains.

Samantha Sterling—a pretty little thing, she was—said to be the daughter of one of the most admired slave owners in the region. She had been on his mind for some months already, specifically across the six weeks she had stayed here in the dull yellow house so close to his dwellings. And for her to be laboring so in the dirt, soiling her beautiful hands when she didn't need to, somehow made her more alluring.

Now and then, she patted her forehead with her fine cotton handkerchief, folding and pushing it back into her long skirt's waistband before setting to again, showing the soil it had to acquiesce because she was not for giving up the fight against it.

And our good Lord knows, thought Richard. *In her hands, I would be malleable too.*

Richard grinned, feeling his dry lips and eyes suffering and complaining.

But even so, he did not intend to move himself from the tree. No, not yet. Maybe not even till Samantha went inside to take tea. For now, his eyes were happy enough feasting on her porcelain skin. Even for her, the late June sun was unforgiving, yet it somehow only enhanced her beauty with that tiny waist pulled in tight in a back-laced dress, the hue of bluebells, and a beautiful smile to make any man cave in. Richard was no exception.

He was helpless in front of her, having yielded to her prettiness long ago.

His eyes trailed up her blue dress to her frizzled half-updo, her hair the color of the packed dirt road between them, enhanced by what he thought could be coppered strands. Samantha had just turned twenty-two, a perfect age, also a sublime juncture at which to show a fine lady how to be treated by an equally fine man. Aye, twenty-two was a good age for him to court her.

He had just completed some business in town—at the Chatham County Courthouse in Wright Square—and found himself still unusually well-attired from visiting in polite company. It might be a most opportune time to present himself again to this fine lady—an opportunity to woo her while she was tending her garden on such a bountiful day.

This was his once-in-a-lifetime chance of being alone with her, a moment he would not ruin.

Standing upright, Richard smoothed down his brown jacket and pulled his white shirt collar straight, promptly swaggering across the dirt road with a learned expression as if he even owned the land on which she stood. He did not own it.

He had merely discovered this attitude wooed ladies; they respected confidence and relished seeing a man who carried himself with poise and looked as if he earned well enough to feed himself and a wife and children. Of course, he *had* done well for himself in this life, enjoying a lavish lifestyle and earning the envy of all those who knew him. Hopefully, his look today would indicate he could afford to be frivolous in the haberdasher's, commissioning his own clothes. To complete his outfit, he wore three gold rings on the left hand and a fine gold watch. It wasn't the best that money could buy, but at a time when frivolities came only at a high price, it was rare.

As he approached, Samantha looked up from her hydrangeas, at first holding a fragile hand to her eyes to block out the sun, squinting into the blinding light upon seeing him emerge.

Behind him, the giant willow tree rustled its dry leaves, swishing as if to chuckle at his antics.

A dull expression Richard could not decipher flashed across the lady's face, but it was brief, instantly replaced with a pleasant, ladylike smile. She laid her gardening tool atop the loose soil, brushing down the voluminous folds of her ankle-length dress.

Why would she do this at the sight of me? I should be rather surprised if she even cares what I think of her. But if she does, then perhaps I have a more than meager chance.

"Miss Sterling," Richard said with a crooked smile. "It is a pleasure."

For the first time ever, suddenly feeling conscious of his teeth not being quite straight, he was not smiling as broad as he would like to. He did not let the wide smile linger, changing instead to something less overt, allowing dimples to form in his cheeks at the faintest upturn of his lips.

"Mr. McLeary," she returned. "Well, well. It has been quite a while since we last encountered one another, has it not? It is a pleasant day we share, don't you agree? See the sun's glow."

He nodded. And so soon, even before he had done more than say the briefest of hellos, she had him alight on the inside as if holding a flickering candle to his helpless heart without even asking for permission. *Quite brazen of her,* he thought. It made him powerless.

The man feared she was driving him toward a terrible affliction: the sickness of adoration.

"I couldn't help but notice you over here by your lonesome," he ventured next.

"Ah, well, you see, I'm *not* alone," she protested in that demure way that could only serve to lure a hapless fellow in even more. "You see?"

She wafted her arm about herself, indicating the fruits of her work. "I have my flowers' company. I'm almost done tending to them, actually. But see how they look up at me and smile? They are a joy and not troublesome to me at all."

Richard grinned at her nuance.

"Then that is fortuitous, and I am gladdened to hear they behave for you. But perhaps you'd like to take a ride with me when you're finished. Plenty of shade down yonder. Enough for two."

Richard pointed to his white horse tied to one of the branches beneath the willow tree. "We wouldn't go far. Just stroll around the plantation, get to know one another. If it pleases you."

"*Your* plantation?"

He grinned. "Yes, ma'am. Over nine hundred acres, the largest in town. And most certainly the best," he boasted. He leaned closer to Samantha, leaning against her fence, lowering his voice. "If you would like, I can offer to share some *management* secrets."

Samantha's lips tugged upward as she stepped closer to Richard.

His grin widened.

She smiled. "You seem to ignore the ring on my finger, and the one on yours for that matter, Mr. McLeary."

Richard slowly placed his hand over his ring. It was to his good fortune that on this day, he had worn several; he could explain they were merely decorative, the same as his watch. "Well, I never see your husband around. I'm beginning to think this beau o' yours is a myth."

"He's very busy." Still smiling, Samantha peered up and said, "Besides, I'm not one for… *business,* Mr. McLeary. I prefer to keep far lighter matters at heart. But perhaps your wife would be more willing to hear about your management techniques." She wiped the dirt from her hands onto her apron. "You're an interesting man, Mr. McLeary, but I'm unsure if you are a gentleman. Rumors are going around town about you and your cruel and twisted treatment of your slaves."

He recoiled as if physically struck. The assertion was unfair and inappropriate. "Is it cruel to take in a stray dog? I house them. I clothe and train them. Feed them. I give them everything and leave them wanting for nothing."

"You should refrain from calling them dogs, sir. They are real people with real names."

"Even dogs have names, Miss Sterling. The way I see it, I'm doing them a favor. Where would they be without the likes of me?"

"I shall tell you where they would be, Mr. McLeary. They would be free, not chained in everything they do. And as for doing them a favor, would you subject your own kin to such treatment? Or is this why you wear a golden band yet try to persuade me to take trips with you?"

Now, his finery and polished speech were beginning to abandon him. He floundered, struggling for a retort. The pretty vocabulary he had worn like a dress coat so far was now slipping away.

He scoffed. "My kin ain't niggers, Miss Sterling. I am sure you know that."

"But you'd be doing them a favor, wouldn't you say?"

Richard briefly narrowed his eyes but caught himself and smiled. "Look, Miss—*Mrs.* Sterling, please understand that I did not come to you to cause a petty squabble of this kind. Perhaps we got off on the wrong foot, wouldn't you agree? This isn't about my slaves, so please don't mind them.

"The slaves are but simple tools like the ones you use in your garden. Do you fret over a plow or hoe? They're nothing but property. Items. Farm equipment acquired to give *them* a purpose and to give *us* rewards for putting them to good use." He paused. "And please, call me Richard."

Samantha's smile flattened as her lips pressed tightly together. "You're right," she said. "Even dogs have names."

Now, Richard wasn't smiling. Something caught in his throat at the insult, but he was too stunned to retort this time around. Samantha collected her tools, swiveled on her heels, and vanished into her house, shutting the door behind her. The hard slam traveled across the fields.

Richard stared for a second as she disappeared behind the door, baffled. When she ignored him, he slapped his hands on his hip, lowered and turned his head, then let out a huff of evident exasperation. He turned to leave, turned back toward her door, and then again back to face his horse.

There he stood, dumbfounded, something tight and burning welling in him like terrible heartburn after a meal with too much fat. He was a businessman, one used to negotiations and deals, one acclimatized to getting his own way, even in the most confronting of situations. He did not know how it felt to remove himself from any kind of argument or negotiation and to come away without achieving what he'd set out for, to return home empty-handed. That sort of poor outcome just didn't happen to a man like Richard McLeary. Because it couldn't.

Only… now, it had.

There was nothing more bitter or demeaning than rejection, especially from a mere woman, and it made him feel both aggrieved and affronted yet also deeply downcast. Women were supposed to be flattered by his attention. They were usually coy and charming and flirtatious, giggly and shy. So what, pray tell, was wrong with this one?

Because quite clearly, she must have had a lot wrong with her to treat his sincere approach in such an offhand and impolite manner.

It wasn't his problem that she was somehow bitter and moody, was it?

Richard *was* a gentleman; he knew he was. More than that, he was an irresistible one—at least according to other women he'd had the pleasure of pursuing.

Hadn't they all told him the same thing, that he was a man of an upright stature, with attractive physical attributes being all tall and broad with a strong square jaw and piercing gaze?

Somehow, Miss Sterling's clouded eyes deemed it all untrue, telling him nothing was engaging about his person. Her eyes told him he ought to be ashamed of himself and that he was an embarrassment to better men.

There was only one thing of which he could convince himself, and this was that perhaps the rumors around her being one of those nigger-loving scalawags were true. He'd often overlook the claims, presuming it was only a jest, a spew of complaints told by men who had failed to win her hand, just as he had. No matter the case, *Mrs.* Samantha's rejection struck a chord in him, and he fumed, tightening his jaw, sighing, scrunching his nose, and kicking at the ground with his fine shoes.

You ought to have known better, his inner voice said. *You should have gone into this conversation with your wits about you, not going off seeking to woo a woman rumored to have abolitionist sympathies despite having a slaver for a father!*

And that was another thing he couldn't quite understand. It was incomprehensible.

Richard returned to his plantation on his beautiful white horse, brooding all the way down its winding road. The plantation, which focused on cotton making, was indeed big as it stretched across the way and boasted about seventy-eight slaves, but it was still not the biggest in town as Richard claimed.

It was actually a little over seven hundred acres, the third largest plantation in Chatham County, and only because one of the richest slave owners had moved out of town, having caught wind of the fact that he could procure an even bigger plot of land upon which he could expand.

So it was in this way that Richard's farm had 'grown'—or rather stayed the same—to become the third largest, and everyone knew how. So they made a habit of ignoring his conceited boasts.

And he did boast a lot.

The largest plantation had over a thousand acres, but perhaps the townsfolk were simply looking at the matter of size in the wrong way; the town could not deny that, even with fewer acres, Richard's plantation produced one of the highest profits amongst others each year.

Richard's face was a blur under the trees' shadows right now, but the shade did not hide his demeanor from his slaves. They could all see that he was clearly upset.

His face contorted in fury as he rode past his cotton fields, by all the men and women he had purchased to work them. The field hands were nearly quiet as the loud sounds emanated from his horse's hooves clattering along the dirt. None dared to look at their master. They knew better by now, aware that eye contact at the wrong moment could bring a punishment, even if only to be made to conduct more lowly tasks than those to which they were accustomed. Yes, the slaves knew better. All but one who dared look Richard right in the eye.

Still lost in his brooding over what it was he had done wrong to the lady, Richard quietly brought his horse to a halt a few feet from the brown barn. On cue, he was greeted by his loyal friend and head overseer, James Walker, another man who dared to fix his gaze upon Richard's own quite openly. James approached him with a warm smile, a habit that had developed over the years between the fond friends.

"Took you long enough," James chimed. "What kept you?"

"Business," Richard said plainly. He was more curt than usual, his expression dour. Usually, these two men enjoyed a pleasant banter as they talked, jousting with words, puns, and jibes. Not so now.

"Care to join me out in the far field today?" James joked, trying again.

"And burn in this heat? Not a chance."

James shook his head as if to say, *Well, what's the matter with you?*

As usual, he held the horse's rein tight as Richard dismounted it. The entire time, Richard looked elsewhere as if intent on sidelining James, eyeing instead the boy over in the cotton field, a young one he'd never seen before, the one who dared lock eyes with him as he rode in. Most likely, the lad was in his early twenties. His dark skin, contrasting against his beige shirt, and his disproportionately large lips were no different than those other wide-nosed niggers on his property. But this one clearly didn't know his place.

"How'd the auction go at the courthouse?" James asked. "Any of 'em catch your eye?"

Richard shook his head, occasionally stealing glances at the bold black boy. He turned to see James with a raised brow again. "What, *none* of them?" he said.

Richard had gone into town to purchase a new field worker to help increase production, but not a single slave seemed worthwhile. In truth, James had made it clear he wanted him to obtain three or four for that reason. The work was becoming far too hard here of late, the slaves putting down tools and complaining of how their backs were sore and their mouths drying up and of how there were simply too few of them to tackle the mountain of tough physical work.

Of course, Richard wanted more slaves to grow his plantation, too;

what planter wouldn't when the growth of a plantation was said to indicate the merit of a man?

But he also had another reason, and this was to show people he had at his disposal more than sufficient money to go out and procure the bunch of niggers in the first place. In fact, he'd said he wanted to buy about seven to ten more workers right away to make the whole town talk about him—though James saw that as far-fetched. It would be hard to take on and train even half that number, and the notion of finding even two of fit caliber was unlikely.

Richard needed the right slaves, and they had to be impressive ones to increase production.

Two birds, one stone, so to speak. The problem was, as every slave owner knew, it was all too easy to take on the wrong men because of the hurry to do so, thus ending up instead with one bird and two stones around his neck. And then it could take many months or even as long as a year to make a trade and move them on, leaving the master back where he'd started but poorer.

"Don't get your britches in a knot," Richard said. "There's word a large auction is taking place at Oglethorpe's Racecourse within the week. I'll try again there. Anyway, who's the brave soul?" Richard asked his old friend, nodding towards the field in the boy's direction.

"That's Micel," James said. "He just arrived from another field, a trade I just made. A pregnant slave for one that can put in the work about the place."

"I see… You think it was a wise trade? He wears a look. An unpleasant air."

James looked back at the young man he'd taken as a slave, the one who did not hesitate to look the master in the eye. Unusual, and no doubt one who'd bring much trouble their way. As for James, he just shrugged. "A wise enough trade, I daresay," he said. "And what's done is done."

Richard smiled at the slave as the boy quickly looked away.

Leaving James with his horse, Richard walked into the fields, his strides long, quick, and vengeful. Others knew to keep working as he strode past.

As Richard approached the young man, he deftly pulled out his knife. The wind kicked up the dust from the dry earth as he stood before the shivering slave.

We'll see just how much you have to be confident about, youngin', Richard thought. *We'll see how much unruly spirit you have in you. Let's see you stare me in the eyes now!*

"Hey, boy," Richard said. "Turn around and look at me."

The boy's hands froze on the cotton. He did not look up this time, freezing in the manner of a rabbit suddenly finding itself stalked by a big cat. Perhaps this was not lack of courage, but simply not wishing to find himself out of a job again so fast nor the recipient of another beating.

Other workers stole glances, but none dared linger, knowing their place.

The young man slowly turned, suddenly feeling the overwhelming pain of his cheek being sliced by Richard's knife. He emitted a piercing scream as Richard raised his hand and struck him again, ruthless as he went about it, making sure to cut against the same spot to make it nice and deep.

"I swear you slice like a suckling pig," Richard said, the blade held tightly at his side. "The knife likes you."

Still, the hapless boy shrieked, almost sounding at one point like an exotic forest bird.

Richard chuckled at the wild antics. His eyes sparkled with amusement, and he grinned all the more, looking around for his crowd of admiring spectators. He jabbed the knife into the young man's shoulder this time, but before he could strike again, Richard's body was sent flying off the boy, pushed into the ground. *The goddamn slave has fought back! The audacity!* Micel would soon regret it.

Then he realized it couldn't have been Micel, could it? The boy had not moved, still crouched there as before, covering his sliced cheek with a hand. Richard looked about himself, seeking out the perpetrator.

He sprang to his feet, furious at the assault. Chest heaving, he now came eye to eye with an older man standing in front of the wounded boy, holding up pleading hands. Everyone froze.

"Massa McLeary," the older man begged. "Please, have mercy. The boy is new to the plantation and doesn't know his place. He will be trained. He's willing and keen."

"Yes, and I'm willing and keen to put an end to you!" cried Richard, still affronted. For a slave to attack a white person—and a master no less—was a poor decision liable to beatings and even execution. But he did not wish to kill the bold older slave because what good would that do? He'd be a man down and would only have lost more money over the fiasco. He'd teach him a lesson his own way.

Two white drivers in the field pointed their guns at the master's attacker. James stepped forward, hand on his pistol, but Richard held out a hand to stop him. As was common enough, the overseer—who was supposed to run the place—was rarely afforded free rein himself. Whenever the slave master was around, his own practices also had to take second place.

The senior slave's name was Charles, and he had been Richard's for a little over a year. He was a stout fellow, occasionally disciplined for insubordination, but this took the cake. To attack his master, no less, in front of his own overseer and employed drivers was unheard of.

And Richard wouldn't stand such transgressions, wouldn't stand to be insulted by any lowly slave.

Not by Micel, and now, not by Charles either.

Richard unbuckled his belt and effortlessly slipped it from the loops in his pants. Partially wrapping the belt around his right knuckle, he brandished the buckle and smacked Charles with an upward swing, striking the hard point of his jaw. Charles stumbled as his head was thrown back, emitting a pained grunt. At the noise, Richard lunged. Each swing was wild with no specific target. The metal thumped along Charles' head, back, and shoulders. Lacerations blossomed on his skin each time the buckle hit his flesh, pebbling drops of blood in its wake. His body folded in on itself as a last resort to protect his middle, raising his hands to block the blows aimed towards his face. But Richard whipped the man until he was flailing on the dirt, his soft whimpers begging for mercy.

There was none.

Richard straddled him, pinning him down by the neck with a tight grip and beating him in an even worse rage. He delivered a flurry of right hooks, his knuckles splitting at the impact. Charles wailed in agony blow after blow until the blood on his face was no longer his own but also Richard's.

The blood on Richard's hands was nothing compared to the pulped and bloodied face of the man who had dared stand up to a slave master. Charles looked half dead, blood pumping from his nose, his eyes, his ears, some having gushed from his mouth. He was soaked in a bath of his own life-giving secretions. But eventually, Richard stopped to catch his breath and held Charles down by the throat. "You shall never lay a hand on me again, you hear?"

Charles was quiet and still. Still as if his soul might have fled his body. Perhaps it had.

But none of it satisfied his master's rage.

Even dogs have names.

Richard rose to his feet as the memory of Samantha's words flashed through his mind again. A fire boiled in his gut like water in a kettle. His face contorted into a look of great bitterness, and in the heat of that moment, his heavy boot dragged along the dirt as he kicked Charles in the head one good time. His head jerked, and a deafening *crack* echoed in the air.

Charles' body grew limp.

All movement stilled. Everyone went silent at Richard's outburst. The sound of plucked cotton and snapping twigs was replaced with a hushed breeze. Even James and his subordinates stared in astonishment—their brows raised, gazes flat and calculating at the sight of white, red, and yellowish brain matter spilling out across the earth.

Richard's expression sobered as his emotions calmed, morphing into regret when he realized he'd gone and done the very thing he'd sworn would be pointless: he'd stolen away his own laborer.

Now, he really had to go buy a new one.

An ear-shattering cry broke the silence as a lithe negro gal zipped through the field, her brown striped dress flailing behind. It was Charles' wife, Rachel. She threw herself onto the ground, grieving over the older man's lifeless body, even stooping over the immobile figure to scoop up the spilled brains in her hands, kissing them, covering her lips and chin in warmed blood.

Richard stood, ignoring the cries.

"Benji, Parkinson," Richard called to his go-to drivers. Benji had since lowered his weapon, but Parkinson still held his tight, ready to shoot at any moment.

Richard pointed to the young man, Micel—or whatever his name was—holding his cut cheek. "One of you take him to the shack."

Parkinson, a towheaded man, immediately stepped forward, gripping the boy by his forearm and yanking him up. "Get up!"

This time, there was no protest from Micel. He got to his feet, shaking all over and never daring to remove his hand from his face lest it should fall apart. A long trail of bright red blood spilled down his arm in a rivulet of red water that reached his elbow before dripping off. The young man looked weak, whether from shock or blood loss. No one could know. But not a single person stepped forward to help him. Many stared, but the wrath of the slave master would stop any of that nonsense where they might show each other compassion. It was simple enough. The boy had been surly, so he had gotten what was coming to him right enough.

All around, the plantation workers carried on toiling in the heat of the day as if some minor incident had just played out before their eyes, and now it was over. Normality resumed.

Richard turned, fixating his gaze on the shack.

The shack was a simple structure of poorly nailed planks but made small, windowless, and tall. It was a dreaded place to which errant slaves were dragged so they may be alone with their thoughts and wonder if they'd soon meet the oak tree where the bodies of those before them would hang until the crows had taken their fill. Perhaps they should look forward to it. At least then, such a fate promised them rest, the one thing they all repeatedly prayed for from the Lord.

Years ago, Richard had originally ordered his workers to take any nuisance slaves and tie them to the sturdy oak tree when the rest went to sleep, so the slaves got to spend their own time there, out in the cold, while others got some shuteye. Tied to the tree, they'd be left there until morning to contemplate their mortality and their good fortune at having found a situation and master so good to them all, a place to call home, so long as they kept their noses clean.

It gave them much-needed time to think about how best to serve the master without giving him trouble. Plus, having spent a cold night tethered to a giant oak with no conveniences, they'd be expected to work without having eaten dinner, which may be the only meal they would get to eat in a day. For a time, it was fair to assert it worked. Yet, for some reason, the shackled men were not always as repentant nor as famished in the morning as he'd hoped. Something was stopping his plan from taking its fullest effect. One day, over at the tree, James looked around.

He eyed the tree: all was well with the fastening for the huge chain.

He eyed the soil, scuffing at the ground with his boots. What was that?

There, hidden among the stubby grasses, lay bones. Thin bones. Wings.

Sure enough, he'd discovered the reason for the slaves not especially suffering when receiving their due punishment. It was lying out on the ground among the earth for all to view.

Chicken bones. Since no chickens lived out here near the tree, the workers' ruse had been uncovered. The ones bound to the tree had evidently been receiving sustenance of a kind from those who were not bound, such that being tied was not much greater a misery than being indoors and getting a normal night's sleep. No doubt the ones who furnished the chained with dinner had also snuck a woolen blanket out to the tree, too. And so it was that each man would have enjoyed a night's fresh air and solitude, well fed and warm enough, thereby going off to work the next day in no worse a state than he ordinarily might have been.

Richard shook his head at the memory, the past anger rising in him once more.

It was all a grievous insult, and the slave owner was livid! More to the point, so was James, as he would have to confess that he'd failed again in his overseeing.

Now there was also a new problem: how did those cunning niggers manage to get hold of chickens in the first place? Their diet was rarely so rich. Only on scarce occasions did the slaves receive a bowl of bone broth boiled out of the birds' innards. They were not given the flesh.

So, the finding of the discarded bones must reveal the cause for the missing birds from the master's coop. The ones put down to stealing by wildlife. Some charlatan had been helping himself to the birds and then wringing their scrawny necks—no doubt envisaging the poor bird was Richard as he did so—and roasting it over a late-night fire.

Then, there was no doubt they'd divvied out the portions among themselves, taking the legs, wings, or innards to the man by the tree. James would have to confess to Richard about it.

In due course, he did, and this was when they stopped this process and erected the shack, merely lengthening the work hours for them all from sunrise to sunset to accommodate for any lacking worker. But now, an undeserving dark-skinned dog could be locked inside the shack with no means of passing in food or any other home comforts while preventing any means of escape, too.

Richard watched Parkinson drag the misguided young man to the shack as James laughed at the boy's ripped-up face. "You feel better?" James said to Richard. "The shack will give him plenty thinking time. Time to heal. Time to repent to his maker. And most of all, to his master."

Richard eyed him blankly.

"No, I don't feel better at all, oddly. Just distracted with inconvenience," Richard said as he pointed to the dead body. "You two," he yelled, pointing to the two nearest able-bodied slaves, who stood as still as a rooted tree. "Hey!" The two snapped to attention. "Drag this mess out west of the forest and dispose of it. Be quick about it, or there'll be more of the same."

The laborers nodded and approached the body, but the cries of the woman simply grew louder. They whispered to her, trying to pull her away, but Rachel's grip grew tighter.

Richard remained there watching the two slaves try to untangle the woman from the corpse. She hollered and wailed, her arms flying wildly about the air as if trying to swat a storm of horse flies, so bereft was she. Her dress was covered in blood, and what was worse, she was using all her work energy on the bitter lament.

What a sorry and pathetic display this was.

"Best you pull back them tears and get back to work," he said to the weeping slave. "Come on now." Nothing. Still, she flung herself back on the still-warm corpse each time she was tugged free by the band of helpers, sweat rolling from their foreheads. Annoyed, Richard sighed and put his hands on his hip. "You niggers really testin' my patience today. Can't seem to organize to get pissed in a brewery. Trying my nerves, y'are. Benji!"

The two male slaves backed away as Benji approached. The woman wailed more, so Benji grabbed her by the arm, forcing her onto her feet. Thrusting her forward, her cries grew distant. But she fell. Kneeling, Benji looked back to Richard for instruction.

"She ain't for havin' it," Benji proclaimed as if the slave owner couldn't see the state of affairs with his own eyes. "No matter what I try, she's fallin' again. Shall we show her?"

With a tap of his foot, Richard gave a simple nod. Benji removed the whip from his side and hovered over Rachel, who was on her hands and knees, crying more than ever.

Benji whipped Rachel along her shoulders, each strike ripping open the back of her dress more and more, such that the poor skin with its copious huge welts and bruises became increasingly on display. Soon, it was also opening and beginning to bleed. Her body jerked with each crack, but Richard remained there watching blood splatter, the flesh tearing on her back as the negro gal continued to cry. The air smelled of blood, her squeals reminding him of a pig heading to slaughter. Richard had a sudden craving for meat.

As Richard and James headed to the white, two-story mansion supported by sturdy columns, Richard asked, "Is Mary inside, by any chance?"

"She's in the library, still hating you as much as you hate her," James said.

Richard chuckled and mumbled, "I hate arranged marriages. 'Tis nothing personal against the lady, you understand. Just that what the ear hears about plans made on one's behalf—and everything that's resulted from this, good and bad—does not always accord with the eye seeing other ripe fruits dangling on the tree as I pass by."

Of course, the ripe fruits to which his mind was turning happened to be Samantha, despite the fact she had most grievously and embarrassingly rejected his attempts to woo her lately.

James nodded, agreeing. "They can be a hassle, these arranged betrothals, but she did gift you with two children. Let us not dismiss the lady as not being good at all."

Richard scoffed. "Indeed, then 'pon your insistence, let us agree that giving me children is all Mary *is* good for."

James snorted out a laugh. "You are a cruel man, Richard McLeary. A very cruel man."

"Daddy!"

Richard turned. The sudden sight of his daughter, soon to see her seventh fall, brought a bright grin to him, almost making him forget about the treacherous day. She was his reason to live sometimes, his little shining star.

She came rushing out with her teddy bear in one arm, hopping down the stairs to greet her father. Richard quickly wiped his bloody hand using his handkerchief before feeling the tight embrace of his daughter, Margret. He leaned over, picking hay up from the floor, and did his goofy bunny impression by scrunching his nose and holding the hay to his head like bunny ears.

It always made her giggle. Right now, however, it did not. The bunny drew only a sob.

Richard froze a moment when he saw that her eyes were red and puffy.

"What's wrong, Maggie?"

Margret looked down, gently kicking a pebble away. Richard asked her the question again, raising her face with a gentle hand underneath her chin. "You look as if you have taken fright. Or has someone hurt you? Or did you trip over the coal scuttle again and stub your toe?"

He was still trying to make her laugh; it was their language, something that united them.

"I'll tell you," she said. "But you have to promise me something…"

"Oh, do I, indeed? This sounds like something I'll need to consider before agreeing to it. Must I consult my lawyer?"

She chuckled, a sweet sound.

"No, Daddy, don't be silly! It's just that you can't be mean to Henry if I tell you."

Henry was her brother and the eldest of the two by three years.

Despite their ages and his son's independence and how the pair frequently bickered and fought and—on occasion—aimed hard kicks at one another's shins, they loved each other very much.

Richard laughed heartily and looked Margret in the eyes that now sparkled. She looked herself again, appearing more like the cheeky, giggling little girl he loved to behold.

"Ah, then that is something I can do. You have my solemn promise I won't be mean to Henry," Richard said.

Margret waited a moment, then confessed, "Well, he did something terrible. Henry drowned a rat he found in the barn. He held it down in the bucket of water no matter how much I asked him to stop. And I did ask him, maybe six times. No, *nine* times! But by then, it was dead, Daddy. It was hanging there like a piece of string when he pulled it out by its tail."

Richard sighed. He kissed her on her head. "That's terrible. Then I do solemnly promise to talk to Henry, but you must also remember that you two are not allowed in the barn."

"I know." She lowered her head.

"For one thing, it isn't safe in there," he said. "There are tools in there and plenty of equipment, and giant RATS with tails longer than your hair, and they'll come out and eat you!"

He surged forward, baring his teeth and putting his hands to his head like rat ears, growling.

She shrieked and jumped backward, crying, "No, Daddy! No! I'll never go in the barn!"

Oh dear. Now she looked perturbed, not cheered. It wasn't what he'd hoped for. The pretense of being a giant rat must have reminded her of what it was she'd been crying about.

Richard exchanged a glance with James, unable to take her sullen face. He leaned in and pretended to look around before whispering, "If you're good, I might leave a treat in our secret spot." Richard tapped the side of his nose to emphasize *secret spot*. "But bear in mind I say I *might*. It depends on your smile."

Margret lit up, smiled, and nodded.

As Margret hopped away and returned inside, Richard looked at James with a proud grin. "Henry will make a fine slave owner one day. I also started out by drowning rats and whatever little blighters I could get my hands on. Preparation, you might say, for having the hardened heart needed to keep the plantations running and the workers in line."

"You gonna talk to Henry about the rat then, or will you let it slide as good preparation?"

"Oh, I *shall* speak to him, but not necessarily about the rat. I couldn't care one way or the other about those things. But I'll speak to him about being in the barn. You know how many times I've had to tell those two to stay outta there? Sometimes I swear they're as bullheaded as their mother. Possibly even as bullheaded as their father."

He smirked; it was something to be proud of.

"And how is Mary keeping these days?" James asked. "And between you two… still akin to sailing the rocky seas or becoming smoother passage?"

Richard's face tightened with distaste.

"Mary served her purpose, giving me two kids. Now I'm stuck living with the shrew."

James smiled. "Glad I was never bothered with marriage."

The sound of a whip snapped in the distance. Before heading into the house, Richard looked back to see Rachel's bare back, watching the rain of blood as it poured down her skin from her open wounds. Her strength had long left her, her face pressed to the dirt and her spittle creating a smear of mud on her lips. The only noise that could be heard with each landing of the whip was her squeals.

"James," Richard said. "What do you think about roast pork for dinner?"

CHAPTER TWO

Word got around quickly when the latest slaves finally arrived for auction at Oglethorpe's Racecourse. In the wee hours of Tuesday morning—three days after the incident—Richard stood, perusing the contents of his wardrobe in his bedroom, waking his wife from a deep sleep. They had been married for ten years, but it seemed that the more the years passed, the more their affection for each other depreciated.

Oddly, one small part of Richard still hoped that Mary found him attractive. It brought a wee pride when any woman's eyes sparkled upon looking at him, even if the woman happened to be one he could not stand to be near. And that was why he spent every morning slicking his thick hair back. Each dark brown strand had to be in place, carefully tied back, and centered as it grazed his upper back. In need of constant admiration by the fair sex, it was a source of much further rancor and grievance to him that she also couldn't much stand the sight of him.

Her shrieking voice complaining to him about this or that—or quite frequently, about both this *and* that—pursued the haggard and beleaguered man throughout the house, the barn, and the fields. She'd whine about what he had done and moan about what he had not.

Such was marriage. Not only for him, of course. Other men suffered from similar entanglements. But so far, he had not met any with a situation as bad as his own about being saddled to one another.

Being the son of a wealthy plantation owner, Richard was always expected to marry into the very limited number of similarly wealthy families in the region.

That was, unfortunately, an inescapable truth throughout his life until it came to fruition. And what was worse was that every wealthy family hoped mostly to give birth to sons who could carry on the family name. Many had been fortunate, and this meant a smaller pool of eligible females to select from—hence how Richard had ended up with Mary, not the cream of the crop.

The expansion of a landowner's empire was important too, in addition to ensuring heirs to continue running it. And in order for Richard's father to expand his land, he had long since entered into some type of business arrangement with another wealthy individual named Nathaniel Trescott living nearby. An occurrence most unusual for the time, Mr. Trescott had sought to give up his land, the reason being that he was getting too old to bend and whip slaves and handle the stress of other business affairs. He wanted to relax in his house without the sounds of horses neighing and slaves crying. He also had no sons, not having been one of the blessed.

So, Richard's father Hayman McLeary had come to an arrangement: Mr. Trescott would give Richard's father his portion of the land, and as a result, Hayman McLeary would give Mary's father a portion of the total profits each year, but only if Richard's father promised Richard would wed Mary, the business partner's daughter.

Well, that was awkward indeed, and it took Hayman McLeary at least a day to think about, but no longer than that; it had been most unfortunate for the then-young Richard that the discussion had come at not the best time. Or at least not the best time for him. He had been quarreling with his father of late regarding his dallying and lack of urgency to settle, thus the elder McLeary did not feel especially benevolent toward his son, who looked as though—without the guidance of a strict woman—he might become fat and lazy as he aged. Thus, Richard's fate had been sealed. Had the two men managed not to argue so much at the time, perhaps the elder McLeary wouldn't have forced the unfitting marriage on him to a woman with a pretty face but a voice that could scare crows.

But as mentioned earlier, she also had good breeding loins, so that was something. Thus, the marriage between Richard McLeary and Mary Trescott had come to pass! And Richard considered he had been well and truly 'done over' in the process!

In due course, Mr. Trescott stuck to his side of the agreement and gave the land over to the elder Mr. McLeary after the marriage was sealed. Upon meeting Mary, Richard noticed how clean and capable she was, and certainly, she could enhance his life in some respects. Like his own father had said, he needed to sharpen up, needed to have more goals, needed to be driven, and needed a good woman to keep him in line, didn't he? And he certainly needed a good woman to bear his offspring.

There'd been a time when he told himself he was quite taken by her excellent people skills. But as the months passed following their betrothal, he quickly noticed her spoiled nature. At first, he made excuses for the girl; what child born into wealth *wasn't* spoiled?

So, she wanted him to do all the work with the slaves, all the work on the business and its accompanying paperwork, fix and mend about the house, and always pay her the finest compliments. She wanted him to buy her fine garments and a better home. She had him warming the bed with the warming pan, chopping meat to make the stew, clearing the pig pens, looking after the horses, even pressing the bedlinen sometimes. She possessed a great hunger for him to behave more and more the landed gentleman, to acquire the richest brocades and fancy ornaments for her. And never was it sufficient! In addition, he was expected to make the most excellent trades in all directions. Trades of men and goods.

And he did try. Lord knew how he tried to do it all to please her. Just to make her praise him.

She rarely did. There was always an objection, a *but*.

"This is all right, Richard, but…"

Soon, Mary always seemed sensitive, bored, and distant, as if she never wanted to be bothered. The older she got, the more bored he was with her too. It was easy for a man's eye to wander away from his own wife when the wife's eye was never upon him in the first place.

She would rather sit and weave or make tattle talk with the other womenfolk than notice the fine specimen of a man who came home to her nightly, bearing meat and coinage.

Mary had always been extremely beautiful, and she was even now, in her mid-thirties, a glow radiating from her flawless skin. This made one wonder why Richard always wooed women even when his wife was prettier. He could admit to that' sure, she was prettier, but over the years, she had gained a bit of weight. Not much, but enough to be noticeable. A tiny waist like Samantha's was a favorable obsession compared to one who had to change corsets to ever-increasing sizes, even asking her husband to fasten them tight. Without that attention, Mary's shape just was not as it used to be, especially after the children came.

Richard knew Mary was well aware of his philandering. Many a time, he had felt her eyes burning into him when he was outside, purportedly attending to a chore. She'd keep her gaze on him to ensure he attended to only what they had agreed, never anything else.

The hairs on his neck would bristle when she caught him out yet again, chattering idly to some girl passing up or down the lane. To his chagrin, there'd been one time she'd found she was missing her favorite ladle and discovered the young lady from a cottage across the fields happened to possess one just the same!

He was wily, right enough. She had long since learned that she needed to keep an eye on him.

Richard figured this was the main reason she must have begun to hate being married to him. As a master, he found it hard to 'obey' anyone, especially a woman.

So he would try to be who she wanted, 'to a degree'. After that, he'd do what he wanted.

So, the more years that passed, the more she recognized Richard as a 'loathsome monster with no gentlemanly quality or finesse to recommend him.'

She always loved taking nips or jabs at him whenever she had the chance, and he did so in turn. Still, Richard couldn't get rid of her now, not only because of the agreement but also because she was the mother of his children, who *adored* her.

Even so, Richard got the feeling that even if Mary could leave, she wouldn't because of her rational fear that he might kill her if she did, or even if she considered it.

In her days together with him, she'd heard tales of how many he had put an end to.

He surely would not think twice if the next killing had to be of his own wife. A public flogging was entertainment to him. A drowning was 'an unfortunate incident', and a man stabbed through the heart was said to have 'passed like a stuck pig.'

Richard inwardly smiled at the thought as he buttoned his brown vest and tied off his cravat, slamming the wardrobe shut. "Aye, that'll have to do," he muttered.

Mary groaned, slapping her hand down on the sheets. "Do you have to make such a ruckus? Do you have to make a spectacle of your dressing? I'm still trying to sleep. Not all of us have somewhere to be, you know."

"Beauty sleep is wasted on you. Closer you get to looking like an old crow."

Mary raised her head to glare at him. "Perhaps that's due to your constant interruptions considering you try to cover up nasty with robes."

It was his turn to glare. Richard purposely re-slammed the wardrobe shut, but Mary didn't even so much as flinch. Nostrils flared, Richard stomped his boots across the room, kicking the empty chamber pot peaking from under the bed across the floor. The clattering only erupted a grunt from his wife, so as Richard set the water basin down roughly on the washstand, he vigorously scrubbed his hands and arms, splashing water around the floor until Mary shot upright, glaring at him with deathly promise. Like most mornings when their usual quarreling began, it started with Mary's whip of a voice.

"Goodness me, Richard. Be less noisy. Keep it down. I am trying to rest."

"Rest, rest, rest," he snapped. "All you do is *rest*. You're a good for nothing these days."

Mary shot out of bed in her shift, stomping her bare feet on the wood floor and up to Richard. The two barked at one another, not caring who they woke in the house.

"Yes, rest I must, too wearied dealing with an infantile, good-for-nothing husband with no desire to ever adhere to or please his wife."

"It's a *wife's* job to please her husband," Richard raved. "But you do nothing but sit around moping in your story books, only dropping smiles for when other men come as company. A loss of loyalty to her husband. Nay, not a loss of loyalty. A demeaning show of disobedience."

Mary's face seared a deep red. Her breathing grew labored when she pointed a finger and yelled, "You wouldn't know a thing about loyalty, you disgusting conceited whoremonger! All *you* do is chase petticoats like an unmated dog! A *dog* you are."

Even dogs have names.

Samantha's words echoed in his head, loud as though she were in front of him, screeching like Mary before him.

Richard's nostrils flared, but only briefly. His reaction to her words was unexpected. He just stared at her for some seconds as though he was going to pounce on her. He imagined himself choking the life out of her, and that thought alone brought a smile to his face. But perhaps in another sphere of his life, he could take revenge on her, his sneering wife. Each time he hurt a woman slave or the wife of a slave, he could impose the vision of Mary's face onto her.

Mary stepped back at the sudden smirk this bone-rattling thought brought to his face. And he lapped up the fear. The way her round eyes gaped and angled lips trembled, she bore a striking resemblance to his son. Richard suddenly grinned.

"I'm taking Henry with me today," he said and left the room, calling James' name as he went to the foyer.

It was 7:00 am., the morning sun barely up. Richard, James, and

Henry headed for Oglethorpe's Racecourse just three miles outside of Savannah so they could replace the property that had unfortunately died. Richard was still quietly gutted to be losing money, time, and effort in doing so; it was as if the slave was getting some form of retribution for the inconvenience of it all. At least now, their early arrival could yield the best outcome. With little time spent, they could select the best replacement before other slave masters had the chance.

Mothers held their children's hands as they walked with their husbands, looking at the fear-filled faces of the latest products available. And products they were too, the vast array not unlike any other of a kind loudly advertised and seen in any store. These were wares or chattel, belongings for better men of a far superior hue to take as part of their estates. Seeking to buy these goods was no different than setting forth to buy a new coat or a piece of ironmongery. All varieties were to be displayed, a feast for the eyes and a challenge to the pocket. If you had a fair sum to spend, you might acquire a prettier one or a younger one, perhaps one without a recent ailment or affliction, or one with vibrant good looks to draw attention to their value.

Young to old, short to tall, and lean to plump, the goods for sale were all shackled to wooden platforms as hands raised their bids on the best-looking ones. This was not about good value, no. It was about showing which man could find sufficient coin to take away the best desired.

Richard, Henry, and James walked down the street, dressed in their finest clothes. Both older men were attired in their sumptuous, gaudy vests of bright fabrics, adorned with a thin, over-dressed neckerchief correctly placed and knotted at the throat. Richard's was striped, James' spotted and vivid, both men almost as if silently calling out, *Here I am, the best, most affluent, and able slave master in town! Look at me! See what marvelous goods my funds shall buy me today!* Though both men had no choice but to also wear their coarse and yet pretentious air by virtue of showing the dull faces they were born with—well, dull in James' case at least—they sought to boast in their clothing.

The young master Henry seemed to have been dressed to be a smaller version of Richard—the only difference being his dark golden hair taking after his mother—and the breeches of all the three were of the finest material and chosen to be bright and gay. However, in the Racecourse venue, many men were similar; these three were drops in a great ocean, alas. Here, most men were ostentatious; all had wealth to flaunt and to spare.

As they scoured the crowd for potential slaves, Richard thought about picking the right, skilled workers who would improve his plantation production while making him look good.

"James, are we on track for an increase in our income compared to last year? And if so, by how much, would you say?"

"For this month, yes, but the totals for all the months up to this point are no more than the year before. It is a moveable feast, should we say. One month a surplus, the next a dearth. Some more, some less, as it goes. Over a year, it evens such that we lose not a disproportionate sum."

It was spoken to sound good, clever words astutely wrapped. Or at least sounding tolerable.

But what it didn't speak of was *we are doing better than we ever dreamed of.* And this was where Richard McLeary always wished for things to be. He frowned and pulled his brows tight together, mulling over every word, long or short, that James had just spoken. All the while, little Henry swaggered along as if intent on buying his very own slave that day with his own funds.

Richard clicked his tongue. A part of his father's agreement in keeping Mr. Trescott's land was that if he incurred losses for three years straight, the land was forfeited.

"Are you saying we have broken even? Or that we are on track to do so when the year is out?"

"To date, even. As for next month or the month thereafter, given the vagaries of the weather and the slow harvest, and the fact we cannot be sure how many of our product may fall sick—"

He was waffling, saying little, yet trying to put into Richard's head that maybe, just possibly, they might lose. A little. Only a little. Not a great lot.

Richard pieced it together, looking appalled.

"Then why did you not say so sooner? Then surely, we need to double our resources."

"Isn't that one of the reasons we're here? I would not venture to say so because one assumes you know the realities as well as I do."

Small Henry looked up, his eyes tracking between them. "Have we not got any money then, Pa?" he asked. "Will we be evicted from our land?"

He piped up his statement in a most grievous fashion, such that all the men around could hear. Richard puffed out his chest and laughed a hearty laugh. "Oh, goodness me, no, child. We merely discuss the ups and downs of our investments. That is what good businessmen do."

Then he whacked the child on the back of the head. Not enough to hurt but just sufficient to say, *Shut up, you imbecile. Think of your father's reputation!*

He turned back to James, looking at him askance.

"Right, but I purchased some slaves last year, and production still managed to go down? It should have increased. Maybe these niggers are slacking, or maybe I haven't picked the right ones. Or maybe you and the boys have been too lenient." Richard paused to think. "We need to double our resources on the plantation by the end of the year so we can get our property back to the necessary numbers. Or should I say, *you* need to get the numbers and the resultant revenues back to the ideal position. I trust that you understand me."

"How? I've already upped the cotton quota from 225 pounds to 250. And increasing numbers isn't possible unless we intend to make them work double as they do now. And they cannot keep on doubling and doubling, for sooner or later, we simply run short of hours to make them work."

"That's as it may be, but for now, so be it," Richard said in response. "Make them start working Sundays. All of them. Every last one."

"You do realize imploring slaves to work on their day off is a crime?"

"It's not a crime, James. It's only frowned upon. Besides, the Thompsons did it. It's just until we get the numbers back up. I am not suggesting we make a habit of it. Try for the next month, see how it all looks, and then after the month, we revisit it."

"And by then, they may be dead. We'll only be down more stock,"

James murmured something or other to himself, barely loud enough for Richard to hear in the loud melee around.

"I'm sorry? What was that?" asked Richard. "It's noisy here. My ears may have deceived me." He couldn't be sure, but it almost sounded like James was making a complaint about how he ran things at the plantation. Surely, the man wouldn't be so arrogant as to think he knew better than Richard himself did.

"Oh, I said yeah, the Thompsons did try it. But do you not recall what happened? Some fell ill with a festering complaint that may or may not have been in their own imaginations, and those not shoutin' about the griping in their guts banded together and revolted. Besides, Mary won't like that. Sunday's the Lord's day."

Richard didn't care too much what Mary thought or about the Lord's day. As far as he was concerned, he was to remain the only deity of those filthy ingrates.

"These niggers ain't hers. Anyway, there's bigger danger in a man letting a wife tell him what he can and cannot do. Men were put on the earth to rule and to sow. Women were given to us to assist us by obeying and reaping."

James sighed. "Just be careful."

It seemed to Richard that James felt there was no point in arguing and that perhaps James found him somewhat pigheaded. But on the quiet between them, Richard would concede that James was often the one with the greater sensibilities. He could usually sense when a bad thing was coming.

The year was 1833, and changes were afoot.

"There's word about an underground railroad. I'm sure you've heard the rumors," James said. "More and more are said to be attempting to escape to the North. And more news about some being successful keep surfacing. I suggest you keep a tight leash on your property, Richard. They break free from their confines and achieve freedom on occasion by sticking together."

Richard laughed, "These niggers think they can escape up North all the way from Savannah, do they? I'll break their spirit before they even think about attempting."

Richard felt a tug on his coat. He turned to see Henry looking up at him.

"Pa, have you ever had a slave try to run?"

"One or two," Richard said. "But they never got far and sure as hell ain't stupid enough to try again. Not from my employ. Maybe from another fool. These niggers ain't got a good head between 'em. You couldn't make a good 'un, boy, even if you added them all together. So don't go worrying about negroes getting out."

Richard recalled the time he'd punished one of his runaways by pulling out five teeth straight from the root. There was also the time Richard beat another before branding a sizzling "R" onto his left cheek. The brand, a raised brown scar, would be a marker for any others should he ever be sold or should be found if he ever ran again. On a separate occasion, Richard had taken to slicing the heels of the same nigger after he ran twice, but only enough so he could still work in the fields.

His slaves should be grateful for such mercies.

If anything, Richard figured his methods were a lot more lenient compared to his father's. His father once suspended a nigger underneath a piece of roasting pork fat so that as it cooked and the fat melted, it dripped down onto the slave, creating little splotches where it scalded him through layers of skin.

Henry continued, "Can I come with you if you ever have to capture a runaway again?"

Richard contemplated for a moment. He thought back to when his father had slit the throat of a runaway. Was this good viewing for the boy?

As a young boy, Richard had been fond of a maid named Abigail who worked in the house, and a specific memory had stuck with him all these years. He'd fallen ill with a fever, tossing and turning in his bed, crying out for someone, anyone. She'd sat beside him all through the night with a cold cloth to his face, humming songs under her breath. He'd wondered for so long if that's what it was like to have a mother—but she must have got in his head because his father flogged her for 'tempting his son'.

Richard grew up in the house, and his father was always out on the field making sure everyone was hard at work, so Richard wasn't very exposed to the cruelty of his father's ways.

So after the incident with Abigail, his father took him to the field each day, slowly turning him into a younger version of himself.

Once, his father had thought it best to wake Richard in the middle of the night when it was announced a few slaves had run away. Eventually, they caught up and cornered the two runaways—one being Abigail, the other her daughter.

"I won't go back," she said. "I will never go back."

With nowhere to go and no one to help her get away, Abigail slit her daughter's throat before attempting her own, but his father's workers swarmed her, grabbing the knife and pinning her down. Young Richard was bug-eyed, his blood running cold from what he'd just witnessed, and there was more to come. He would always remember the slow thump of his father's boots as he approached Abigail, pulling her head back by the hair and taking the knife.

There was a certain look in his eyes that night as he slowly slit her throat, never taking his eyes off of Richard. To punish him? To punish her? He didn't know.

It wasn't until Richard had children of his own to think about that he understood why his father had chosen to end her life that night instead of keeping her. "Never grow fond of a pig," so his father said.

Once a worker tried to escape or to turn on an employer, that was it. They were called to God. The question was, how much of this should a young boy see, and when? Richard had to decide if he'd expose the young Henry to what happened to escaped slaves at the earliest possibility. Or would he wait for the boy to become a less tender age?

His father had later died of tuberculosis in his fifties, leaving Richard the plantation. His mother had died in childbirth, so Richard had been an only child left alone to manage the entire place. James was perhaps the closest thing to a brother. Still, Richard wouldn't have been able to run the plantation right if it hadn't been for his father. It was only because of him—everything he'd done, advised, taught, and shown—that Richard knew how to handle the workers and put the fear of God into them. Even so, Richard believed he'd been unduly scarred back then because he wasn't mature enough, so a part of him felt that perhaps it was too soon for Henry to experience the same thing. It made a difference whether a boy was scarred or encouraged by what he witnessed. In youth and adulthood, it could make him a man or a coward.

Richard remembered the screams of the softspoken black servant after his father found out about his fondness for the girl. He remembered the look in her eye upon her dying breath, even how it appeared her spirit must have risen from her body when the blood drained free, because one moment it was there, a fire in her eyes that let everyone know *I am Abigail!*

Her big black eyes were still open during and after death, so she ought to have looked just the same, really. But then, as she took her last breath, they showed a shell.

'Abigail' had vacated the corpse. So where was she now? What was 'Abigail' such that she could shine from the eyes in one moment and vacate the corpse the next, showing it dulled?

And even now, he could never understand why a mother would slit the throat of her own child for such a foolish reason, and he'd seen that too, though so mercifully fast that the child wouldn't have known a thing. He still had nightmares about all of it sometimes, and a part of him didn't want his son to be as tormented as he was.

Richard finally said, "Going to the market is the closest I'll allow you to be when looking for slaves."

James gave a curious expression as if to say, *I thought you'd say the opposite. I thought you'd love for him to embrace the sight of beatings and death.*

It was not enough for the boy anyway. Henry looked up at Richard with a gleam in his eye that spoke to him as a father. It was unwavering determination mixed with that bit of disappointment that sat heavily on his heart. The young boy tilted his head up as if to say, *I'm old enough to handle it*, yet his lower lip had begun to protrude and quiver. Richard sighed.

"Fine," he said. "I'll take you next time."

"You promise?"

"I promise."

Henry gave a gleeful smile, saying, "Huzzah" under his breath. Richard's son's cheeriness made James offer a faint smile, but Richard remained hard-faced. He'd let Henry have his moment and hope for a next time.

Though, he'd make sure there was no next time.

Richard took a swig of whiskey from his flask as the three passed two slaves that stood alone, apart from the main event. One was an older woman, the years having carved deep and unforgiving lines in her face along with bags of exhaustion, poor nutrition, and hopelessness under her eyes. Her hair was brittle, fragile looking, as though a single touch would cause her to be bald because she must have suffered some appalling affliction on her body.

But the boy—no more than twelve and just a few centimeters taller than Henry's ten-year-old frame—who held her hand, hiding behind her, showed potential to Richard.

A young boy could easily be beaten to become an exemplary worker.

Henry tugged on his father's brown coat and asked, "Pa, why would you be interested in a slave so weak and worthless?" Richard smiled, turning to his son. Henry's eyes were fixed on the boy now, focused. His son paused, tilting his head. "He looks like me."

And by default, that meant he also looked similar to Richard. The boy's eyes seemed to implore his father to agree. Richard did not agree; how could he?

He frowned and shuddered; perish the thought that there were *any* similarities between his son and this boy. It was a vile and preposterous notion.

He turned away, now seeing an old man with the slaves' chains in hand, sitting on a bench, hiding in the shadows from the burning sun.

"Excuse me," Richard said, approaching the old man. "How much for the child?"

The man looked up slowly, giving Richard a once-over. "350."

"That's a bit pricey for a child, don't ya think? I'm used to buying three for that."

"Thelma and Solomon are sold together. The price for them both is 350. So y'either buy them both or move on."

Richard knitted his brows. The two slaves must have been related. Was this old fool trying to foolishly preserve the slave family intact? If so, then it was pointless and a ridiculous notion because sooner or later, one of them would fall prey to a flogging, an illness, or just die from overwork in the searing heat. Was it not better that the remaining one didn't have to live through that? Separate, the pains were less, Richard was certain.

As though reading his mind, James asked, "Why both?"

"My daughter kept them together, so they are sold together. Thelma here is a medicine woman with great knowledge of herbs. She understands English but does not speak it too well. The boy, her son, speaks for her."

Medicine woman.

That must mean Africa, surely.

Wasn't that illegal? As a slave owner, Richard was conversant with the law—specifically, the act that prohibited the importation of slaves. In the back of his mind, the thought came that maybe the two had been illegally smuggled in; there was no support for importing Africans—it was indeed illegal—because of a law passed thirty-five years ago in 1798.

Hearing that actually made the two a lot more attractive to him. It would mean him having rare, valuable commodities. Illicit things always brought a certain appeal to most slave owners, increasing their reputation and mystique. And he wouldn't have imported her himself.

Something forbidden. James must have read his mind again. Perhaps the two were worth 350, after all. He considered it, wondering if anyone else might be listening in. If they were, and if he drifted away from the slave owner to ponder on it, the likelihood was he'd return to find the boy and woman both gone, purchased to make someone else's glory shine.

James turned to Richard and whispered, "You do know the old woman could be helpful in the home if you really want the boy. If I were you—"

Richard just turned and slightly nodded, enough to convey they were thinking along the same lines. Then Richard asked the old man, "Why is your daughter selling them?"

The old man said, "My daughter and son-in-law lost their plantation to a fire and need the money. The flames took the whole place, top to bottom, the barns too, and the land is parched. They have to start again from the ground up. It ain't easy."

"Well, no, I should imagine it's not easy at all," Richard conceded, almost feeling a stab of empathy for a change. Almost. Feeling sorry for a person was not in his nature. A person had to take their lot in life and make the best of it, like he was doing now. But just this once, he was determined to make an exception.

Richard fumbled in his pocket for his coin purse, deciding to buy the pair, but instead of paying $350, he gave him $400. "Keep the change," he said. "Use it to lift your daughter's spirits and make her more pretty than she sounds. Maybe get her a nice dress, something her husband would be happy to come home to after a long day."

The man huffed out a mock laugh. "I'll do that."

The man wrote up a bill of sale and handed it to Richard, who made a mental note of the seller's name: William Bennett. It was a familiar name, one Richard thought he'd heard or seen before. He stared at the careful scrawl for a moment, trying to pinpoint where or when, but when nothing came to mind, he folded the bill and tucked it away. As the old man passed the chains to Richard, he clapped his hand hard on Richard's shoulder, looked him in the eye for a moment, and walked away.

"What the hell was that about?" James said.

"I haven't a dang clue. Just something, that's all."

James shrugged, casting a look as if implying that one day, but not anytime soon, he would begin to comprehend Richard. Richard ignored it.

Still feeling unfulfilled, Richard and James continued their shopping. They could already see some slaves in chains waiting to be sold as they walked along, but none of them appealed to Richard. It was an ongoing problem. They had grown from three to five, the new property being something of an encumbrance, plodding slowly, not daring to pass any comments but giving looks to the other slaves. None of them appeared worthy.

When his two new possessions cast a look or a wink to another when they moved past, what was the meaning of it? Were they encouraging the slaves to hide so they wouldn't be chosen, or were they saying to puff out their chests and stand tall so they would? Which one was it? Some might well want to be selected. Maybe it made their small brains feel better than they were for a few moments. Or perhaps it would get them released from a master who hated them and a slave owner who had already decided they were no more use to him.

Who'd want to stay under these circumstances? *Certainly not me,* Richard thought. He decided the looks being thrown by the two new niggers must be to encourage the others to look better than they were. *Well then, I'd better be on the lookout for that. Don't want to buy any useless stock.* He always went for men who had sturdy bodies rather than ones who appeared like they had been starved or gotten sick in their previous homes. But now, there was more than a chance they would try to look healthier for just a few minutes for the trade to initiate.

Perhaps these two, the woman and the boy, were related to others and so wanted to see them do better and end up together on the one plantation. He'd keep an eye out for this, too.

In the distance, a man with a thick, handlebar mustache announced that auctioning would begin. He stood atop an old wooden crate that looked as though it bowed from the weight of him. He waved people over with the rumpled handkerchief from his pocket and the promise of worthy goods.

"Richard!" a hearty voice boomed. Richard groaned and rolled his eyes, preparing for what was to come. How could he ever mistake *that* voice? He turned around.

"Clinton," he said. "How pleasant to meet you."

Pleasant, it was most decidedly not. This was Clinton Appleton, a wide, bawdy man who always wore a size too small, such that Richard wasn't sure if the man's clothes had shrunk or Clinton had put on weight and then fallen on hard times, unable to replace his clothes.

The latter was a consideration merely in jest as Clinton had everything—and everyone knew it. It would never come to pass that Clinton couldn't afford *any* item—at least if you were to believe the words that spewed from his mouth, anyway.

He was always mitigating and raving, comparing whose horse was bigger.

Richard hated him passionately and believed he must be cursed to see him there. But it shouldn't have been a surprise since this man wanted to flaunt just as much as Richard to prove he was better. That he always had something more.

Clinton tipped his top hat.

"James."

"Clinton."

"And little Henry!"

"Good morning, Mr. Appleton."

"Well, always the polite one. What are you all doing here?"

"Well, I suppose we're here for the same reason as every other man walking these tracks," Richard said with a fake smile. "Seeking to acquire new, to replace the old, dead or useless."

Clinton laughed and stepped up to see Thelma and Solomon in chains standing behind them. "I thought you had plenty of slaves running your plantation. Didn't think you needed more. Especially not… ah… Especially not of their ilk either."

He was at it already, sizing up, judging, proclaiming himself better by far.

"There was a… mishap with one of them. Just replacing them."

"Replacing them with an old hag and a boy?"

"Discounted. I was doing a man a favor."

"Always the generous type. But what to expect? You are known to run your slaves with an iron fist, even taming the most unruly of the bunch."

Clinton cleared his throat, spitting into a handkerchief.

"So Richard, when are you gonna join our gatherings? With a man who prides himself for being a nigger breaker, there's a lot that can be done in our neighborhood, and a hard-fisted slaver such as yourself would make a great contribution."

Richard sighed. Clinton was part of an organization where he and chiefly other middle-aged slavers would come together to share ideas on better ways to tame slaves, the best places to buy them, and even the best methods of breeding and trading. It was in this group that Richard's father had met with Mary's father, and they'd made that deal later on.

But Clinton's little organization had a habit of participating in indulgences, leaving trails of mulatto bastards wherever they set foot. Richard wasn't too fond of being a part of it, let alone being in the same room as Clinton.

Richard smiled. "I already have a lot on my plate, Clinton. Don't see a reason to add more."

"Nonsense, sir. No time at all to offer wisdom and insight? To enlighten us on the best ways to manage our property? To give advice on disciplining and breaking them? To show us how the master does it? Well, well, then, that's a disappointment since I had long believed you were among the best. 'Tis a shame now to learn it isn't so and that you've naught to show us."

"What is there to show? We both know how lazy blacks are. They'd never work a day in their life if not for the whip. Simple. So, I'll give you that little nugget of learning for free, Clinton. As I said, I have a lot on my plate, and if I say I cannot come, it is because I have better things to do with my time than entertain you with snippets."

"Come on now. You don't want to miss out on all the fun, do you?"

The corpulent and opinionated man was relentless. No doubt now, he'd go back to the next gathering and say Richard McLeary's business was on the slippery downhill slope, and therefore, he'd declined to come because he was too busy sorting his meager affairs.

"I'll think about it."

"Don't think too long. The spot might be taken soon." He glanced at James. "And you should join us too, James."

James nodded.

The clatter of the crowd raved around them. Richard smiled. "I think that's my cue. If you'll excuse me, I have to make my way to the auction. I do believe it has begun."

Richard made his way towards the auction stage in the distance, posthaste. He stood in the back of the large mob, surly among many who were there to buy today. The soaring voice of the auctioneer cut through the clatter of the crowd.

The first item brought up was a frail man with graying hair and too-thin limbs. Richard scoffed and looked at James as if to say, *This is what they are selling today?* The old one didn't sell for much—a mere $175—and Richard couldn't understand what a weakened slave could do for production.

The second was a woman who looked corpulent at first glance, but the announcement that she was pregnant brought a hungry gasp from the crowd. She sold quickly, but the idea of her squeezing out the bastard on his land made him curl his lip in disgust. It was any slave owner's goal to increase his stock, sure, and Richard set aside only a specific amount of his nigger gals for breeding, but the expenses to raise the little scoundrels and to make up for the slack of the mother were detrimental, especially when it came to his father's deal with Mr. Trescott. It was better to trade and have another owner handle the care. And best to bring them back when the babes were older and able.

Brought up on stage next was a tall one with thick arms, a broad-shouldered slave built like an ox. Yes, now this was a nigger worthy of his coin. He'd be good for heavy lifting, doing the hard labor that a lot of the skinnier ones couldn't. But the murmur in the crowd wasn't fond of him, and when he was slightly turned to the left, Richard could see why. He had an "R" branded on the side of his neck. A runner. He let out an annoyed sigh for the loss of what could have been.

After a few more unsavory slaves graced the stage, Richard perused the line of niggers in chains. He was akin to auctions, how the best products were always saved for last, but none of the ones he could see caught his eye. He was about to leave when an eruption of hoots and hollers from the large crowd suddenly caught the three's attention. Men were huddled together in front of a slave showcase.

Richard and James struggled to make their way to the front of the group, Richard holding Henry's hand as they pushed through the crowd. Clinton was there a few men down. Richard did his best to avoid eye contact with the bastard. But when he looked at the platform, he froze.

A female slave was being brought up.

He laid eyes on the fine woman and couldn't help but gawk in admiration. The slave wore rags with a slit on the side, but Richard couldn't help admiring her long, thin legs, strong muscles, and no doubt soft and supple breasts. She looked to be in her thirties and wore her hair in two thick braids tucked under, different from the usual plain hair pulled back among his other female workers. And she had the darkest, glowing skin.

Something about her awoke a predatory and raw tendency inside of him.

It stirred like a dormant beast, roused from its slumber by an irresistible scent. A scent it craved. Perhaps this was merely a sign, a gut instinct for exceptional goods. Richard dared not acknowledge it as anything more.

But his gaze lingered, betraying the sudden, unsettling hold, even as he tried to push creeping thoughts aside. However, her high, upright posture pulled him back in.

The way she stood, there was nothing fragile about it. It was damning how much her stance commanded the room like she was better than the other niggers. Like she wasn't a slave to be sold. But the thought was surpassed by the intrigue that bubbled up when her undisciplined eyes filled with mirth as she looked every man before her directly in the face.

He noticed a scar on her right thigh that would have looked ugly on someone else, but it seemed to blend with her undeniable fiery personality. She didn't seem ashamed of it or try to hide it.

"Don't let the scar fool you, gentlemen. This is a strong, fine, healthy negro gal in great condition, a black pearl of few words, and a jack of all trades with few flaws," the auctioneer shouted. "Great cook, cleans, will pick better than any negro male. A woman of few words and good ears to listen with. A good investment, gentlemen! The bid starts at $450."

Richard threw his hand in the air.

"I thought we needed a strong male. Why are you bidding for

this girl that'll be little to no use to us?" James asked, shooting him a confused look.

He thinks I'm easily influenced and don't know my own mind, thought Richard. *He thinks just about anything with pretty features could have me wandering off course at a moment's notice like a stupid hound after a hare. And he's probably right… but what harm in it? Mary's not here.*

Richard ignored James and continued to bid. But the bids kept growing higher.

"I hear 550! Do I hear 560?"

Richard threw up his hand and shouted his bid again. He had vowed to own the girl no matter what, already picturing her making the most striking pair alongside the purchased boy. Now, seeing that many other slave masters were bidding for her, this only made his determination all the greater. He heard someone call out a thousand dollars, double the amount of a very strong-looking male. Richard turned to see who it was. Clinton stood with a raised hand, a small smirk on the corner of his lips.

Richard clenched his jaw in frustration and ground his teeth together. Once again, Clinton found a golden opportunity to gain footing against him. In his eye was that same gleam that Richard likely also had while looking at the slave. But Richard would not give up so easily, not to the likes of Clinton.

The auctioneer called out the hand that raised the bids higher and higher.

But when the beautiful woman looked fiercely into Richard's eyes, her gaze targeted as though calling to him, he raised his hand and bid too.

"$2,500!"

The crowd of bidders froze in silence, all hoots and hollers stopping. Everyone stared at him in shock. No one else could bid past his price, including Clinton himself.

But Richard didn't give a rat's ass.

The auctioneer called "Sold!" on Richard's proposal, declaring him the winner.

A clamor of dismay, sour moans, and growls of defeat echoed through the crowd. James spun to look at his friend with wide eyes, his mouth hanging open in shock. "Richard, what the hell are you thinking?" he protested. "We coulda got at least four to six skilled niggers with that kind of money."

But Richard simply grinned. "Stop throwing such a fit just because you know that if you were a slave, you wouldn't have been sold for more than an eighth of that amount." He laughed as he patted James' shoulder, but James did not look amused.

Richard released Henry's hand and shifted through the crowd alone, going behind the podium to seize his purchase. As the auctioneer's helper handed Richard the chains, violently tugging the woman, Richard looked her up and down and asked her, "What is your name?"

But she didn't respond; instead, she looked Richard dead in the eye, a look of confidence but not of arrogance or impertinence. Well, the auctioneer had spoken true; the girl had good ears to listen and rarely answered back. In short, she was a dream.

But that didn't excuse her from answering a simple question from her new master.

Just as Richard stepped closer to his hard-fought prize, ready to show her the consequences of disobeying her master, he heard a man's voice say, "Nini." The woman still only gazed.

Richard turned to the young man. "Why doesn't she speak?" he asked.

The bidder assistant simply shrugged and said, "She's mute." Richard glowered at the boy, a feeling of being cheated bubbling to the surface, but then the boy said, "Auctioneer did say she was a woman of few words, but don't fret, sir. She's mute, but her fine ass makes up for her lack of voice."

CHAPTER THREE

Back at the plantation, Richard was washed up and cleaned. Beads of sweat cut paths through the thick dirt on Nini's cheeks as she worked in the cotton fields, her new—new to her—bluish-grey dress and cream apron swaying. Richard watched her from atop his white horse with a grin across his face. She could no doubt feel his piercing stare but kept to her work. Richard knew the normal him would have slapped the girl for shooting deadly glares at him, but for some reason, he let it slide. He couldn't explain it. James kept shooting glances at him to do something about the girl, but Richard pretended not to notice him.

He remembered James asking him why he had purchased her soon after the auction. In fact, Richard wasn't sure why he had. Just something about her eyes that needed taming. When they arrived at the plantation, Richard told Nini she would be working in the cotton fields with the others. She had to meet the same quota as all the other field hands or would be punished severely.

Then, Richard himself gave her a tour around the plantation, dismissing the helper tasked to do so. With a hand banded around her arm, he took Nini around to show her where she would spend her nights. As he did, he explained everything, including how the slaves began work at daybreak and how there were no days off. He even stood at a window and pointed at the cabins on the side of the house where the domestic house servants resided.

James questioned Richard about why he was doing all this; that was typically his job regarding new slaves on the plantation. In fact, James wouldn't bother with something so trivial as a tour. He'd have another nigger do it. And why show her the inside of the manor when she was to be a field nigger? Richard reassured him that nothing was different. Why would it be?

Indeed, why would it? His roving eye had nothing to do with it.

Even now as Richard watched Nini at work, there was just something in her that needed taming. Her features slightly reminded him of Abigail, whose throat had been slit by his father. But her attitude, the way Nini carried herself, was incomparable, and perhaps that was what drew him to her. She had a quiet inner wisdom about herself, also an air that said she knew who she was. It also spoke of being untamed, that no one had ever got the better of her, no one had broken her despite many savage beatings, sometimes meted out only to try and do exactly that.

Perhaps that's why he wanted to be the one to tame her and show her her place. Perhaps this was also what his father would have felt in regard to the maid, a thing he'd never grasped.

James and even a few of the other employees on his plantation were not hesitant to give Richard questioning glances, but he chose to ignore them too.

Come lunchtime, Richard sat on his porch, watching his recent purchase work the fields with enjoyment. James walked up the creaking wood steps and sat beside him, taking a handkerchief out of his pocket to wipe the sweat from his forehead. He removed his hat to fan himself, revealing his short, wavy, brown hair, trimmed perfectly, complementing the short growth of darkened fresh stubble adorning the lower part of his face.

"You think the girl's really mute?" Richard asked James.

James shrugged, settling into the seat adjacent to Richard. "You don't typically oversee the field yourself." It was a statement. But it still expected some form of a response.

Richard knew he was right; he hated going so far out to the field and looking over his slaves because it was always so damn hot. James typically handled the affairs and directed the daily work of the slaves. He was used to being alone out here most days. He also liked it this way.

James knew how far he could question the slave owner and where his interrogations had to cease, a skill honed over a long period of working together with a respect that was mutual sitting between them both. He had met Richard at an auction years ago, one at which he'd advised him on which slaves to buy. James' keen eye had impressed him.

He had noticed that a slave girl Richard wanted to buy was actually in an early pregnancy. It would have been a waste of money to purchase her now and would have given Richard another mouth to feed that would've been useless about the place for another decade at least.

Richard kept in touch with him, and they'd kept on going to auctions together until Richard finally saw sense and offered him a job. What else would he do? The man was simply right for it.

James was a big contributor to Richard's plantation's success. Because of this, he trusted James and left a lot of the tasks to him with little supervision. They had also become close friends, explaining why James thought he could question and doubt Richard's buying decisions. James—who'd always been in situ as the overseer—and some of the other managers lived on the plantation, and he often dined with Richard and his family.

So, it was very rare for Richard to be out in the field or even to think about coming out.

"What tasks did you give the other two?" Richard asked, changing the subject to hide that he was looking specifically at Nini.

James noticed the change but played along. "Thelma was tasked with cleaning, making beds, and mending small wounds. I made Solomon tend to the horses for today, but I'll get him started working the fields soon." He paused, looking out at the field. "That auctioneer was right. The girl's a good picker. Basket's already damn near full. I suppose it's because she doesn't talk."

Richard nodded, not that what James had said made any sense. "But we don't allow them to talk while they work so I don't follow how you mean that's why she's different."

"Well, if ya don't talk, you also get used to not letting your mind wander off. Focused."

Now, that did make sense. "I think you're right," Richard said. Yet again, James had picked up on something he would never have discerned for himself. The man was a treasure.

James told Richard something else. "You need to look at Nini closer," he offered.

Richard was taken aback. "Look… Look at her closely? Why? Something's amiss with her?"

"No. Just look."

Both men looked, both noting her slender body and beautiful figure. Richard saw the reason for James' infatuation. James saw the reason for Richard's too.

James then said, "She could be used for breeding. That or she might make for good comfort during the night." He turned to Richard with a certain knowing look in his eye.

Richard paused, contemplating taking her out of the cotton fields. He had put her in the cotton field as default from James' suggestion. But it was true; making her a comfort girl for those lonely nights was something to consider.

Yet a part of him didn't want her as a comfort girl because others would have access to her.

He was surprised when another part of him wanted to lash out at James because of his previous statement. But just as Richard had seen something raw and untamed in Nini, was there something just as unbridled in himself? Something that made him make this visceral response to the suggestion? Yes, he was feeling territorial when it came to her, something incomprehensible.

Even if she were to become a comfort girl for Richard alone, Richard had multiple white workers on hand already, if for no other reason than to prevent an uprising. And several of them lived on his plantation, a few in his own manor, several in league with Mary too, frequently sharing tittle-tattle. With the workers living in the manor, hiding Nini's role as a comfort girl might be hard. He needed to keep up appearances. Still, Richard had never lain with a nigger before, although the thought had passed his mind briefly.

He was toying with the idea, and his father's voice judged and insulted him, but now, he clutched onto the notion. Richard's thoughts strayed. He imagined touching her brown skin, the color staining his own. For a moment, he pondered. How would life have been if his skin were brown, if he had been born a different person, and black?

It was a strange thought indeed, sickening him to realize that allowing his mind to meander into wondering about being a product of color had weakened him. It had even, for the most fleeting of moments, taken him to a worse place: that of wondering how it felt to be a slave.

He felt nauseous at it, feeling the upsurge of a roiling in his gut. He wanted to heave.

Slaves weren't people. They were property, and he could do whatever he liked with it. Everything except to gain feelings and sentiments and sensibilities! He could use them, abuse them, hang them, flog them, and drown them. He could beat them, starve them, bake them in the midday sun, and watch their skin darken even more before it cracked and bled and festered.

But he could not, just could not, feel for them or with them. He was now repulsing his own self. Richard sprang up from his seat and quickly walked the fields, cussing as he went.

With his hand on his holster, Richard called out to Nini and beckoned her with two fingers, demanding her to follow him. For a moment, Nini stood still, her back straight and her chin up.

He called for her again, yet she didn't move. Richard couldn't hold back his smile as he walked up to her and grabbed her arm, pulling her towards him.

"Are you deaf too, girl?" he asked. While dragging her from the field, he added, "They don't make them like they used to. When my father was an owner, slaves dropped everything to answer his call. You won't be the first to think you can defy a master. You won't be the last."

He roughly swiveled her to face him.

Nini looked down to the ground now, hiding her angry eyes in which fury burned. He had already recognized she was not like the others, yet at this moment, he chose to forget it again. Now, he was treating her the way he would the rest. Richard placed his hand under her chin and forced her face up.

"Unless you want me to rip your hair from your head as I drag you to the whipping post, then I'd suggest you not upset me. Do as I say. Now turn around so I can examine you. I need to know which work is most suitable for you," Richard told her. However, she remained still. "Come on, now."

Nini didn't budge. Despite his warning, she looked into his eyes with fire and defiance. Richard's hand swiftly struck her across her face. The ring on his finger split the corner of her lips, and blood slightly trickled down. Still, she did not budge, standing as if unfeeling and rooted to the spot.

"Trying to be a bull-headed nigger will get you nowhere here. You are my property and will do as your master tells you, you hear me, girl? You're nothing, just property," Richard reminded her. "Now, I have a new job for you. You'll be working in the house, and I expect you to answer when I call anytime. I said anytime. D'you hear?" He pushed her hand to her face.

"Blood. Clean it up," he ordered.

Nini slowly wiped the blood with the back of her hand and spat out the rest of it at Richard's feet. She fearlessly raised her face to his, daring Richard to do his worst. Her fierce, upturned eyes were still strangely enticing, maybe more so.

Richard's hand twitched, ready to deliver another blow. But instead of hitting her again, he stared back at her. Her audacity. Her entitlement. Her sense of superiority!

She gritted her teeth as she glared at him. Angry, he grabbed her by the hair and pulled her neck back, reminding himself of his father again with Abigail. Despite her efforts to hide her eyes by blinking and glancing to the side, Richard noticed the tears pooling inside them. She began to tremble. Her throat bobbed as she swallowed roughly, and her hands clenched at her side so tight that her dry knuckles began to crack from the strain. Her lips quivered, but she bit down on them, and at any minute, those tears would finally spill down her cheeks.

A slow, subtle grin braced Richard's lips.

He loved that she was scared, and he had finally gotten the better of her. But he also loved that she was defiant. He did not know which way was up or down. The woman was entangling his thoughts and confusing him. It was a new sensation. An interesting one.

He got satisfaction from this bizarre in-between. Richard wanted to throw her to the ground, but whether to hurt her or devour her, he wasn't sure. However, he remembered the property that had died on that very same soil, and he restrained himself because what use was she if she was dead? Especially after how much money he had just used to purchase her. A ridiculous sum. It was preposterous now that he thought about it. James ought to have stopped him.

Then, in the next breath, he recognized he was asking the impossible. No, even James could never assert any kind of authority over him, not even when Richard was engaging in activities fit only to ruin his own self, the plantation, and all that went with it. No, he had to control *himself*.

No one could do it for him.

And right now, he also couldn't do it. Richard noticed a sudden throbbing between his legs. Her fierce gaze and rage had tightened his britches, his breaths deepening, his blood rushing quickly down like a stream into an undoubtedly, tumescent erection.

He released his grip on her hair and tried hiding his situation by sliding his hands in his pocket to mask the bulge, giving Nini one final scathing look before walking away.

This one would need to be broken. He could only hope he wouldn't give in to his base desires and break her in the wrong way—a way that could possibly bring harm to his success.

CHAPTER FOUR

Richard found it challenging to see and count the number of fresh bruises on Nini's soft skin.

But with each passing day, he and other white plantation workers, such as his drivers, Benji and Parkinson, couldn't seem to tame Nini's silent defiance. Now, he was aware of several of her obstinate behaviors: she refused to bathe before working in the house, especially around their food; she avoided meeting Richard in a room when he called upon her; she intervened to protect Thelma from being hit when the old woman broke a vase; and she almost struck a plantation worker while escaping up a tree because he flogged her too hard.

Two weeks had passed since Richard had withdrawn Nini from the cotton fields.

He continued to beat her, and without really observing it, he had established a pattern of personally overseeing her tasks. Over time, Nini upset Richard and other plantation workers and got punished numerous times by being starved, beaten, and even suspended by her wrists from a high place.

Eventually, James and other plantation workers brought to Richard's attention that he was going easy on Nini, that he seemed more lenient with her, and that he was losing control of his slave. Annoyance fell over Richard for people even considering such nonsense. And he was annoyed at himself for entertaining the idea. Richard was known for breaking slaves.

Whatever was the matter with him that he was letting the nigger get away with things?

He couldn't mention the embarrassment he felt from others' judgmental gazes of not being able to control a simple, mute girl. But taming Nini was like trying to tame a bull; you wanted it to comply, but there was no chance of achieving it. Besides, there was fun in making it angry.

However, Richard denied the thought that his hate for her rebellion had soon turned to quiet admiration and intrigued Richard the more. He refused to realize his fondness for her and berated himself for even considering it. He would not fall prey to a slave. Instead, he'd teach her that she was nothing but a submissive animal who belonged to him.

She would work and obey his instructions. It did not matter how he got there, but he would.

Now, Richard tightly grasped the handle of a leather whip as Nini stood nude before him, her lithe, soft arms tied to a post as the high noon sun burned her skin. Richard snapped the whip against her bare back, and the sound of the whip crack made Nini's fellow slaves jump as they were forced to watch. Nini let out a small cry, her nails digging into the palms of her hands as she felt the brutal sting of the whip again. Richard's fellow white plantation workers laughed and mocked Nini's suffering as Richard swung the whip back and forth repeatedly.

"You gon' listen now, huh, girl?" one shouted.

But Richard was taking little enjoyment from Nini's suffering.

Unsatisfied, Richard told two of his slaves to cut her loose. All watched Nini fall to the ground, struggling to hold back her tears. Richard threw the whip from his hand as he fiercely strutted over to the sobbing girl, pulling her up by her hair and proceeding to drag her to the shack. The small hut door squeaked open, grinding against the packed-down earth.

All Nini would be able to see was darkness, only small beams of sunlight shining through the seams of the rotting planks as Richard pushed her inside. He watched her crawl to the corner. Her knees pressed against her chest as he closed the door and locked it from the outside.

Richard's angry footsteps stomped as his fist flew violently at his sides. He turned to see the field hands standing with furrowed brows and pursed lips, the worry deeply etched into the aged lines on their faces.

"What're y'all doing just standing there? If y'all don't want to join her at the post, then I suggest you move your goddamned asses!"

Everyone moved at once, quickly getting back to their tasks.

Richard returned home while Mary sat in the living room, reading a book. She wore pale lipstick, light-brown eyeshadow, complementary blush, and a slightly off-colored facial powder. And oddly, no jewelry besides the gold ring on her finger. Without looking at him, she asked, "So, do you feel satisfied after beating the helpless woman?"

Mary had always considered Richard a cruel owner; in fact, Richard's actions had increasingly repulsed her over the years. Her father was a good owner, according to her. He didn't treat slaves like his equals, but he also didn't treat them like dirt. He treated them harshly only when they had been delinquent time and again and only after many warnings.

Having been selected for her by her father, she had thought Richard would be the same, but he was a monster in her eyes, and her statement showed just that.

Richard reminded Mary, "That *woman* is my property."

Turning a page, Mary said, "Yes, well, your blood—and my own, for that matter—is the same color as that of your property. You're no better. I suppose you would even flog *me* if you could."

Yes, perhaps he might.

The blood in his veins, whatever color it happened to be, was boiling. Her comparing him to slaves was a clear insult.

Richard rushed to Mary and hit the book out of her hand. She quickly stood to meet his glare.

With a smile, she said, "Need I remind you how good you'll look among your peers if I were to be bruised?"

Richard raised his hand but stopped himself from striking her.

"You do remember our little agreement, do you not, dear husband? Or should I say not so much our agreement but the one your own dear papa struck with Father?"

And she was right. His father's agreement—their marriage—was the only reason he held all the land that he did. The two things that would break the deal would be if Richard incurred losses for three years straight or if harm were to come to Mary. Richard tolerated her because he was afraid of her father. Afraid of him taking back the land. The bitter truth, it was.

Richard lowered his hand.

As he strode away, Mary called out to him. "You should be more watchful of yourself, Richard," she said. "The way you look at Nini, you seem to have a fondness for that nigger gal's deviance and defiance. Mind yourself. It could get you into trouble."

Richard scoffed and smiled darkly.

"Yes, I seem to have developed a fondness for her neck: to break it."

Mary's smile faltered. She shivered at the statement as Richard held her gaze with terrifying eyes. And she froze. He could tell she wanted to look away, anywhere but at him. But Richard held her there to send the final message of who was in charge. To remind Mary why she should be afraid.

With brief satisfaction from seeing the flash of fear across Mary's face, he walked away in angry, purposeful strides to his backyard, cursing angrily at the remarks of the terrified woman.

However, while his wife felt that the cause of his rage was because she had triggered a feeling of disgust by stating his desire for a slave, Richard's anger was actually because he realized Mary's words were not far from the truth.

The music of a summer night chimed as Richard sat on his deck, rocking in his chair as he sipped his whiskey. The moon outlined the shack, and his thoughts wandered to Nini. The way she had sobbed that afternoon at the whipping post. The way her smooth back was riddled with lashes. Her smooth legs. The way the sun shined on her buttocks… His thoughts festered.

He thought of her beautiful breasts, wondering how she would feel under him, how it would feel being inside of her. All he could think about was Nini down on her knees with her dark-toned thighs, her rounded buttocks up in the air, eager for him to penetrate her from behind. And then he'd turn her on her back because of her eyes—he wanted to look into her defiant eyes.

His thoughts were vivid, as though he would suffocate if he didn't have her immediately.

Wonder became determined as he made his way to the shack to whet his desire. Fiddling with his keys, he swung open the door to find Nini standing, her back pressed against the splintered wood. Richard took the lantern hanging on a wooden post just outside the shack door and brought it before him. Nini's dewy skin glowed in the gentle light as she shielded her eyes for a moment. Richard found a bent nail from which to hang the lantern and closed the door with a grin across his face. Slowly, he made his way across the room as Nini pressed her back closer and closer to the wall. He danced his fingertips up her arm, moving to her face.

He slipped his finger under Nini's chin and lifted her head to meet her gaze.

Nini recoiled, no doubt tasting the sudden sting of his whiskey as Richard forced his tongue into her mouth. Using all her strength, she pushed Richard away. A brash smack of their lips parting sounded as he stumbled back, hitting the opposite wall. His face flushed with crimson.

Richard lunged at her, his hands comfortably fitting around her slender throat as he threw her to the ground. He climbed on top of her, feeling her tiny body squirming under his weight as he undid his belt. Nini's heart pounded against her chest. She struggled for air as she felt the pain of Richard's powerful thrust.

He let go of her throat and used the weight of his body to hold her down, thrusting deep inside her, pinning her hands down as she used whatever strength she had left to try and break free. Moments felt like forever until Richard finally lifted his sweaty body off of Nini's.

Still, he fixed his gaze on her. Still, she refused to meet it. As stubborn as ever.

She tried to catch her breath as tears cascaded down her temples, her nails digging deep into the soil as she curled herself up.

Richard took a deep breath, exhaling with satisfaction as he tightened his belt back up. He took his flask out and finished his whiskey as he left the shack, taking the lantern with him.

"I hope you get everything you deserve."

Richard stumbled upon hearing the small voice. He looked back, wondering if Nini had spoken, but the words were so soft—like a faint breeze—that he figured it was the whiskey talking. He shrugged off the thought and left.

CHAPTER FIVE

Richard slept in later than usual. And it would have been longer if not for the clacking of shoes disrupting his sleep. *Mary*, he instantly grumbled. Who else would have been trotting around so early?

"Damned woman. Shut up!" Richard yelled before throwing his water glass from the night table at the door, not purposely trying to hurt her but just to give her a little scare.

There was no response.

Richard opened his eyes, a nudge of apprehension coursing through him as his groggy mind contemplated the possibility that he might have actually struck her. Instead, he saw a terrified Thelma standing in his doorway cradling white bed sheets, the broken bits of glass only a foot away from where it had collided with the wall.

"What the hell are you doin' in here so early?" Richard asked.

In broken English, Thelma said, "Master, it nearly noon." She presented the sheets in her arms. "Come to change sheets but did not know Master in bed still."

Richard squinted hard and twisted his face, taking a moment to figure out her words through her thick accent. He groaned and sighed, the memory of Nini's warm body underneath him suddenly rising to the surface of his mind. He thought briefly of last night—how his muscles stretched and pulled as a result. They had yet to be accustomed to not only his age but also her defiance. However, the soreness only proved their time together was not a figment of his imagination. He let the memory ruminate before flashing a satisfied grin. He told Thelma, "Go on. Get to it," as he meandered out of bed.

The morning sun seemed warmer than usual as Richard prepared for work.

Mary was already out of bed, prepared, most likely in the library, wasting her day away in another book. He kicked at some of his clothes on the floor as he stretched. He looked at the shack from his bedroom window, sitting without shade from a tree. As Thelma—who now wore a headwrap upon Richard's orders to cover that unsightly mane— slowly fixed the sheets, Richard turned to her and said, "Let someone know to get Nini out of the shack, and I want you to tend to her wounds. I expect her to be ready by tonight. Understand?"

Thelma froze a moment, wrinkling her brow as she quickly glanced out the window, seemingly surprised, but Richard wasn't sure about what. Eventually, Thelma nodded.

Richard left to start his day.

As usual, James and Richard sat on the porch, watching Richard's property work the cotton fields. And Benji, the driver on duty, sat atop a brown horse nearby as he also kept his eye on them, occasionally scratching his friendly mutton chops. The field hands who were too slow or collapsed from the heat—or seemed to be taking a break or slacking off—were to be whipped until they rose to their feet, continuing to work.

Richard looked at the slaves' cabin a few times, antsy. His thoughts wandered to Nini, how good she had felt pressed against his body, feeling her racing heartbeat against his. He hadn't seen her all day. He also hadn't seen Thelma all day, either. It couldn't take that long to fix up a few scratches on a mere girl's back, could it? But deep down, he knew even the toughest male slave took time to regain strength to work again after a whipping. How much had he hurt Nini?

No, he thought harshly. *She brought it on herself.*

He'd expressed civility, and she'd turned him down. She was his property, and she should have been honored that he stepped so low to attempt knowing her. But as the sun set, a beast growled inside Richard, and he wanted to spend more time with Nini again.

The cotton for the day was turned in.

Richard went to the slaves' cabin. The dwellings here were primitive, fitting for their needs, at least offering a roof over their heads. The place had dirt floors and poor, crude, wooden structures. Although on some plantations, slaves lived spread out in a cluster of single cabins, here, there were two small communal cabins where they effectively had a shared space.

Richard rarely, if ever, visited the slave quarters.

He'd wondered why Thelma had chosen the field hands' dwelling to tend to Nini when she could have easily done everything in the domestic residences by the main house. Forcing their master to make such a long journey… Richard fumed, assuming this must have been a pathetic attempt to avoid him. To hide Nini from him.

He stepped inside and saw Nini lying on a makeshift mattress—a large sack filled with corn shucks—and a simple pillow made of straw tucked under her head.

Thelma was finishing redressing the wounds on her back.

As Richard entered the room, the slaves scattered, moving as far as they could from him, avoiding looking his way. But Thelma stayed by Nini's side, even when Richard told her to move away.

"Not done," she said.

"What do you mean you're not done? I gave you damn near all day."

"Hard," she said. But Richard didn't understand. "Hard," she repeated.

"The wounds are severe."

Richard turned. The boy, Solomon, sat cross-legged on the opposite side of Thelma and Nini. His broad nose was pointed up, large eyes focused as he gazed upon his master. Somehow, he looked out of place.

Richard's gaze fell on the herbs and a bowl of red liquid at the boy's side.

"The wounds," the boy repeated. "She says it took a long time to clean and wrap. She had to gather herbs to do so, sir. The girl keeps on plenty bleeding. Lucky she didn't bleed out."

"No. Her time is up. No more dressing. It's done."

Richard tapped Nini's wrapped ribcage with the tip of his boot, nudging a little harder when she remained still. "Get up," he said. "Time to return to the house."

When Nini didn't react once again, Richard heard hushed murmurs from the others cowering in the corners of the cabin. Feeling his cheeks turn red, he grabbed Nini's arm and yanked her to her feet, ignoring Thelma's protest and futile attempt to stop him.

Nini pushed away, trying to reclaim her arm from his tight grasp. Richard's blood boiled as he raised his hand and felt the sudden sting from slapping Nini. Her head jerked to the left, but Richard gripped her by the jaw and forced her face to his.

"Don't be daft!" he spat, his voice growling dangerously. "You are my property, and you will listen to your master. I'll show you what happens when you defy me."

Tears welled in the corners of Nini's eyes as Richard prepared to drag her off.

But Thelma stepped closer to Richard, her hands in front of her, but before she could attempt to calm the situation, Richard punched the older woman in the stomach with the side of his fist when she refused to move out of his way. It was a hard punch, too, the sort a man would take.

Richard watched her stumble backward, gasping for air and coughing violently. He suddenly heard those once hushed whispers become louder and feet shuffling.

Sweat started to bead at the top of Richard's forehead. He grabbed his pistol and pulled back the hammer, pressing the trigger in the air. Everyone recoiled. "Now, all of you stay where you are!" he warned the others. "I'll shoot anyone stupid enough to move any closer."

From the corner of his eyes, he saw a brave soul challenge his claim.

He turned his gun before him.

A sudden, hot liquid flicked at Richard, sizzling his skin and dripping down his face and neck as he pulled the trigger again. The boy, Solomon, fell, crying as he held his knee.

Thelma rushed to the boy, embracing him, but Richard pointed his gun at her, forcing her to step away.

The cabin door swung open as James and other plantation workers rushed in, pistols in hand. The slaves again coiled back to the dark shadows.

"Richard, what's going on?" James asked.

But Richard was too preoccupied, grasping the side of his neck. At some point, he released Nini, who was by Thelma's side. Richard peeled his fingers away to see red coating his fingertips. "What'd did you just throw on me?" Richard asked the boy.

No one responded.

Richard raised his voice, pointing his gun. "What you throw on me, boy?"

Thelma raised her hands. "Chicken!" she cried. "Blood. Chicken blood!" The substance thickened and tingled against Richard's skin.

James stepped closer. "Richard, what happened?" he asked.

But Richard, filled with anger, just stared at the boy clutching his knee with tears streaking down his face. His eyes seemed to plead for mercy, and the wails of his mother echoed around him. But Richard would have none on this day.

"Lynch the boy."

Thelma wailed, throwing Solomon behind her and sinking to her knees, pleading with Richard. Hers was the only voice speaking up for the helpless boy among the faceless mass.

James waved his gun at Thelma. "Shut up! Or the boy shall only get it worse!"

But she didn't.

"Hush up now and stop that cryin'," he said again, gentler this time for some reason. Perhaps James was able to feel something, some sort of hidden emotion Richard lacked. This was a mother and her child, after all. Was it not natural she would protect her boy?

But when Thelma threw herself between her son and the overseer trying to take him, James pointed his gun and yelled, "You stay back!"

James cocked the gun, prepared to fire at Thelma, but Richard said, "That's enough, James."

James stood back as if recoiling; did Richard truly speak those words?

Thelma looked up to Richard with slight hope in her eyes. "She'll hurt more when she sees Solomon's body hang off the oak tree branch," he said next. "I think we will save her for that."

All hope fell from Thelma's eyes. But after brief sadness, her eyes darkened, shrouding with anger. Deep whispers spewed from her lips.

"Speak up," James told her.

And she did.

She spoke in a language the white men couldn't understand. Louder and louder, her voice grew. Even some of the slaves seemed confused, some frightened. Soon, her words echoed from the shadows, seemingly just whispers from nowhere that grew to deafening heights. The chants were not from the slaves' mouths, though Richard believed they were coming from them. That was until he realized their mouths weren't moving.

The hairs on his arm stood. He looked around frantically.

"What's wrong, Richard?" James asked.

But the chants only grew louder, more chaotic and disorienting. Yet no one else reacted. It seemed Richard was the only one who could hear the cacophony of the shadows, the many voices coming from one mouth. No, it couldn't be.

"Enough!" Richard yelled. And everything besides Thelma's mumbling fell silent.

It took a moment to compose himself and come back to reality.

James prepared to fire at Thelma, but Richard stopped him by raising his hand, fearing the slaves would soon rise if Thelma was killed. They were not prepared for that; besides, it would be a spectacle that would only draw the wrong kind of attention to the plantation.

"Get my money back for her by selling her at the Chatham County Courthouse next Tuesday," he told James. "Sort it today. Get her listed and speak to the auctioneer. She must go, whatever the sale price. I'll not tolerate her sort around here."

Richard fixed his gaze on James and other plantation workers, then cried out, "And take that surly boy to the oak tree. Right now. Spare him no mercy, you understand?"

And, of course, they all did understand.

The boy needed a public flogging before his evident demise.

Solomon was pulled from Thelma's arms, kicking and crying for his mother. Richard turned and looked at Nini, who was holding Thelma back. There was so much he wanted to do to her right now, so much pain he wanted to inflict, but with all that had just occurred, with all the witnesses about, now wasn't the time. The time would come again after dark, with no prying eyes.

Richard stumbled as a voice he could have sworn was familiar whispered, "I hope you get all you deserve."

He flinched, his blood running cold.

Last night… had he not heard similar words then, too? Words he wasn't sure of?

And like last night, he questioned himself, wondering if those words had somehow come from Nini or if he'd imagined it once again. He stared at her while leaving, wondering if it was only his own mind playing devious tricks, the same way he'd determined the chants must have been.

The door slammed behind the men. All around, he could hear their crackling laughter between the boy's screams. Soon, they became distant, and suddenly, nothing more was audible.

CHAPTER SIX

Richard took a moment, tucking in his kids for the night, making sure that he gave his daughter her teddy bear. "Daddy, what was that gunshot from earlier?" she asked, snuggling deep in the covers.

"Oh, most likely some useless property getting what was comin', like what will be comin' to you if you don't mind your own," Henry teased.

Richard gave him a look. "Henry, don't talk to your sister that way," he said as he put Henry's blanket under his arm.

Margret asked, "Daddy, what happened to your face and neck?"

Richard touched it. After the incident, he'd gone to the closest mirror to assess the damage. Red blotches from the chicken blood were scattered down the left side.

"I touched something very hot," he told her. Margret reached out to touch it, but Richard kept her hand away. "Still stings a little. Now, be a good girl and just go to sleep."

Margret put her hand atop the blanket on her stomach. But still, she eyed the burn as though studying every blotch on his neck. She seemed to be assessing him, keen to understand.

"Daddy, why do you never tell us stories?"

Richard knitted his brows. "Now, why would you ask a thing like that all of a sudden?"

Margret pursed her lips.

"Maggie?" he coaxed.

She slowly raised her teddy bear, hiding her lips behind its scruffy head. After a pause, she said, *"Thelma* always has a story for me."

"What?"

Margret nodded, slowly revealing her face. "Thelma and I talk while she folds the clothes and does some of her chores. She tells me stories of the magic and miracles she's seen."

Richard tightened his jaw. "Does she, now?"

She nodded cheerfully. "But I hadn't seen her all day. When I found her, she seemed upset. So I haven't heard any stories. And I do hope Thelma won't be so upset she goes away."

Richard tightened his grip on her blanket, angry that the old hag was conversing with his child. And not only that either; he also knew now that if Thelma were to be sold, his child would suffer. Perhaps that had been Thelma's ploy all along. He fumed at the thought. And it struck him then—the realization that perhaps this was how his own father felt when he'd interacted with Abigail.

But he calmed himself, deciding to let it pass since Margret seemed so happy. He knew Henry never wanted to play with her, so Richard had always worried she'd be lonely. It seemed Thelma being around had helped somewhat. But she would still have to go. He'd find a playmate for her somehow. But it couldn't be another slave. The risks were far too high.

Suddenly, Margret asked, "Daddy, do you believe in magic?"

Henry balked. "Are you so stupid?"

"Henry!" Richard snapped, giving his son a look that made him shrink back. "Mind your sister."

Henry mumbled, retreating into the sheets. "Sorry, Pa."

Richard's stern gaze lingered for a moment. Then, he turned and nodded for Margret to continue. "Why?"

"I hear some of the workers in the barn talk about it a lot. They say there might be a witch among them. A witch who can cast spells and everything."

She sounded excited. This was the problem with having children near niggers. Their dirty color spread by way of equally filthy black rumors and stories, affecting the children's minds.

Richard sighed. He had warned his daughter so many times to stay away from the barn, yet it was like beating a dead horse.

It was dangerous for his children, or anyone else's children for that matter, to wander the plantation alone because he figured wild slaves could harm them. But he supposed the fault would lie with whoever was to watch her. He'd have to deal with them later.

The barn was at least one field away from the house, with the slave cabins for the field hands being farther yonder, quite some distance.

Before James had come to work at the plantation, Richard had made the house slaves live outside in the cabins with the field laborers and other slaves.

However, the slave cabins for the field laborers were sited so far away from the manor house, so it made sense to have some of the house slaves reside on-site. This way, they were there on hand if Mary or Richard needed them to do something, rather than them being sent for from a distance away, which could take far too long. Sometimes, Richard had caught Mary completing a certain chore herself rather than waiting for the house slave to arrive and do it. It irked him too much, which was one reason why he'd prefer the house slaves to have better access to the house.

But he'd picked them with care. Richard only had a select few residing in or close to his home. And even then, those slaves lived in a particular part of the house, downstairs next to the kitchen and other rooms where they did most of their work. It kept them out of view, too. After all, didn't he see enough of their brown skin out in the fields? It would make him sick if he had to encounter it in his own house at all times of the day and night. No, they would stay invisible.

Though the field workers lived yonder, a majority of the domestic servants had quarters in small cabins on the side of the house, and Margret wasn't far off from exploring said quarters.

If she did, he'd have to tan her hide, which was something he didn't want to do. So best cut it out before it festered. "Margret, how many times do I have to tell you to stay out of the barn?" he scolded. "You're not allowed in there."

"I know," she said, looking down. "But the slaves bring up that they believe in magic, just like Thelma."

He sighed again. He really was going to have to nip this in the bud. "There is no such thing as magic," Richard said. "And it's time for you to sleep."

"Then maybe the slaves believe in magic and witches from the storybooks," Margret said.

Richard scoffed. "Maggie, there's no such thing as magic or witches, and them niggers can't tell a word from cotton. Now, if you don't go to sleep, I'll get a real witch on ya."

He pointed to Mary's room.

"Pa," Henry groaned, a ghost of a smile on his face.

Richard chuckled. "Time for bed now."

"Wait!" Margret grabbed his hand. "Could *you* tell me a story?"

"Not tonight, sweetie."

She frowned, looking down at her pillow.

Richard sighed, unable to bear being the cause of that sad look on her face. "I have to think up a good one for you. How's about I tell you one tomorrow?"

Margret beamed. "Promise?"

"I promise. Now, sleep. The both of you."

Richard kissed his children as they all exchanged goodnights. He went to his bedroom as Mary was still getting ready for bed. Richard could have slept apart from her, but since the house housed a few of his plantation workers, he'd continued to sleep in the same bed for no other reason than to maintain appearance. Especially for his children. There were some mornings when one child or the other, or both, would surprise them. They loved to jump on their bed and wake them up with noises or walk in at night when having nightmares, and they'd start asking questions if they missed Richard in the bedroom.

Richard removed his wedding ring and slid into bed, and Mary soon followed, their backs to each other.

"Margret told me that one of the slaves was crying in the kitchen," Mary said.

Richard shifted in under the sheets, rearranging his pillow. "Don't worry about it," he said.

He thought about what had taken place in the slave cabin. He couldn't explain the strange whispers he had heard; were they imagined? But Richard didn't believe in superstitions and decided to let it go, putting the night firmly behind him.

He drifted to sleep without a second thought.

Richard struggled throughout the night, his throat and face where the blood had touched burning like fire. His stomach ached and cramped as his brain pounded against his temples. Mary lay still, undisturbed. Unable to take any more discomfort, Richard decided to leave the comfort of his bed and wash his face using the basin on the dresser adjacent to it. He stared at himself in the aging mirror, watching as water dripped from his stubble beard and thick mustache. Slowly, his body began to sway. The world started to blur and darken, going black a moment later.

The sudden sound of glass-shattering screams woke Richard from his deep sleep. He opened his eyes, his vision slowly coming into focus, realizing they were Mary's shrieks of fear. They were horrifying, the sounds of a woman plainly scared out of her wits. He turned to the terrified woman, her face pale in horror as she cowered at the far end of the room. She was afraid of something right behind him. He turned and looked—but there was nothing at all.

The dark had given way to the day by now, and he could see perfectly well, even if it wasn't quite light yet. It must have been the early hours, perhaps five or six o'clock.

Mary, you're having a nightmare, stupid woman. Go back to bed!

She only shrieked again, this time even worse. She stared as though he was an apparition, forming her face into a terrible sight all of its own.

"Who are you? I beg you, don't hurt me!" she repeated.

What has gotten into her? To be acting like someone mentally deranged so early in the morning wasn't doing any favors for his throbbing head. Still groggy from sleep, he wondered if he was still dreaming or not because he couldn't explain her panic. Why would Mary be asking who he was? Perhaps she'd had too much to drink.

But no. That wasn't Mary. Certainly never so early in the morning.

Richard picked himself off the floor, scrambled to his feet, and balanced himself using the bed. Then, as he stood looking around, he caught a glimpse of something heinous; there, right before his own eyes, was a tall and wizened black man standing in the room. If the good Lord had blessed him with half as loud a voice as his wife's, he would also have screamed the place down. But right now, he had no voice at all; it had been jolted out of him from the sight before him. Startled, he quickly grabbed his gun from the holster he hung on the side of his bed every night and pointed it at the black, but the nigger only seemed to mimic his movements.

The action made Richard pause. *What am I dealing with here? Has the man lost his wits?*

He stared at the stranger, then cocked and aimed the gun—at his own face staring back at him. His hand visibly jittered as if trying to escape his own skin. The figure jittered, too, the same way.

Richard knew he was seeing his own self, except that right now, here in this moment, it was not his face he viewed. It was him all right because each tiny movement, each tremor, each breath, each flick of a finger, was mirrored by the man in such fine detail that he would have had to be a mind reader to get the actions correct. It was indeed a good thing he had not fired in the panic of the moment; the ricochet from the mirror might have blown his own head off.

Oh no, there was no mistaking that Richard was staring at his own fair self, except that he was no longer fair at all. Not fair, but dark, a black man, in fact, a negro, a nigger!

His skin color was one of the darkest he'd ever seen, even on a black man, and his usually tidy, slicked-back hair stood kinky and unrecognizable.

This isn't real. This can't be real.

By now, he had laid down his weapon, and his hands were busying themselves on top of his own head. His fingertips were feeling around, touching the curls on his pate, taken aback by the rough texture. Disgusted by his appearance. *No, no, this is just a dream. A nightmare I'll wake up from soon. That's not really me.* But he paused again. This black man's face and neck were burned too, livid burns that looked as though they would never heal. And he could swear they were in the exact same spot the blood had hit him the day before when that vile wretch had flung chicken blood while the crazy nigger woman chanted. He touched his neck.

The devil himself had been at work here.

Yes, for sure, the devil, with his evil ways, had only gone and turned him into a black man!

By now, his wife had fled, and her panicked tones reached his ears, jabbering to someone loud and animated, interspersed with the howling cries of a woman in fear for her life. Then came a deep voice, a resonant voice… familiar.

Whoever it was, a man seemed to be here in the house with her. She must have fetched help.

He grabbed hold of his gun again as the bedroom door swung open, and Richard saw James standing in the doorway in a nightshirt carelessly stuffed in dusty britches, his gun drawn. "Your name, sir! Right now, or I shoot!"

Richard tried frantically to speak, his mouth opening and closing like a fish on dry land, but the only sounds he could make were mumbles and gasps. It left him only able to raise his hands, flailing his arms in the air, pointing at himself with wild and insane-looking gesticulations. *Me, me, me! It's me! I am Richard. Richard, you blind fool! Can you not see who I am?*

Fear and confusion engulfed Richard as he couldn't explain what had happened to him or why he was unable to speak. It was as if his tongue had been cut from his head, leaving a weighty void in his mouth. Mary rushed to stand behind James.

"What's going on? Who in the Lord's name is that?" James asked Mary. She was standing away from the door, as far away as she could while still viewing the intruder, saying a quiet prayer into the room as if it could clear the atmosphere of a spirit.

"I don't know. I woke up, and he, he was just lyin' on the floor," she cried.

"Where is Richard?" James demanded. "And why are you sporting Richard's attire? Answer, boy! You are a ruffian and a thief! People like you get to hang! A scourge on society!"

Richard pointed at himself again as he mumbled loudly. Soon, other workers, including Benji and Parkinson, ran into the room, stopping in the doorway at the sight of him. "Christ," Parkinson said. "Who gave a nigger a gun?"

"One of you go get Richard," James said.

One man quickly ran out of the room, crying out as he went, "I will, but where is he?"

Nobody could answer. Indeed, where had the slave owner gone?

"I haven't seen R-Richard ever since—" jabbered Mary, stabbing a finger in the man's direction.

I'm right here! Richard screamed in his head as he hit his chest. He tried to form the words, but none would leave his lips. He looked around the room. *A pen. I just need a pen.*

James turned to Richard. A few men advanced on him, but he remained still, not sure what to do and certainly not in any way accustomed to fleeing. He owned this place and every man in it!

He thought of fighting back, but James still had a gun pointed at him, and Richard didn't want to shoot his friend either. *Have to stay calm, stay calm, Richard,* he told himself. But Parkinson and Benji lunged, disarmed Richard, and beat him about the head with heavy wooden stakes before grabbing him on both sides. He cowered, holding his hands above his head.

At this time, the man James had sent out rushed back into the room.

"I couldn't find Richard anywhere," he said out of breath.

"Did you check the stables?"

"The stables, the office, the backyard, everywhere. He's nowhere to be found."

James pursed his lips, huffing out a frustrated breath through his nose. "Then go check the slave quarters. He's here somewhere. This bastard will have tied him up. Better not have shot him."

The man nodded and rushed back out. James approached the apparent black man.

"Where's Richard?" he asked. "Where have you taken the master?"

I'm right here! he screamed, but still nothing escaped him.

When Richard didn't respond, James hit him hard on his face with the barrel of the gun. It was hard, yet not hard enough to break a bone. Not yet anyway.

"Speak," James admonished, "or I'll put a bullet between your eyes. How did you get into Mary's room? And where is Richard?" Again, he couldn't respond. James whipped the pistol through the air and hit the side of Richard's face harder this time. "Answer me!

"I'll kill you, nigger! Coming out from nowhere to abduct the slave master and now daring to come back here to do more vile deeds? Oh, so you think you dare, do you?" he shouted, spittle flying from his mouth onto Richard's face.

He stared hard at Richard's shirt. "Wearing the master's own garbs? So the very least you'd come here to rob and steal, tryin' to pass yourself off as the master. Why?" He sneered and leaned closer. "You came here for Mary, did you? You wanted her, too? Well, she's fortunate to have woken before you could have your way with her, you filth!"

James pressed the barrel of the gun against Richard's neck. "One last chance. Where have you taken the master Richard McLeary? One. Last. Chance."

All the while, Richard couldn't speak.

James' eyes were deep-set, piercing, and black. Richard recognized the undeniable murderous intent from a previous debacle when someone had challenged his friend's leadership, but he wondered what had brought it about this time.

James wasn't the type to kill a slave so easily, but something had him really riled up more than he would have been. A black man, or what appeared to be one, was in a white woman's room. Richard's heart raced, terrified beyond belief.

He's really gonna kill me.

Richard made a noise, something he couldn't recognize himself as he tried to form words. His neck quivered as his vocal cords strained and produced nothing but the slightest of feral grunts, the same sound the genuinely mute slave might make. It caught everyone's attention.

James scrunched up his face in bewilderment. Then he leaned forward for a better look. And he jumped a little as if receiving a jolt of some kind. There, on the black man's neck, was an odd burn mark. He moved Richard's face to the side with the gun barrel to get a better look.

"Well, I'll be damned. Look at this."

"What is it?" Benji asked. He looked to where James was pointing.

"The one person who might know what happened is mute," James said, letting out a frustrated sigh. "But look. This scoundrel bears the same marks on his neck that were inflicted on Richard yesterday. Something is afoot here. Never have I seen such a thing. Not in my lifetime."

"So?" Parkinson said. "Just ask what they are!"

"*So* we can't get any real answers from the nigger. You didn't happen to notice that for yourself? Are you so stupid?"

"We could put the mysterious fella in the shack until we find his owner and find Richard," Benji said. "Or we hang him upside down from the tree. He already looks in bad shape, so that'll bring something out of him."

I am Richard! I am!

James nodded. "Take him outta here. Either of those possibilities will suffice."

The men hoisted Richard by the arms, his feet dragging through the halls as they brought him outside. But before Richard was removed from his home, he passed the children's room. Henry and Margret peeked over the corner, Margret holding her teddy bear. James followed closely behind the men.

"You two see branding on him?" he asked.

Parkinson yanked up Richard's shirt. "No, nothin'," he said. "He's not marked. Unless those things on his neck are some sort of brand. Could be."

James nodded.

"Would be nice to have free stock to add to my cotton fields," James admitted with a chuckle, forcing Richard to bite his lower lip. "Especially after that stunt Richard pulled off at the auction. Cost us way over the odds and we still got no useful hands from the trade."

They dragged Richard past the cotton fields, past the fearful looks of the slaves he usually beat daily. James swung the shack door open, tossing Richard inside.

He hit the dirt and watched the door close behind him. The shack was pitch dark, but he knew someone else was in there with him; he could hear the dirt moving under the body as a hand extended toward him. Richard quickly slapped the hand away.

Don't touch me! he thought. The nerve of a slave to touch him.

The man seemed to be taken aback. With Richard's eyes slowly adjusting, he realized the man was only making gestures. And he was attempting to help.

"I have never seen you before," the man admitted. Unable to speak, Richard tried to point to the main house, but the slave simply pointed to Richard's chest, then placed his own hand to his, repeating the gesture. "Friend," he said. "I care for friend."

Well, in a different place and a different lifetime, Richard might have felt moved by this. As it was, he felt only revulsion. *Yes, well, get away from me. You'll soon see I'm not your friend.*

CHAPTER SEVEN

Richard furiously banged on the shack door for what seemed like hours, at least according to his growling stomach. It was not hours. Not yet a quarter of the hour, to be precise. After but a few minutes in the dark, critically observing his body after being thrown in there, Richard perused his mind to know how the hell he'd ended up the way he was. His mind had taken him to a very bad place. One to which only bad men went, not a man who did nothing but tend to his workers and look after his family. No, Richard was sure he was a good man and true, not deserving of it.

It was his own mind playing tricks. Though *why*, he couldn't know.

There was only one other possibility, and this was that he really wasn't Richard at all.

Nothing else in his new body proved that he was, except his memories. His hands were weather-beaten, his knuckles wrinkled and gnarled, and his fingers sitting crooked. His arms and legs were wrinkly too, undernourished, looking dry and dehydrated. His toenails seemed to have been attacked by some sort of a white fungus or an unpleasant affliction, and there was jet-black hair sprouting from his body—on his chest, his arms, his legs.

His face was rough and itched like insanity itself, while a straggly, unkempt beard matched the coils of unruly and disgraceful black hair atop his head. This was not Richard.

Somehow, the memories and sentiments of the plantation owner had been sucked into the body of a black man, he thought. This happening was a crime, a revolting affront.

The black man—if he was one—felt most grievously affronted to find he had a white slave master inside of him, like the very worst possession. The white man was revolted to discover that he inhabited this black and voiceless, powerless, unhygienic, and stain-infested body.

However, deep inside, Richard knew the two were one and the same. His new body held no nigger's memory, and the slightest things betrayed him. Richard felt at the faint indent on his finger where his ring used to be, then the crooked teeth he had tried to hide from Samantha days before, and finally, he touched the tender skin on his burnt neck. This new body? Was it actually his? No, it couldn't be. And the thought of admission only made him more disgusted.

Either way, it couldn't work. The man was afraid of his own skin. Of his own color, no less.

A few hours in, Richard had yet to work out or to believe what had happened to him. And his overseers looked set to kill him, blaming him for the disappearance of his former self.

At some point, Richard remembered the mumbles Thelma had spoken on him the previous night—or what he thought had been the previous night. His thoughts were melding and merging now, becoming fuzzy with the unrelenting blackness of the shack. But there came a vague recollection of the words spoken in some foreign tongue, a tongue from the continent of Africa, so he believed. He thought he recalled seeing her head down, but eyes upturned, shadowed by the heavy furrow in her brow. He was locked in place as the bright whites slowly seemed to become black voids, sucking him in deeper and deeper, as though his soul was being pulled from his body as she incanted.

Her words had come fast and furious, her tongue moving a thousand times a second, her body attaining a rhythmic sway. And finally came the appalling boy, flicking that redness at him. Since then, he had only washed and slept, and when he'd awoken, there it was. The affliction.

And the redness he thought he had washed from his throat had stained him, the mark of some kind of a vile curse from the dirty habits of the country from which the blacks themselves came!

Figuring Thelma must have had something to do with his situation, he banged on the door. He needed James and the others to call for Thelma so she could undo what she had done to him, removing the spell and returning him to normal.

Margret had been right after all. There was a witch among them.

So he stood, and he banged. And he stood. And he banged. And no one came.

No one even said a word, though he was sure he heard a shuffling noise outside.

For now, he was stuck in this skin as dark as night, with its fattened lips and curly hair.

"I don't think I've seen you before," the man in the shack said. Even after Richard's eyes had fully adjusted to the dark, he still couldn't see the man's face clearly, but the slave introduced himself as Pico. Richard knew him well. Pico was a hard worker, one of the best, in fact, one who seemed to keep the other niggers in line and docile, even suppressing many a rebellion or uprising.

Yet Richard would never trust having black slave drivers, even at James' request.

Lord knew he didn't trust them niggers to run things or look after themselves.

Nevertheless, James had insisted on a trustworthy driver to be a bridge between white and black, making it easier to keep slaves in line. At one point, Richard and James considered making Pico a commandeur, but he was a cheeky fellow, lying often to get others out of trouble, taking it upon himself to bear the punishment. So, after some talks, they'd decided against it.

Richard continued to bang on the wooden door, ignoring Pico's banter, too preoccupied with trying to get someone's attention.

At first, when Richard had entered the shack, Pico spoke to him using single words and gestures, in short, treating the master as if he was unable to comprehend even the simplest of terms. As if he was an imbecile or mentally retarded. But the sole reason had been because he wasn't sure that Richard understood English, no one getting a reply, no matter who they were.

He'd even tried speaking in a language Richard couldn't comprehend, a language that, at its utterance, offended Richard's ears; he stomped his foot and thumped the wall with a fist as if to say, *No, no, don't make me listen to that!* It also sent confused and intolerant glances Pico's way. When all that failed, Pico finally asked, "Tell me, do you understand me?"

Richard gave a brisk nod. Ever since that, Pico hadn't shut up. Pico now knew that Richard followed his meaning, so he started with his banter and lengthy conversations.

"What is your name?"

"Where are you from?"

"Why don't you speak?"

"What's that mark on your neck?"

"Why do you wear the massa's clothes?"

"Are you a new purchase?"

"You don't need to be afraid of me. Why do you flinch when I come near?"

If he wasn't out of his mind before, Richard certainly was now.

Even now as Richard furiously banged on the door, Pico *still* had something to say.

"You should stop making noise," he said, tucked away in the farthest corner of the shack. "You'll anger the massas and end up punished if you don't. You're new. You don't know yet."

I don't know? I don't know yet? I own the place! Richard thought.

Moments later, Richard heard keys unlocking the door. And outside, he saw the colors of twilight. Four men stood at the entrance. Two of them—Parkinson and Benji—walked in. Parkinson immediately locked eyes with Richard, sparing no time in coming forward and smacking him in the face. Richard stumbled sideways, nearly hitting the wall.

"Knock it off!" Parkinson yelled. "All that ruckus… Damn near made my ears bleed."

Richard rubbed the side of his cheek and clenched his fists. He had barely been here and was already tired of being hit in the face.

As he gathered himself, Benji pointed to Pico.

"You," he said. "Your time's up. Get back to the field. I better not catch you sneaking food from the other fields again. Next time, it'll be more than just a whipping."

Pico took himself from the corner of the shack. As the other workers dragged him away with one man on either side of him, Richard attempted to leave as well, desperate for the sight of the sky and to feel the air against his skin. But Parkinson pushed Richard back inside.

"That wasn't an invitation for you. Stay put."

But Richard didn't. He tried again, lunging for the door. Somehow, he had to let them and James know his situation, but Parkinson blocked his path, and it took the two to throw him to the ground. Now that they had him subdued and where they needed him to be, they kicked and beat him worse than Richard's memory of a drunken brawl he'd had in his twenties when he foolishly picked a fight with the biggest bloke in the tavern, all to impress a lady, no less.

He thought back. Much of what he'd done had been to impress someone or another. Whether it was to impress the ladies, his family, his father, or the society in which he moved and mingled, his whole life as a man was all about impressing. Yes, he'd tried to impress the whole lot of them, and now look where it'd gotten him. This impressed no one.

Not even himself. *Especially* not himself.

Their fists were heavy, not holding back. Once they were done, Richard was left on the ground. Parkinson and Benji turned to leave, Parkinson spitting at the floor. Richard painfully moved his body and reached for the door, but it closed, locking again behind them.

How could they leave me like this? No, more than that, how could they treat me like this? Can't they see who I am? Don't they know I am their master? This is a terrible crime, and when I get hold of them… Then he realized. He had no way to get hold of them. He was at their mercy.

Richard fell to the ground. Lying on the dirt floor injured, he wished only to feel warm again, to feel fed again, to feel empowered. Right now, he was none of these things. He was a wounded animal, left to rot in here, nobody caring. He curled into a fetal position, hoping sleep would take him to a better place. But there would be no sleep. Everything about his body ached, and he was cold and starving. How could sleep ever come in such a predicament?

They were treating him worse than he'd treat anyone.

Then a thought came: *Except I treat my slaves this way. But only as they deserve it!*

Suddenly, in the next moment, there were voices. Richard groaned as he dragged himself upright again and pressed his ear to the door. He spotted a narrow crack in the wall, but it was large enough to faintly see Parkinson's and Benji's backs as they walked over to James.

"Nigger's got some fight," Parkinson said, his voice in the distance.

"Yes, well, I'm fixin' to break his fingers if he keeps at it," James said.

"Don't worry," said Benji. "Parkinson took care of it."

"I've never seen a nigger pitchin' such a fit like that one there," Parkinson said. "Whoever the boy's master is didn't do a good job wit' him. Seems to think he's someone."

James nodded. "Any updates on the current situation regarding Richard's disappearance?"

"We've thrown multiple search parties since yesterday mornin' to find him, but none have been successful. And it's nearly too dark out now to continue lookin'."

"I ruled out kidnapping," Benji said.

"And why's that?" James said.

"Well, Mary said she went to bed with Richard at her side. If there were a struggle, she surely would have woken."

"Couldn't he have just gone out for a walk or somethin'? Could have been snatched up that way," Parkinson said.

"You think Richard's the type to go on early morning walks? He doesn't even like walking the fields," James said. "If he went out, someone must've carried him. Bundled him up and borne him out in their arms. I know it sounds humorous, but that's how I see it. He wouldn't walk. And not before he's had breakfast, for sure. Has anyone checked? Did he eat?"

Parkinson shook his head. "Didn't eat. There's his bread roll on the side. He would've—"

Benji cut in, "Have we heard anything from the mute's owner yet?" Parkinson glared at him for the interruption, but Benji ignored him.

"No," James said. He moved his mouth, churning his jaw as though chewing. He always did that when in thought. "Two mutes on the plantation… What are the odds?"

"You think we should question the other slaves? See what they might know?"

"Why don't we just question *him*?" Parkinson asked.

They paused. "He's mute, remember?"

"Yeah, but he got fingers, don't he? Make him spell it out."

James and Benji just stared at Parkinson as though he'd just used a hammer to pick his teeth.

"That's if he can spell," James muttered.

Richard shook his head. It was very well known that slaves were not literate. It was a shame he had to make it clear to the men; it just showed they were not too bright either. When Richard returned, they'd have to set about hiring again.

The reality was that the slaves could speak, sure, because of hearing conversations here and there and being raised on the plantations, but how would they ever be able to write? It was against the law to teach niggers, and for good reason. The more you taught them, the more likely you were giving them ammunition to rise up.

Sure, Parkinson could hold his own in a fight, but brawn didn't make up for brains.

"…educate… very much doubt…"

Richard couldn't hear what James was mumbling now; it was too quiet. He couldn't help but wonder if James' babbling was aimed at him or Parkinson. But he could see the man shrug and shake his head.

"Have you forgotten niggers can't read or write? What good would havin' him 'write' in the dirt do? Even if he could write, his fingers are—"

Parkinson thought for a moment, stroking his peach fuzz as if straining hard to even think. Then he interrupted.

"Could… Could he draw pictures?"

James, Benji, and even Richard himself rolled their eyes and groaned collectively.

"What?"

"You ain't the brightest, are you, Parkinson?" James said.

"Yeah," Benji agreed.

"Hey, I'm just throwin' out suggestions here."

"Well, he won't be writing or drawing any masterpieces in the soil with the state he's in," Benji said. "You're talking as if you never saw him. It's gibberish you're spoutin', the ramblings of a delirious man. He's deadbeat. So *I* suggest we start questioning the others. They're bound to know somethin'. Maybe he has a lover among the batch."

James shook his head. "How? Richard doesn't let 'em leave, let alone interact with outside slaves unless they have to. Hell, he rarely allows the select few to go into town to run errands with a pass leave. Besides, if we start lettin' the other slaves know we don't know Richard's whereabouts, they might start gettin' funny ideas. Best keep 'em productive."

"Then what are we supposed to do? As far as I know, this nigger just came out of nowhere."

James sighed and put his hands on his hips. "It does seem that way." He churned his jaw. "How about we discuss what actions we can take?"

Parkinson suggested, "Well, he was found in Richard's bedroom. I think he should be castrated and lynched. Ain't no way he didn't try to force himself onto Mary. At least castrate the bastard and hold him up as an example to the rest."

Richard gulped. Unfortunately, Parkinson had finally birthed what might seem to all the others his best idea yet. Richard knew how James especially would think. And in his own absence, there was pressure on James to act in such a way that'd please him on his return.

Unfortunately, this likely meant that James would act more ruthlessly than usual.

It was not his normal way, but he'd want to keep Richard happy and show how he'd managed the plantation and the slaves in the master's absence. He'd want to excel.

Richard's guts churned. He was about to vomit.

James' brows furrowed as he stared Parkinson down, a look of disgust and—was that anger? "If Mary's safety was in jeopardy, that nigger should be killed if he tried that. If he's touched the master's own wife, he's signed his death warrant, I can tell you that."

Benji gave James a questioning look. "Why are you so worked up all of a sudden?" he asked. "I didn't think you were so close."

James snapped back to attention. "We're *not* close, and I'll thank you to keep your unwanted opinions inside that thick skull of yours. But I'd be damned if I'd let Richard's wife suffer in his absence. You know about his father's agreement. I'm responsible for that now that Richard's away."

Benji and Parkinson seemed satisfied by his answer, giving him quick nods in agreement.

James cleared his throat, changing the subject.

"Anyway, I don't think the mute should be emasculated," Benji continued, countering Parkinson's suggestion. "Castration reduces a man's strength and that'll make him useless to us when we're short of hands. And lynching should be out of the question for the time being since we don't know whether someone owns him or not. If or when his owner gets him back, he won't want him without his balls intact. We'd have to pay for him."

Richard released a relieved sigh he didn't know he held.

"So…" Parkinson said. "Castration's been ruled out?" He seemed terribly disappointed.

"He's not our property. And as much as it seems likely, something tells me he's not a runaway."

"Come on, now. Surely he's a runaway."

"Why the hell would a runaway *run away* straight into another plantation?"

"He could have gotten lost. The nights are dark."

"So lost that he wound up in Mary's bedroom? That's quite a problem with his direction."

Parkinson shrugged.

Benji scoffed. "Fine, say he's 'lost?' It would still be lawful for any *decent* person to apprehend a slave whom they believed or suspected to be a runaway if they couldn't present their freedom papers. Not go around damaging what isn't theirs."

"Says the guy who stomped into his ribs."

"Says the guy who couldn't bring down one simple nigger by himself."

"I was handlin' him just fine!"

"Enough!" James said. "Runaway or no runaway, we are obliged to return him to his original owner. Now, we just gotta find out who that is."

Parkinson smacked his lips.

"Oh, hush up, Dwight. If you wanna castrate someone so bad, go buy your own goddamn nigger."

"Maybe I will."

"With what money?" Benji said.

"Now lookee here—"

"Fellas!" James scolded. "The owner?"

Benji and Parkinson exchanged daggering glares. "We could bring him to the local authorities to do so," Benji said. "The fees incurred for taking care of the runaway until he's found in the process have to be repaid by the owner…"

Benji's words trailed off, and James seemed to notice. In fact, the two men suddenly brightened at this realization. Their voices dropped. Richard moved, trying to better hear his workers' conversation some ways beyond the shack.

"Benji," James said, doing his chewing motions. "How much did Mr. Edgar get for returning a runaway? Can you remember?"

"The reward started at 150. But the owner got real desperate when his runaway didn't show for nearly three months. Raised the reward to a thousand dollars. So…"

James nodded, a hint of a smirk on his lips. "Hmm, so…"

Everyone was thinking over the options, and one in particular seemed alluring.

Benji Cohen seemed to like the idea too.

He was the son of the overseer who worked for Richard's father. He was forty-five, only older than Richard by three years, and he was intelligent, an opportunist with the instincts of an animal, partly why Richard had hired him years ago; Benji's hunches were rarely wrong.

The dark-haired man was docile and assertive, not at all abrasive compared to Parkinson, but he was always calm and logical, always assessing situations or managing to spot any situation that could rule in his favor or that was the more just and righteous route. Unfortunately, he had the nasty habit of being a borderline pacifist. He wasn't against the discipline of slaves, but Richard got the feeling that, like Mary, Benji didn't always agree with his harsh and brutal methods.

"Mary says she woke to him passed out on her floor, right?" Benji said.

"So? What's that got to do with anything?" Parkinson asked.

"What about the likelihood of the boy ingesting some type of poison that confounded or confused him? Would explain why he was so disoriented to have found himself in such a situation. Besides, the boy looks strong and should be put to good use in the fields. He could replace the other one." Benji nodded towards the oak tree.

For a second, Richard asked himself what 'other one' he meant, then remembered Solomon.

James nodded in agreement with Benji's suggestion. "After that stunt Richard pulled at the auction a couple of weeks back, we need all the help we can get. While waiting to get word from his owner, we could get free labor and possibly compensation from his master. Better still, the longer we hold him, the fatter the payout. Even if the owner never shows, we'd still get a free slave out of it. It's a win-win, wouldn't you say?"

Parkinson, finally seeming to catch up to what the other two were talking about, asked, "Well that's all fine and dandy, but who will run Richard's plantation while he's gone? I vote me."

James gave him a cynical but amused look.

"What?" Parkinson said. "Y'all get too soft runnin' these niggers sometimes. They need an iron fist like Richard's."

"An iron fist, not a joker," Benji scoffed, raising a brow before shaking his head.

"You were the one soundin' like an idiot, sayin' the mute wasn't a runaway."

"And what exactly have you accomplished that makes you the next Isaac Newton?"

"I've done plenty."

"Name one thing."

"What's going on?"

All three men turned, looking behind them to someone Richard couldn't see from the crack.

"Mrs. McLeary," Benji greeted, tipping his hat. "How pleasant to see you. We were just discussing who would run the plantation in Richard's absence. The debate got a little out of hand. I'm very sorry if you had to be hearin' it."

"I see," she said. "Oh, believe me, I get to hear a lot worse, especially when my husband's about. So think nothing of it. But I suppose there hasn't been any luck finding Richard yet?"

"No, ma'am."

There was a slight pause. Richard wished he could see her face. Though he couldn't, he imagined her feeling enthralled at the news. If he went missing permanently, she could become a wealthy woman. She'd either have to take a new husband for herself after he'd been missing for some time, or she would have to sell up. His blood ran cold at the thought of her selling off his livelihood and everything his own father had worked for and given to him.

"In that case, I think James should be acting master for now. He *is* Richard's secondhand and closest friend after all," his wife proclaimed.

Parkinson and Benji groaned.

"Well, you heard the lady," James said, turning to the two men with a victorious smile. "Shouldn't have been a debate to begin with. But now that that's settled, it's time to get to it. You two, carry on searching for Richard. You'll hunt night and day till he's returned to us. Dead or alive."

Eventually, they parted ways.

Richard sank to the floor in anticipatory agony. Thinking about being flogged at the slightest provocation, the overworking every single day except for the Lord's day, the Sabbath!

Then his heart sank even further; he'd also just remembered he'd removed Sunday days off.

Richard thought about the boy hanging at the oak tree. Would he end up like him? His mouth felt dry. How much was he about to suffer? He refused to be subjected to the life of a nigger! Slowly, Richard began to understand that his life was going to be in disarray from now on.

He needed to fix this, and soon. But the problem was, he just didn't know how.

CHAPTER EIGHT

All of his energy was gone, spent on banging the door of the shack. It was hard for Richard to know how many days had passed since he'd been locked inside. In that time, Richard contemplated the few ways he could explain his situation to James since he was mute.

If James knew what had befallen his friend, he could haul Thelma forth and get her to remove the wretched curse she had applied to him.

Yes, that was it. That was the solution! Just tell James!

If only I could get a pen and paper, I could—

But he stopped himself. How the hell would he acquire pen and paper? It was against the law for niggers to be literate. Being caught reading or writing could earn him one hundred lashes. And after one hundred lashes, since he didn't have one-third the bodily strength of the niggers who were so accustomed to manual work and getting the lash, the flogging could kill him.

Even if he managed to procure paper and pen, Richard had a strong feeling that wouldn't be enough. Who would believe anything a nigger had to say? Who'd even bother to read what he penned?

Richard cursed himself for even referring to himself as a colored man. The whole thought of it twisted his thoughts as well as his guts, constantly threatening to make him sick. And if he were sick, then this space was so small and so cramped that he'd be made to lie in and smell and see his own vomit. And, of course, this only made him feel all the worse.

Out of ideas, he tried to speak on occasion to test his voice but abruptly stopped, hating the humiliating, undignified, and degrading grunts and sounds that he produced.

But he couldn't help it. Now, a terrible thought came: was this how Nini had felt when he'd forced himself on her? He had listened to those same unintended moans and grunts of despair.

And he had done nothing to help her, only thrusting into her even harder, enjoying the noise.

The darkness overshadowed the small beams of light passing through the splintered wood as it quickly faded away. As Richard lay on the floor, feeling a slight breeze pass through the gap between the ground and all, his angry, empty stomach cramped and growled as his mouth felt dry and his throat sore. Familiar voices started to approach closer to the shack, then Richard heard their footsteps, and the shack door swung open.

He coiled back from the bright sun, covering his eyes.

James and Benji stood in the doorway, pulling Richard onto his feet and out of the shack.

"Looks like I have myself a new slave," James chimed. "Be grateful. You get to work out in the cotton fields with the others. It's good work. Healthy work. You get to breathe clean air."

The two dragged Richard some ways beyond the shack before shoving him forward as he stood before them.

"Strip," James said.

Richard hesitated. He looked at the gun cozily holstered at James' side.

Another in his hand casually pointed to the ground, perhaps a precaution from him banging on the door so much and trying to break his way through. Richard remembered how easily James had resorted to wanting to kill him after that incident in his bedroom.

After hesitating, flushing top to toe with awkwardness and

embarrassment, Richard removed every last shred of his clothes. If he played his cards right, it should be simple to keep out of trouble since the field slaves only usually got in trouble for disobeying or not pulling their weight. So he just had to do as he was told until he figured out how to remedy the situation. *Simple enough.*

But one question did remain: would he be able to work as hard as the others? Or would he be singled out for trying to make things easy on himself?

He stood nude, his clothes tossed lazily to the side, feeling somewhat humiliated. Richard never was ashamed of his body, but standing in front of his peers and being told to strip was a different story. As a white man, Richard had sun-tanned skin, a well-defined waist, and broad hips. As a black man, Richard was tall with broader shoulders and strong, sturdy legs.

But on the other hand, as a white man, his skin had been largely unblemished, soft, and supple, and had always been protected from the harsh rays of the sun when it was at its peak. As a white man, he applied creams, lotions, and potions, bandaging up his skin when he became even slightly injured. He'd also worn a wide-brimmed hat to protect his face and eyes. But now, as a black man, his sturdy legs, wide back, and muscled arms were pitted and bruised, marked top to bottom in welts and unhealed wounds and thickened ugly scars. They'd clearly received no protection from anything—not from the rain or the sun, or a good thrashing. But his neck remained unmarked, perhaps the only parts not reached by the beatings.

"Turn around," James said.

Richard paused a moment, giving a soft, annoyed sigh that made James squint that same look of when a slave was close to stepping out of line. Richard caught himself and turned slowly.

"No scars besides the one on his neck," Benji said. "Not a single mark or blemish besides the ones from the beatings. You'd think he'd led his life as a prince."

"No wonder he's so unseemly. Show me your hands."

Richard lifted his hands.

"Palms up."

He turned them over.

James scrutinized them. "Flawless," he scoffed. "This man has never done a day's hard work in his life. But that'll all change very soon. We'll soon give him scars, right enough."

James nodded toward Benji, who turned to retrieve something.

As Richard waited, he saw Solomon's body swinging in the background. Well, there was no way he'd ever end up like that boy who'd been foolish enough to attack his master.

Richard reminded himself that if he played his cards right, he'd be fine.

Eventually, Benji returned with a set of clothes in hand. The soft thud of the clothes landing in the dirt at his feet snapped Richard's attention back into focus.

"Some proper clothes," James said, pointing. "Put them on, now. Cover your ugliness."

Richard stared at the clothes—one pair of plain, sturdy, unblackened leather shoes without buckles, breeches, and two long-sleeved shirts made of osnaburg. Richard looked into James' eyes, appalled at the idea of having to wear the same clothing as his property. But James squinted back in his familiar way. It was a manner Richard had seen many a time when James eyed a worthless slave.

"I don't know what plantation you come from, but you listen here, cuz I'll only say this once. You need to keep your head down. You hear?"

James' voice was low and dangerous. Richard looked away.

It's rude not to look someone in the eye. That's how you assert dominance.

His father's words rang in his mind. Yet there he was, averting his eyes like a common thief caught in the act. It was intolerable. Undignified.

In his absentmindedness, Richard studied James' boots, moving to his rolled-up white sleeves and brown vest before his gaze flicked to Benji's dark coat. Richard blinked his urge away but ultimately locked eyes with James again, only for a moment, because the room spun as his head tilted from the force of the overseer's hand.

Richard's head was knocked to the side, and a burning sensation warmed his cheek. His hand came up to rub the spot, and he noticed James lowering his own. He'd slapped him faster than his brain could process. As a master, he was to make eye contact. But when he was the opposite of a master, to lock eyes meant being insubordinate to the worst degree! The very same problem Richard had encountered in Nini, in fact.

"Don't look me in the eyes, boy," James said. "You'd be wise to remember it next time. Now, as I said, get dressed."

Richard stared at the dirt, angry, wishing he could speak. He picked up his clothes from the ground and flushed top to toe yet again to be so berated. Now, he was forced to dress as the other two watched. Perhaps this wouldn't be so simple after all, to try and do as he was told. He had seen how the drivers loved to play games with the slaves, one man giving one instruction, then a second saying another that contradicts it, as if trying to draw them into conflict to be worthy of punishment just to punish them in the end.

"Too bad we don't have a name for him yet," Benji said. "What do you think we should call him?"

"I'll think a somethin'. There's a few names coming to mind already. None of them nice."

They laughed, and poor Richard felt the burn of their collective ridicule; it seemed he couldn't do right for doing wrong! No matter how he behaved or tried never to argue back and always to follow the ever-changing 'rules', even just the act of breathing and living was already drawing him into trouble. They seemed to deem every small thing he said or did, or any look he gave worthy of either their scorn, punishment, or both.

Richard finished up by tying his pants with a single knot. Once dressed—the coarse and ill-fitting clothing chafing his delicate skin already—Richard was shoved to the fields. This was most peculiar; his skin and body looked tough and well-seasoned with hard work and long days of exposure to the worst sun. Yet he felt so weak, so incapable, and his skin was so tender.

For a moment, he stood, looking around, unsure of what to do. Some field hands stole quick, curious side glances but were swift to continue their work.

Everyone around knew better what to do.

"Stop your lallygagging," James called. "Move!"

The blistering sun beat down on Richard as he struggled to figure out quite how to pick the cotton. Telling him to do it was one thing, but he had no idea how! He'd been on the plantation his whole life with his father having passed down these cotton fields.

But despite his life experience running the fields, he had never known how to pluck the cotton from the stem. In fact, he'd seldom watched them; in any case, watching and doing were two different things. Richard tried to observe the others, but they moved too fast for him to keep up.

A sudden, gentle hand touched his shoulder, causing him to jump. But when his eyes looked into the kind eyes of Nini, a look from her he wasn't used to, his worries seemed to drift away.

Richard figured James must have moved her from the house to make her a cotton picker again to get the numbers back up. Still, without speaking—and with a soft smile—Nini showed him how to work the cotton. With careful, nimble fingers, she dug at the base of the cotton mound, curling her fingers around it. She gave it a small twist until it gave a little snap and pulled it from the boll. She dropped it into the basket and then did it again, but faster.

Did she, and maybe other slaves, not suspect it was him? But then again, why would they? They probably just saw him as another purchase as Pico had. Just another chattel.

When the two heard horses' hooves, Nini quickly slipped away, returning to her post, but not before dropping a warm smile for him, a genuine smile, showing a full row of white teeth. Richard might have been a slave to them, but he was still Richard at heart. As Nini left, he stared at her back, something sour churning in his stomach. He clenched his jaw, inflamed at the fact that Nini was showing such kindness toward the black version of himself, but never to him as Richard, never to the white man.

James approached Richard, looking into his basket with a hardened gaze to assess how much cotton he was picking. Soon, Richard saw that gaze assessing his slave skin. James roughly grabbed hold of one of Richard's thick hands, running fingertips along them before commenting, "Baby soft. And unspoiled."

But they really were not; the biased overseer evidently chose to see whatever he liked in a slave. In reality, Richard's hands were rough and pitted in places, at least compared to before.

But he thought that, no doubt, James wanted to see him put in some hard work.

He invariably craved to see welts and calluses developing on the soft nigger's hands, even if he had to whip them into shape to get them looking so.

Well, at this rate, it'd have to be the latter. Richard wouldn't get the toughened, shiny palms that the others had by hard work if what he'd picked so far today was any indication.

Nini had helped Richard in more ways than one, adding cotton to his basket instead of her own. But it hadn't been enough.

A quick snap of the whip hit Richard's back. He'd felt the sting of a belt before from his father, as most young boys did, but this was a lot sharper, more painful than he'd ever felt.

"Move them fingers, boy!" James said.

Richard tried to yell, but no voice could be heard as the whip snapped again, sending a spasm of pain through his spine. He could feel the slow warmth dripping down his back as he tended immediately to the cotton, remembering what Nini had shown him.

Her lesson had at least made the grueling task a little easier.

The hours passed. Richard's stomach growled. He was starving since he hadn't eaten in several days of being locked up in the shack. He felt as though he'd pass out, but the fear of being whipped again kept him on his feet. But Richard knew the day would end when the sun started to set. Then what? Where would he stay? The questions echoed in his head. Nini was already done, allowing him the chance to watch her confident walk back to the slaves' cabin.

Richard followed the line of slaves with their baskets and bags filled with cotton while his barely reached the edge.

Feeling a nudge in his basket, he looked down. Cotton was being slipped into his basket from behind again and again. Richard watched as other slaves slipped cotton between them, moving up the line and placing their share into his basket. Now, his basket was full.

These sneaky niggers, Richard thought. *How long have they been doing this? And right under our noses! No wonder production fell short.* But he was conflicted. He wanted to curb that behavior when he was normal again, but at the moment, he needed the aid. It also struck him how the niggers helped each other out. It wasn't a thing he was accustomed to in his own world.

As the white man, even as the master, no one came forward to offer help to him without first engaging in some sort of a discussion about a trade. If he gave this, what would he get back in return?

There was no time to stand and ponder on it all, however, as Richard was next in line, pouring the contents of his filled basket into the barrels in the cotton shed adjoining the gin house.

A familiar voice carried across the field, reaching Richard's ear. He looked to the door, his heart warming. There in the distance, near the porch steps of the house, was his daughter, wearing a pink ribbon.

Margret looked in all directions to see if anyone was around before peeking into their secret spot. The first step of the porch was the loose tile on the step that he'd caused when he was younger. It creaked more but didn't open unless moved a certain way. Richard told Margret about it, so they'd made it their secret place to hide goodies.

He did this when Henry took her candy, so it was just the two of them who knew about it. A couple of weeks ago, he'd left her the pink ribbon she was currently wearing in her pretty hair, putting it into their secret spot along with some peppermint sticks.

He'd left a bag of lemon drops there, too. Now, Margret was peeking under that step to see if perhaps her father had left anything for her. Then he saw her let out a sad sigh. She closed the lid of the step, disappointed to find nothing. Disappointed to know that her father had gone and abandoned her, leaving her sad. For a moment, his shoulders slumped, and he closed his eyes with a sigh, but he quickly tried to shake the feeling, thinking it better not to focus on how his heart felt tight in his chest.

As Richard turned, something whipped across his vision before landing with a sharp crack against his face. His eyes instantly began to water as he let out a pained grunt. Stumbling back and holding his bleeding cheek, he felt warmth drip down, this time between his fingers and down his neck.

As he fell to the ground, a kick to his stomach knocked the air out of his lungs. James looked down at him, a tight hold on the whip handle. James was only a few inches short of Richard's six-foot frame. But in that moment, he felt larger, towering over him.

Until now, Richard had never realized how intimidating James could be.

But why? What had he done wrong now?

"Mind your eyes," James warned. "Never look at the child again. If I catch you bravin' a look at the master's children, I'll take this knife and drag it right across your eyes. You hear me, boy? We all know what the dirty colored types do to children."

James kicked him in the chest. Richard painfully gasped for air as his nails dug into the earth. His natural reaction would be to fight, but he reminded himself what would happen if he did, and he wanted to reunite with his daughter again. Someday, he hoped it would be so.

James demanded two slaves bring Richard to the cabins, roaring, "Get him out of my sight." Two black men helped Richard up and brought him past the cotton fields away from the house and to the cabins. There were two small cabins in total and a small camp in the center of the buildings with a large cooking pot in the middle dangling over a fire.

Richard was taken to the farthest cabin.

The two slaves ushered Richard inside as he held his bleeding cheek, trying to fight off the stinging of tears. His eyes met Nini's the moment he stepped through, and she let out a surprised gasp, but the surprise quickly dimmed, replaced with a saddened yet casual look, no different than a doctor used to seeing a mangled body. She got up and pointed to the floor where a pillow and lantern lay unused. He didn't hesitate and lay down in defeat, rubbing at his sore chest, which was sure to bruise by morning. Kneeling beside him with a rag in her hand, Nini inspected the new wound he bore.

So she treats wounds too, Richard thought. The man who had sold her to him had been right about her being a jack of all trades. He wondered what else she could do, what else she was hiding from him. But then again, was she hiding it, or had he just not seen it? He didn't know, but right now, he was simply aware that whatever he needed, she seemed to offer. She was simply looking out for him, seeing how things went, helping without a hope for anything in return. Warmth and kindness oozed from her. And he loathed her for it.

So, I see your game, being all generous of spirit with the dark-skinned ones, the unpleasant ones. Never with me, Richard, your lord and master. Well, we shall see about that.

Richard sat up as best he could, but she held up a hand for him to take it easy. Her gentle touch made him recoil at first, mostly because of the painful sting, but a part of it was because he was still mad that she was treating *this* Richard better than the white one.

Nini grabbed his chin and wiped away the blood from the lash. As he looked into her eyes, Richard saw how soft they were. He was so used to seeing fire behind her glare, the sharp slants of her brow, but now, they were loose. Soft. Kind. Giving. She was silent as she cleaned his wound, as she always was. He wondered how she'd become mute. Was she born that way? What would her voice sound like if she hadn't been? Maybe he was just in his head too much.

As Nini tended to his wounds, a young-looking man knelt by Richard, offering a bowl of water. As soon as he spoke, Richard immediately knew who he was.

"I am Pico," he said, introducing himself again in what Richard could only describe as some distorted African Creole dialect. It was a common Creolized language arising amongst plantations, but only his older slaves had heavy accents. "Remember me from the shack?"

Hard to forget, Richard thought as he scooted away as best he could, albeit very little.

"It's all right. We are not your enemy. Here. Drink." Pico nudged the dirty water at Richard, offering him a drink. Richard hesitated. The disgusting smell from the water made his stomach turn, but after days of no food and water, his thirst outweighed the disgust.

Nini and Pico smiled as their new 'friend' drank, though Richard saw them as the furthest thing. Still, Richard hated when she'd finished with his wounds and pulled away. Nini finished wrapping Richard's back, the bandages covering his waist and stomach. She gathered her things, dropped him another smile, and moved on. Then, she left to tend to other slaves.

Pico handed Richard some food, and on receiving his dry bread and sauce, which looked like loose human feces, he contorted his face in disgust. Even in his hunger, he couldn't get the supposed sauce past his throat and only managed to eat the bread.

All the while, he wondered if this was really what his own slaves' food was like.

As Richard devoured his ration, idle chatter among the slaves resonated through the cabin—a mix of murmurs and banter he didn't care for, too focused on being rid of the pain in his gut.

"Massa McLeary."

Richard stopped chewing. He looked up from his meal, desperate to find the slave who'd called to him. But then another called his name. And another, no one sparing a single glance in his direction.

That's when he realized: the slaves weren't calling to him, they were talking *about* him.

Richard started chewing again, slowly, honing in on the conversation centered around him. They discussed among themselves how they hadn't seen Richard and speculated if their master was missing. If so, where could he be? Maybe he was away on another trip. Some spoke in another language, which he hated, some English, and others both.

Either way, he focused on the conversations. They were curious about his absence; some even relieved the "cruelest master" had gone missing somehow. Richard wished he could punish all of them for speaking so ill towards their master, the one who had given them everything.

Was this idle and vicious chatter what they always did? This was the disgusting way they usually behaved when the overseer and master were out of sight?

That would have to be corrected as soon as he was back in charge.

"I hope he never comes back," one of them said. Her mumble of the words drew Richard's attention. She was staring down at her feet, picking at one of the calluses on her toe. He was sure her name started with an A, but he couldn't recall the rest. But why bother remembering when the only thing that mattered was that his slaves did as commanded?

The girl continued. "No good will come from his return."

"I wonder if any of this has to do with Thelma," one said.

"Perhaps he's away to another auction," said another. "Picking up more pretty boys and girls, no disrespect to you, Nini, because you're wonderful, you work hard… But he has an eye for you."

"I feel sorry for whoever else he purchases."

They quickly glanced at Richard.

"Some believe you are a new replacement," Pico suddenly said. "Are you?"

Richard shook his head.

"I see. So just a new purchase. Then I must warn you, it's best to keep your eyes off the Massa's children. What Massa Walker did to you was light punishment compared to what Massa McLeary would have done. Massa Walker's touch is soft compared to his. Massa McLeary, he takes a cruel interest in makin' you hurt as much as possible."

Richard opened his mouth to speak but froze, remembering he couldn't. *A cruel interest?* He only handed out punishments as deserved! It wasn't as though he went around daily choosing a slave or two to beat as though he was picking an apple to enjoy.

"Will you tell me your name now?" Pico asked.

It was instinct for Richard to try and speak, but knowing he couldn't, he thought of other options. He raised his finger to write in the dirt but quickly stopped. Writing would draw a lot of unwanted questions. And he knew from years of experience that some in the bunch had no hesitation to rat out their peers who weren't a proper fit.

Instead, Richard tried to speak, but still, no words passed his lips. Finally, Pico understood.

He placed his hand on Richard's shoulder, at which Richard stared as though it were shit on his boots. "Silence is best in the cotton fields, but at least you're not alone anymore," Pico reassured him. "You're in a family now." He gestured around the group. "We're your family."

Richard inwardly scoffed at the saying, but then he thought for a moment. He looked around but didn't spot who he was searching for.

"What are you looking for?" Pico asked, furrowing his thick brows.

Richard pointed outside the cabin to the main house, but Pico didn't understand.

When he pointed to Solomon's body hanging on the oak tree, Pico simply shook his head. "Poor Solomon. Thelma is heartbroken."

But Richard didn't care about that. He pointed when Pico said, "Thelma."

"Thelma?" Pico repeated.

Richard nodded.

Finally understanding, Pico said, "Thelma works in the big place away from here. She sleeps away from us all with the domestic servants."

Richard clicked his tongue. On second thought, maybe he didn't understand.

"That might be a good thing," Pico reassured, about to say something with more meaning after all. "Thelma is a medicine woman, but some believe she's an enchantress."

He leaned forward, whispering, adding extra emphasis to the *sss* sound on *enchantress*. Making it sound like a stealthy snake in the jungle.

But Richard didn't care what she was. He only needed to make sure he could get to her before James took her to the courthouse on Tuesday. If she was sold as Richard had commanded, his fate in this place, this life that was no life at all, was sealed.

But he still had time to reverse things. He needed to make Thelma fix this.

CHAPTER NINE

The blistering sun beat down on Richard as his fingers fumbled with the cotton plant, trying to collect the puffy flower from its stem yet again. It was harder work than anyone had ever told him as a plantation worker. The pricks of the plant stabbed the tips of Richard's fingers to the point of numbness. At one point, Richard pricked himself so badly that he got angry and hit the cotton, forgetting where he was. A driver came over and threatened to whip him if he didn't curb his attitude. That's when Pico snuck over. "Showing emotion is bad. Will get you in trouble," he said before going back to his area. "Keep yo' head down. Avoid trouble."

It wasn't just how the picking hurt his hands that got to him. His tongue was swollen and bleeding at times, starved of water. His eyelids adhered to his eyes. Now, he felt more than tired, too; sleeping was extremely difficult for him because he had never in his previous life had to lie down on the cold, hard floor surrounded by other bodies, let alone on uncomfortable mats filled with corn shucks. He kept tossing and turning so much that he even disturbed some of his sleeping neighbors. And when he awoke in dire need of a cold shower to rinse off his sweat and grease or for water to drink to replenish his dried body, there was none to be had. None till morning. Anyone would've thought the water famine had come, but oddly enough, he knew it wasn't so since only just across the way, over the field, there was plenty of water in his own house.

The house of the plantation owner. The house that had everything.

As he worked, Richard searched for Thelma, yet couldn't see her.

Usually, he'd see her occasionally out washing or hanging the linens. Richard looked at the house. To the left was a smaller slave cabin where Thelma lived when she wasn't working in Richard's home. Usually, Richard wouldn't have this knowledge, not out of ignorance, but rather from lack of caring. He left James in charge of the slaves' sleeping arrangements. There'd never been a need or a desire to know where those dirty blacks lived.

He only knew now where Thelma was housed because Nini had tried to sleep there until Richard moved her. Knowing James, he'd probably removed Thelma from working the rooms in the house because of her defiance, not wanting Richard's family to be vulnerable if she decided to avenge Solomon, and also because she was being sold soon.

Suddenly, Richard was gently bumped.

He turned and saw the scarred face of the young slave he'd attacked after failing to capture the attention of Samantha's eyes. Richard had forgotten the young boy's name but frankly didn't care. The boy's face was almost healed, but the young man would forever be reminded of Richard's cruelty. And Richard, in seeing him, would forever remember the boy deserving it.

The young man didn't look at Richard as he plucked the cotton. He didn't even apologize for bumping into him, leaving him wondering if the young man recognized him. But Richard remembered what he'd looked like and figured it was unlikely.

The sun began to set, and the slaves duly turned in their bounty. Richard was still barely meeting the demands of the plantation overseer, more so his own demands, but he inwardly blamed it on the fact that he'd never picked cotton before, unlike the workers he purchased.

"I expect you to do better tomorrow," James said, and Richard was pushed out of the way as other field hands behind him turned their cotton in.

As the last slave entered the cabin, Richard watched them share food, making sure everyone had a few pieces of bread and peas. No person went without or was deliberately given less, and sometimes, they would even count out the peas to make sure nobody went short-changed. From the thinnest to the plump, the tallest to the short, women and men, they were all given the same. This was something Richard had never seen before. The only times he'd been with men of his own kind—the whites as he still thought of himself—a fight would almost break out each time there was a short supply of something everyone craved. Not so here.

Even more astonishing was that after the fair distribution of the food in which the thin, the weak, the females, and the old were given the same amount, a strange kind of barter began among a few. "Give me your bowl," commanded one, receiving the bowl of another across the dirt where they sat cross-legged. "Here, take this. And eat it all up."

The vulnerable were now being given extra from the plates of the others. Had Richard owned any organ resembling a heart, he might have wept at the compassion in the room.

But instead, he chose to think, *Ain't no accounting for stupidity. The strong give away their replenishment such that they'll soon become the weak. Must be weak in the head already.*

Richard watched as a few slaves spoke in different languages, including English.

These conniving ingrates, Richard thought.

He'd beat them for speaking that gibberish if he were still white. It was seen as a threat to owners like him because there was always a possibility of a conspiracy to revolt, organize some form of resistance, or some such, which was unacceptable.

Richard spotted Nini as he looked around the room.

No doubt she could see him peeking at her from where he was. It wasn't until she nodded to him with a smile that he realized he was doing the same.

"Not that one." Richard turned to see Pico shaking his head. "Feisty. Always in trouble with Massa."

Yes, and I would know.

Richard trailed Nini, watching her pass out food. Eventually, she handed a bowl to the young man from the field, the one with the scar who'd bumped into him.

Richard looked at him. The boy had a wide face with a cleft chin layered with stubble, a small nose, small ears, hollow cheeks, and large lips. His brown hair was short and knotted. Pico sat next to Richard, taking his hand and giving him two small slices of bread and a bowl of mush. He closed his fingers around Richard's hand, the bread encased in their joined grasp. *Eat*, is what the gesture said.

Richard eyed the food distastefully, but his hunger got the better of him. He knew that if he refused food the same way some of his past slaves had done to hasten death rather than continue working for him, he would join them underneath the earth. He knew to eat no matter what it was. Only those without intellect would do anything else. If it were said to have even an ounce of nourishment, the slave ought to be thankful for it and cherish it. To refuse was to die.

While eating, Richard, who wondered why Pico kept choosing him to sit with in particular, tapped Pico's arm and pointed at the young man.

"Oh, that one. That boy name Micel," Pico told Richard in his Creole. "He no longer speaks because he fears the white men."

Richard smiled upon hearing that, watching Micel eat while keeping his head down, his head almost touching the plate. Stooping like that, the boy couldn't meet anyone's eye.

Then Richard thought of James smacking *him*, ordering Richard to keep his head down if he hoped to avoid more beatings the same as the last, or worse. Richard dropped his smile, took a bite of his bread, and looked at the scars on Micel's face. They'd healed well but they were worn like war wounds, Micel no doubt never forgetting the battle. Then Richard thought of how he scarred the young worker before immediately moving on to the next, forgetting instantly. But as he always told himself when these intrusive thoughts popped up, *He deserved it.*

"His scar is almost like yours," Pico suddenly noted. Richard was unsure how to feel about it. Pico touched the burn on his nose. "See. Scar too. We all have scars. Massa, no scar."

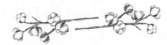

Richard remained awake when all fell asleep from a long day's labor in the fields. He rose from his mat and tiptoed over the plentiful bodies huddled together. But the sound of whimpering caught his attention. He looked down to see Nini shivering, but not from the cold. Her lip was quivering, and he could have sworn he saw something glint on her cheek. A solitary glistening tear. A nightmare, perhaps? But he didn't have time to wonder.

Richard snuck out at nightfall, knowing the path to avoid the plantation managers as he made his way to the smaller cabin tucked away at the side of his home. He rattled at the door handle, finding it locked as always. But there would be a window. Thelma's. In her room was a small dogleg alcove not visible from her bed, and by now, she should be sleeping. That window, he knew she kept it unlocked because late at night, he would sometimes see her tip ashes out. This was her weakness and his gain. He crept stealthily to the window and gently lifted it. The small but wide sash gave way, rolling upward with an obedient and smooth rumble. And he was in!

Thelma was sitting up as though she knew he was coming, yet oddly did not flinch. Her gaze gave him pause. She did not look afraid or surprised. She did not look—conscious.

Richard accidentally knocked a bowl over. Thelma slowly turned her head as if not with him in this world, as though she must be some other creature, one never unnerved; the gentle orange glow of the dim light deepened her wrinkles and showed the lackluster of her skin, her head wrap tightly coiled around her head. Richard crept up to her and looked her in her cold eyes.

She looked deep in thought as though looking through him. She sighed. Richard shook her as she woke up, seeming to snap out of her trance. She looked up and smiled at him. But then, Thelma looked confused, looking over his face as though unable to recognize him.

She did and yet did not, all at the same time.

Angry, Richard pointed to his burn scars and blotches, then pointed to the house. For a moment, Thelma held her curious brows, but then they raised. A smile stretched across her face. Richard waved his arms, pointing at himself and the house once more. She reached out her hand without any semblance of a delay or trepidation, running a crusty, aged fingertip across his neck.

She whipped his head to one side, and somehow, he obeyed. He didn't care what she saw or what she would make him do, what merry dance she might subject him to so long as she recognized who he was.

Thelma stood from her bed and approached Richard.

She looked him over, looked at the burns on his neck, looked at the scar on his cheek, still smiling. But when she looked into his angry eyes, she frowned.

"That look," she growled. "No guilt. Not feeling bad."

Richard stepped forward, breathing heavily, his nose nearly touching hers. In his head, he bitterly thought, *Why have remorse for a worthless monkey? I would lynch your nigger boy again and again and have you watch, you black bitch.*

Thelma saw the brazen look in his eye, and her frown deepened. "No guilt, no heart," she said.

She took his hand. Richard looked at it in disgust, trying to pry it away, but she gripped him tight—her strength surprising for a frail woman—and brought him to the doorway of the small cabin. From here, she pointed to the dehydrated and decomposing body of Solomon hanging from the oak tree. In broken English, Thelma whispered, "Feel what I feel. Feel it!"

Something came over Richard, something he couldn't explain other than how he had felt the night he'd heard those whispers. Whatever it was, it brought him pause and sent a chill up his spine, but before Richard could plead, the two heard the voice of a driver.

It was Parkinson, drunk as all hell. Thelma grabbed Richard by the collar and repeated her words, "Feel what I feel," in a raspy voice, and pushed him out of the cabin.

Richard fell onto the ground and looked up to see James standing over him.

"Well, now," James said, looking to the others. "Looks like the mute here was looking for some sweetness without permission."

James poked fun. Richard could tell from his slurred speech that he was intoxicated as well.

He kicked Richard in the face, causing him to taste the blood from the steady stream coming from his nose. As Richard rolled onto his back, a sudden pressure pushed down on his chest from the boot of another employed worker.

"Is this why you stumbled your way to the plantation?" James jeered. "Unfortunately for you, your little sweetheart is going back to the market tomorrow."

James stomped down hard on Richard's chest before taking a swig of his drink.

Parkinson kicked Richard in the ribs before James pulled Richard up, dragging him back to his cabin and throwing him into it. He nearly landed on a young woman. The taste of his blood stung his mouth as he watched the gleeful men walk away.

Richard looked at the other slaves. Some woke, sitting up at the melee, looking to see what had happened, while others remained still because the white men were near.

Richard didn't move, afraid that he had screwed up yet again. There seemed to be no way to win. No way to break through to become what he knew he should be.

Because he had been made black.

CHAPTER TEN

With a swollen nose, and his chest still hurting come morning, Richard slowly picked the cotton. He had tossed and turned all night due to his injuries. Nini and Pico were now noticing him wincing in pain as he bent over and put the cotton in the basket. Richard could see them rush around, hiding among the cotton and helping him pick, quickly filling his basket before the sound of the horn echoed in the air. Nini and Pico returned to their stations, slipping away with the cotton as their shadows. It was as if the two aides had never even been there, so cleverly had they disappeared.

It was past noon now. Richard had hit his target yet again, glowing inside to think how the overseer would be pleased with his work coming along, even while knowing much of the final weight was not his own. There was a sudden warmth in his chest as a subtle smile braced his lips. For just the briefest of moments, he felt a twinge of gratitude for the help so kindly rendered to him. Then it faded. His smile vanishing as he tensed once more.

Such idiots to waste their own energy to save another man's skin, he thought.

Richard snuck a wary glance at James perusing the fields, remembering his words from last night. He had been absent for nearly half the day, and it made Richard wonder if James might have successfully sold Thelma. Since she was an older woman, not many people would be willing to purchase her, so Richard had some hope that she'd return even if she had been offered. But at the same time, he also knew that the nuisance value of the woman would surely mean James would sooner have taken a low sum than returned with someone who could cause disruption.

James also had a knack for entrepreneurship and haggling; he could sell hay to a farmer. Richard's hope dwindled at that thought, but he shook it off.

He'd be damned if he gave up before seeing any proof.

All the cotton pickers lined up the same as the days before. Richard noticed an older slave, slightly hunched over, a few places in front of him. His name was Jackson. Richard had known the man for most of his life because he had been passed down to him by his father.

Jackson was one of the better pickers, always making quota and then some.

Even in his mid-age, he still outperformed some of the experienced pickers. The way he aged seemed slow for some reason. But now, he was in his mid-sixties. He was still trying, aiming high, but as the years passed, his numbers dwindled. Now, he was low on cotton. Richard was now sure he knew how ol' Jackson was making his daily quota.

Sure enough, the slaves were hiding their sharing, passing cotton bundles up, a field hand adding another to the bunch. But when it was Richard's turn, he shook his head and held a hand over his basket, refusing to pass the bundle. So, with a censorious leer, the slave behind him quickly cut in front of Richard to continue passing it up. Still, it wasn't enough. Not on this occasion.

Jackson presented his basket, and James sighed when he saw it was only half full.

"What's happened here? A little low, if I am not mistaken."

Jackson kept his head low. "I'm sorry, Massa Walker," he said. "I just wasn't feeling well today."

"Don't give me that drab. Being behind seventeen pounds isn't feeling unwell. It's laziness." Shaking his head, he turned to Parkinson.

"Take him to the whipping post."

The older man dropped to his knees to beg.

"No, no, don't do that, none of that," James said. "You'll only make this harder for yourself."

When Jackson didn't comply, James took out his whip and thrashed the man across the chest. The whip violently snapped back as James hit him again. Jackson clutched his chest, gasping for air.

"Take him to be whipped," James repeated, but Jackson raised his arm to him, pleading.

"Please," he said. "It won't happen again, sir. I ask for forgiveness. For mercy."

"Get up!" Parkinson snatched up the old man's wrist. With a violent yank, a sharp *pop* reverberated, the man's arm wrenching out of its socket. The ensuing screams clawed at Richard's ears as all remained still.

While others looked away, Richard watched, glad he hadn't donated any of his cotton, or he'd end up like the poor fool crying on the ground.

"God damn it, Dwight! I need a working nigger!" James said.

Benji, who was keeping records of the cotton, stepped forward.

"Should I call for a physician?"

Richard noticed the slaves around him tense up, holding their breaths.

A dusky-toned woman—Philipa? Or Phillis, if Richard recalled—quickly stepped forward. "There's no need to trouble yourself, Massa Walker. We promise we can fix him ourselves."

"Step back, girl!" Parkinson said.

James held up his hand. "What could you possibly know about fixin' a dislocated shoulder?"

"Thelma has done a lot for us, including showing us how to treat one another. We've seen her do it once before for Benjamin after that accident with the horse."

James made his chewing motion, sighing, frustrated by the situation. He turned his head to Benji, speaking in hushed tones. "The man's getting old. Shows in his work. Richard should have traded him a while ago." James weighed the situation. "If what the girl says is true, this is medical attention I won't have to pay for, especially after Richard's purchase."

Richard waited, wondering what James would do. To him, it was obvious: get a physician. Why trust the niggers to do a doctor's work?

Suddenly, James locked eyes with Richard, who scrambled, wondering if he should look away or not. "You and you," he said, pointing to Richard and another man. "Bring him to the cabin and fix him up. If he's not able to get back to work cuz you messed him up more, I'll have all your skins, you hear? Now move!"

Choosing the side of Jackson's dislocation, Richard tried his best to wrap Jackson's arm over his shoulders gently, but the man screamed wildly, his entire body flailing.

Damn, I'm already mute. You gon' make me deaf too? Richard thought.

"Not to worry, Jackson," the man holding the other arm suddenly said, some ways away from the cotton shed. "We won't let them doctors poke and prod you about, tryin' this an' that."

Richard followed closely behind as the others poured into the cabin. Older men and women spoke in their native languages, the women pointing to Jackson and the floor. After putting him down on the earth, Richard watched as one man held Jackson down while Phillis took his arm.

She braced herself above him, using her fingers to find the joint that had slipped its place. With a grimace, she jerked it back, attempting to set it, and he screamed out in pain. Phillis chewed her lip and began to press around like she might try again, but she failed.

Richard scoffed, figuring the woman must have obviously lied to James. Still, he was just glad it wasn't himself on the ground.

Nini quietly ventured close to Jackson's side, attempting to soothe the older man. She brushed her hand across his sweat-slicked forehead with a rag, but then Richard saw her steal angry glances in his own direction. He frowned, lines of confusion etching across his forehead.

What's got her all riled up?

Just as Richard took a seat, Nini rose furiously, taking long, angry strides his way. Richard looked up just in time to feel a sharp sting across his scarred cheek from Nini's heavy slap, stunned. Instantly, Richard shot to his feet, ready to retaliate with a habitual backhand, but Pico quickly stood between them.

"Share cotton!" Nini yelled, pointing furiously.

For a moment, Richard's anger stilled. He was shocked, not just from the slap but that she'd just *spoken* plain as day. *So I didn't imagine it.*

Richard looked to Pico to see if he expressed the same shock, but he was thrown yet again when Pico didn't show a hint of surprise. Why would Pico and the slaves not appear thrown that she had finally just spoken up? *Did they know she could all this time?*

Anger welled up in him again, and for a moment, Richard breathed heavily, exhaling harshly through his nose. He was ready to pounce but stopped himself.

All remained still while Richard forced himself to walk away, sitting in the farthest corner of the cabin.

As Jackson's screams continued to echo throughout the hut, Richard touched the cut on his left cheek. To his profound dismay, it had opened back up, the wetness of blood pooling to the surface. Richard tried to wrap his head around his own slave—and a *woman*, no less—not only hitting him but getting away with it! And he still couldn't wrap his head around her talking. What else was this whore hiding from him?

Richard watched their poor attempt to reset Jackson's arm, his annoying screams cascading along the wooden walls. *They'll mess up a perfectly good cotton picker by messing up his arm further,* he thought. *These niggers don't know what they're doing.*

Richard had even needed to set a few bones in his day, such as when James had taken a bad tumble off his horse, or when Parkinson got reamed trying to pick a fight with a wild boar. And Richard knew Jackson still had a few good years in him. He'd hate to waste the product.

Tired of watching, Richard shoved the woman attempting to fix Jackson's shoulder out of the way and grabbed the older man's arm. With a pull, Richard heard his arm snap into place. The cries of the slave started to die down as he took sips of dirty water; Jackson soon smiled.

"That worked a treat," the man said, addressing his indirect gratitude to the others who had tried and failed to help. "Never even saw it comin'."

There. Satisfied? Richard thought while looking to Nini as he nonchalantly waved a hand.

"Don't have to be so rough," Nini said in broken English.

Richard waved them off before going back to his corner.

Not even a thank you.

Pico walked up to Richard, who scooted away from him, still sulking. But Pico placed a hand on his shoulder and took Richard's hand, bringing Richard to Nini, who sat across the room. Pico brought him down to her level, taking her hand as well, and made the two hold hands.

"Friends," said Pico to Richard with a nod. He turned to Nini. "Friends, Zora."

Richard knitted his brows. *Zora? Perhaps he misspoke? Or he must have them confused. Thinks Nini is someone else.*

Nini turned away, refusing to look at Richard.

"Zora," Pico repeated, more forcefully this time. Richard's brows raised. His lips parted as he blinked at Pico, glancing from him to her and back again.

Zora? Was that her real name?

Eventually, she turned back to look at Richard and nodded, taking her hand back. "Sorry," she said stiffly, pointing to Richard's cut cheek. "Meant to hit other side."

CHAPTER ELEVEN

Richard looked around the plantation towards the house. He hadn't seen Thelma since the night he'd visited her cabin. Where could she be? Richard's worry increased, wondering if Thelma, his only hope to be turned back, had been successfully sold as he looked at Solomon's body, crows gathering and pecking mercilessly at the decaying skin. He tried to hold onto hope, but it wavered so much. What would he do if she had truly gone?

A few employed men to whom James spoke started for the road toward the willow tree. Richard noticed that the search for him was still ongoing, but his trusted ally, James, seemed unpleasantly comfortable with his absence. He no longer heard James repeating the importance of the lengthy searches for him nor of efforts to enhance the slaves' discomfort in case it might result in a slip of a confession stating what had become of the master.

It was feeling as though no one much cared. No one was missing him.

In the morning, as Richard followed the rest of the pack to the fields—he hated the long walks in the heat and wished he had his horse—a sudden pull on his arm took him out of the line. Richard turned to see James.

"You'll work in the barn today, complete some farm chores," he said.

Richard suspected as much. The slave who usually did these chores couldn't work.

Earlier, he had heard James tell Benji, "The dislocation and bruises aren't life-threatening, so there's no need for the treatment to be followed by a physician's checkup."

But they knew even a dislocated shoulder needed time to recover and that he'd be far slower picking with one hand in the field. So, they planned to move another slave to the fields as a replacement, filling in for the one whose arm just got messed up.

Richard was slower at picking cotton than him.

The dust from the hay tickled Richard's nose and stung his eyes as he moved the cut hay and made the stubby stalks into bundles. He found it less grueling than being pricked by cotton stems, and it was a welcomed break from the burning sun. Richard looked up from time to time, watching other slaves move the hay around. Suddenly, he heard the hums of a lullaby he used to sing to his children. When he looked over, he saw Margret playing with her teddy bear, making bunny ears out of hay and a bowtie using the pink ribbon he had gifted her. Richard let out a defeated sigh. She, too, looked and sounded happy.

It really was the cruelest twist of fate.

He'd always told her to stay out of the barn, but she usually never listened. And sure enough, here she was again, defying him. *Or perhaps her young mind has simply forgotten me.*

Richard stopped working for a moment and looked at his daughter's joyful eyes, wishing he could hold her one more time. But he didn't know how long he'd be stuck in his current predicament. His chest suddenly tightened. That thought brought slight panic to him, forcing him to take a deep inhale. Richard turned to his work to distract himself, trying to shake the thought from his head, but then he saw another slave take notice of Margret.

The man started to approach her, extending his hand. Fearing for his daughter, Richard pushed past the pile of hay and lunged, tackling the slave to the ground and straddling his chest. The man grunted, trying to push back, his arms swinging wildly but never connecting.

Margret let out a high-pitched scream and ran while Richard repeatedly hit the man in the face, the crunch of bone likely splitting his knuckles. Another slave tried to pull Richard off, but Richard elbowed him in the nose, sending him back. Richard's hand went numb as the world became a blur. He continued to swing his fist. Soon, the slave beneath him stopped moving. His face fell to the side, and his eyes closed, covered in blood. Richard heaved lungfuls of air, fist still raised, and only lowered it once he realized the man was unconscious.

"Well, would ya look at that."

Richard looked over and saw James and other white workers, slimy grins across their faces. Richard shuffled to his feet and quickly looked down, cursing himself for the submission.

James walked over to the man on the ground and tapped him with his foot.

"What happened here?"

"He asked you a question!" A carpenter demanded answers, but Richard could give none other than point. Margret had dropped her teddy bear before she ran. Richard pointed to it.

While no one seemed to understand him, James shook his head and picked up the teddy bear.

"Someone go get Margret," he told the others.

The men nodded and went out of the barn, calling for Margret. All the while, Richard could feel James staring. Angry or amazed? He didn't know; he couldn't tell from his quick glances up.

When they did bring Margret in, James approached her, handing her the teddy bear and resting his hands on his knees.

"Margret, what happened in the barn?" he asked softly.

Richard slightly lifted his head.

She was still shaken up. Margret was pursing her lips, holding her teddy bear tight.

"I won't be mad at you," James said. "Just tell me what happened."

There was a brief pause before Margret looked at Richard. "That slave," she said timidly. "He attacked the other one when he started comin' towards me."

"That one there approached you?" James pointed to the unconscious man on the ground. Margret nodded.

She turned to look at Richard, burning her gaze into him.

For a moment, Richard wondered why. Perhaps she was simply afraid of him. He did beat a man in front of her, after all.

"His neck," she said.

James briefly looked back to see what she was talking about. "What about his neck?"

"Daddy had a burn on his neck. That man has the same burn as Daddy."

Margret cocked her head to the side, analyzing Richard's face. She turned to James. "Don't you think it makes him look like Daddy?"

Richard looked up.

James scoffed. "I know you miss the guy, but that coon looks nothin' like your daddy, crazy girl. Now come on, you know Richard doesn't like you playing in here."

He ruffled her hair with a caring touch, bringing the sting of tears to Richard's eyes.

Richard watched Margret steal glances at him as she was ushered out of the barn. When James turned to him, Richard instantly looked back to the ground.

"Obviously, I need to keep a closer eye on you," James said, slowly approaching Richard. "You're trouble, boy. Maybe more trouble than you're worth. I suggest you fix yourself before I do. Still…"

He looked at the unconscious man on the ground, an amused smirk gracing his lips.

"Considering the circumstances, I'd say you did good, but next time, remember not to knock my nigger out cold."

James grabbed Richard by his collar and tossed him out of the barn, demanding he return to work in the cotton fields.

"Someone bring me another nigger," James demanded. "This time, a good one."

Richard walked out of the barn, rubbing his knuckles. When he turned, he saw his daughter watching him from way back, trailing him with her eyes. He wished he could cheer her up or keep her from being afraid of him.

Wait a minute...

Richard smiled. He formed impromptu bunny ears with his fingers to his head—something he always did when he didn't have hay or props—then scrunched his nose into a goofy face. Margret's mouth dropped open, her expression shifting to curiosity and surprise.

Richard held his expression until he heard James, then he quickly threw his hands and head down toward the ground and returned to his toil in the fields.

Some degree of feeling was returning to Richard's bloody fist as he sat in the corner alone, his once flawless hands now rough with cracks in them. Richard's knuckles felt like they'd shatter as he struggled with the cotton after that debacle in the barn.

Most of all, the other slaves feared being near him.

The now conscious man who Richard had beaten had a swollen face, nearly unrecognizable. The man pointed to Richard; it could only be deciphered as a threat.

"Why'd you attack the man?" the others asked him, but Richard couldn't respond.

Man, she says, Richard thought. *The* boy *should have stayed away from my daughter.*

In no time, the cabin filled with heated babble, the words "mute" and "dangerous" being tossed around.

"He's gonna get us all in the massas' bad graces."

"Maybe he should have *his* face beaten in," another said. "He's strange. Doesn't act like us."

Richard turned to the one who'd made that threat. The first thing he noticed was a branded "R" on his left cheek: Isaac, a particularly broody man who was the loudest in his complaints. Richard had purchased him less than two years ago, and he considered it a bad investment. Isaac had turned out to be problematic, always scowling at his master and overseer. But he was strong and useful, so Richard had made it his own business to beat the fight out of the man, and as usual, it'd worked for a while.

They'd kept a close eye on him, especially since he was the one Richard had branded, slitting his heels when he tried to run away.

Isaac spoke up, speaking straight at Richard. "You're a liability. You want to fight back so much, why not turn that anger to the barbarians keeping you shackled? You should go kill the white man. Or maybe you're just another submissive nigger who loves licking the boots of your white masters."

Rage flooded over Richard at the thought that a nigger himself was daring to call him one. He clenched his fists, preparing himself for a brawl, but Pico, slightly taller, stood in front of him.

In his native tongue at times and at others in his best Creole, he said, "Everyone, listen." Richard was amazed when everyone did. "I understand your fear and anger, but no matter what, all need to remain together to survive. If we start going against one another, what would we have left that they haven't already taken from us? It is just another submission. It's another way they defeat us. So, it was wrong for him to beat his own, but it was equally foolish for Adam to approach the massa's child."

Isaac flared his nostrils. "I'm fed up with the white man's cruelties. Just look what they did to Jackson." He pointed to the man James and Parkinson had beaten, the poor man with the dislocated shoulder. "You say we need to work as one, so why don't you tell *him*?" He pointed to Richard. "The mute never shares, and that's how Jackson got the way he is."

"And what about you, Isaac?" Pico said calmly. "Do I need to remind you of what happened to you over a year ago when you tried to run? I need to remind you how many people were punished because of your selfishness? You got off easy, acted on your own accord. We need to remain together. Only then can we survive."

Isaac said nothing more. Hushed whispers were traded among the slaves as Pico sat beside Richard, offering him some of his bread and a bowl of peas, beans, and rice. To Richard's own surprise, he didn't shy away from Pico's company, even in his anger. In fact, he didn't want anyone else by him *but* him, at least at that moment when the room still held tension.

There were conflicting emotions about it, about him. Things were changing, the air becoming diffused with tension, an electricity of unease and pent-up anger.

Richard and James had always known the other slaves put their trust in Pico, and now Richard could see why. Pico was one of the people he could trust. His ability to somehow maintain order and remedy a chaotic situation was almost enviable. He was wasted here, his talents sometimes driven underground by circumstances. He should have been a diplomat. Just a shame he was altogether the wrong color to qualify to become one. Such was Life's lottery.

"Isaac's hatred for the white man is strong, festering, but you cannot allow yourself to reach that point. I know you are angry," Pico began, "but don't take anger out on friends." Pico pointed to Richard's chest, then placed his own hand to his, repeating the gesture. Richard waved off his hand and shook his head. *You niggers are not my friends. I despise the lot of you.*

The others in the cabin ate with little hushed chatter, some stealing glances at Richard as if they considered him volatile, waiting for the gunpowder to ignite again. But he paid them no attention. Instead, he noticed Nini—or Zora, he supposed—slip out of the cabin with a lantern. *Where is she going?* he thought. It was nearly curfew.

He tapped Pico on the shoulder and pointed, but Pico merely shrugged. "I don't know where she goes at night," he said. "But we all have our secrets. Let me tell you somethin', boy," he went on. "We don't need to know everything in this life. Some things we learn in the next."

It was the first time anyone had called Richard *boy*. At least, in a friendly tone.

If ever he did hear it, it was always scathing and cynical.

But he and Pico were the same age or thereabouts. Part of Richard was angry about the insubordination of this Pico calling him *boy*. The other part was amused.

He quite liked the notion in a way, missing being a young man with few worries.

Pico had not finished what he had to say yet. There was always another opinion to give, then another. It was awkward to admit it when they all made sense.

"You remind me of my brother Limbani, you know. Bold. Reckless. Stupid."

Richard scrunched up his face, close to punching Pico in his, tired of listening. Being mute meant everyone could just carry on talking until they were done.

But Pico simply laughed.

"The actions. Not the head. He would always look out for others and protect who he could. And I protected him. My brother was a fighter. Like you. That's why I say you are like him."

There was a brief pause. Richard noticed Pico was still, not taking a single bite of his own gruel. Suddenly, he began to speak again but in a wistful way. "I had a family once…"

Usually, Richard wouldn't care to listen to his story either, anecdotes being cheap, but there was something about Pico's tone that gave him pause mid-bite. He stared at Pico's lean face, the small eyes seeming distant, distracted.

Pico said nothing more for some time until he noticed Richard staring. At first, he spoke in his native language. Richard couldn't understand a single word. It would have been smart to let Pico ramble as usual, but he was curious. Richard tapped Pico again and tugged on his own ear. It didn't take long for Pico to understand. It had to be in English.

"Oh. You were not raised on a plantation, not always a slave? Sorry, I thought you'd understand my few words," he said, then going back to speaking his Creole. "Then let me tell you Pico's story. My father was taken from his homeland many years ago and bought when he was young. His massa bred his slaves instead of buying them. He kept only boy children, the girls he traded. When I was born, my father was overjoyed. But mother… she died while giving birth to my brother Limbani. How my father mourned."

Pico's eyes looked distant for a brief moment.

"Father was proud when I was given a woman to make more sons. Told me she reminded him of my mother. Oh, I loved her. Sometimes, I forgot that we were slaves when I was with her, with my son.

"When my father grew old, he fell sick. Over and over, wasting away before us. But the massa, he did not bother to call for a physician because he was—and I remember these words—'too old to be useful anyway'. Well, my younger brother was hotheaded. A fighter, as I said. I had always kept his temper in check, but this day, he could not bear it. We argued as we never had before. I did my best to calm him, but I was asleep when the boy sneaked out to threaten the massa. Because he was going to help our father, you know? It did not help my father. Instead, my brother was killed—hung—and my father died from shock. As punishment, my wife and my child were sold away, and then, so was I.

"So the way I see it, if a man keeps quiet in disagreement, it might help him. So now, I am alone, and I still blame myself for my brother's death. That's why I try to stay near you. So that your temper isn't the end of you, too."

Richard remained still, unsure what to think.

"So much has been taken." Pico sighed. "I miss my family, my wife, and my children. I plan on staying alive, hoping to see them again... someday."

Richard couldn't help but think of his own children. His own father. But he stopped himself, shaking his head. *Don't fall for the sentiment,* he told himself. *You're nothing like Pico.*

Richard resumed eating, but his mind was so preoccupied he could barely taste what little flavor was there. *I'm nothing like your brother,* he told himself. *I'm nothing like you, either. You cannot even imagine how different we are.*

CHAPTER TWELVE

The sun started to rise. Morning meals were prepared and would be consumed at daybreak in the slaves' cabins. And soon, it would be another day in the brutal heat, fumbling with fluffy cotton and always at risk of receiving a beating.

As Richard sat up, he saw a small group of slaves huddled in a circle, speaking in low whispers in what he figured was a mix of English and some other language he strained to hear. Curiosity got the best of him as he gently pushed past others, only to see Isaac holding a rusty chunk of metal shaped into a blade, a blazing look in his eyes. Richard would always remember that angry look. It was the same angry, determined stare Isaac had also given just before he'd decided to run away nearly a year ago.

Richard feared for his white friends, wondering what was best to do in this situation. For now, he told no one; perhaps he'd lose his nerve and do nothing. Besides, could he even be sure those white men remained his friends these days? It seemed they'd accepted that he had gone.

After yesterday's incident, Richard worked in the fields as James believed he needed to be supervised. This time, he worked next to Zora. He'd caught her giving him side glances a few times after the cotton incident and even more after he'd beaten up Adam, but she still kept her head. But after Pico's little speech, she stopped giving him those glances. She seemed to have grown approachable again.

Wait, approachable? Richard thought. Why did he feel she wasn't approachable? He was her master, for Christ's sake. He could approach her whenever he damn well liked!

Richard took a moment from time to time to admire her gentle smile and beautiful eyes, and then he remembered *that* night. Reminiscent thoughts went through his mind.

He recalled touching her soft skin and feeling her warmth.

Had one of her previous owners given her the name Nini?

Richard thought of Pico's story and how it filled in a multitude of questions. Well, he had plenty of these when it came to Nini, too. Or about Zora—or whoever she truly was.

He was suddenly curious to know more about Zora's background, thinking of how she kept sneaking out at night and returning. Where did she go? What did she do? And why did she only speak at certain times? Did she want him, James, and the others to think she was mute?

If so, why? If she wanted that, it must be because she believed it helped her. He just couldn't see how that could be so since he'd give anything *not* to be mute.

But Zora snapped Richard out of it with a touch to his shoulder and pointed at the cotton. Richard returned to work but inched closer to Zora, answering his desire to be near her.

Richard noticed Isaac two men ahead of him as the field hands lined up at the end of the day to turn in their labor. He looked at him over the shoulders of others, moving his head around with urgency to see if he could find the weapon.

Then Isaac stepped up to James and suddenly dropped his basket.

Blade in hand, Isaac swung at James, a great blow as if his own life depended on him putting every last bit of strength into the swing. James stumbled back, barely missing the blade as he struggled to get his gun. Isaac took the opportunity to swing again, but Richard, dropping his basket, barged through the workers and grabbed the man from behind, pulling his arms behind his back. James stood up as other drivers, Benji and Parkinson, rushed over, taking hold of the renegade slave.

James straightened his jacket. "Bring the nigger to be lynched," he ordered the men. The two gave quick nods before leading Isaac away. Appearing to calm himself with a slow exhale, James looked at Richard and smiled. "As for the rest of you, return to your quarters. I warn you now, you will die if I see any of you out."

All of the field hands scrambled, getting back to their cabins as quickly as possible. Richard looked back, watching Isaac kick and thrash as the men dragged him to the oak tree.

For a moment, Richard inwardly chastised himself for his fleeting thought. *Why should I be caring about a slave being lynched? This new look must be messing with my sense of reasoning.*

Richard wasn't sure what Isaac's plan would have been once James was stabbed. It seemed like a suicide mission. Hell, it *was* a suicide mission. Even if he'd managed to stab James, then what? Were they all planning to revolt? Maybe he was trying to take advantage since the master was presumably gone. Richard couldn't comprehend why he'd make such a sacrifice. He would sacrifice himself just to kill one overseer? *Foolish.*

As Richard stood in the cabin, the many angry eyes of his fellow captives seared into him. And for the life of him, Richard couldn't understand why. If Isaac had managed to wound James, all of them would have succumbed to punishment. One of the men from the huddle that morning approached, pure anger in his unfamiliar eyes as he stared Richard down. His breath tempted Richard to turn away, but he fought against it, refusing to yield or show weakness, even as the man inched closer.

Pico rose from his place, and without even a word, he gently eased Richard back, taking his place in front of the slave. The man yet again backed down. All whispered as Pico talked in their language, a soft lilt to his voice as if soothing a frantic child, leaving Richard wishing to understand what he was saying.

Secretly, he would like to learn some of Pico's skills.

Then, Pico spoke in his Creole, "One dead saves us all." The whispers became silent as all turned in for the night. Once again, Pico had tamed the wild crowd.

But wasn't Pico twisting Richard's original intention?

Richard had stopped the slave from killing his friend, and it had nothing to do with saving them all. He'd have punished them all for such a foolish ploy if he had been white. But the thought crossed his mind that any day he, himself, could be the one lynched.

Perhaps that was why he had that empathetic feeling. The truth was, at times, he couldn't understand his own mind these days. Sometimes, his mind was white, and he was the plantation owner again. Other days, he was black, wondering if today would bring another beating.

Richard shook his head. *I'm not one of them,* he reminded himself. *I refuse to be.* But in his predicament, he was finding that harder to believe.

CHAPTER THIRTEEN

It was at least a half-hour before the slaves returned to the fields. But when James and another entered the cabin, all woke up and crawled to the corner in fear as if simply being there, all huddled together on the floor, would provide protection. The reality was that nowhere was truly safe. There was no genuine hiding place for the slaves. It was as if holding onto one another was like having an anchor to make them unmovable. Fingers dug into shirts and feet planted firmly on the ground to root themselves in deep. Some stood in front of others, careful to avoid gestures that might draw attention, yet their stances were resolute, almost as if to say, *Take me first*. Their eyes were wide and flitting back and forth as though looking between multiple things. Richard turned to see what was scaring everyone. His stomach dropped, churning when he saw that familiar smug face.

Clinton.

What's he doing here?

Richard's surprise turned to curiosity when Clinton looked over the cowering group like a fox hunting chickens. After a moment, another familiar face—a plantation owner he wasn't entirely acquainted with—walked in and stood behind James. Like Clinton, the slaver scoured the group.

The nameless plantation owner looked at the women all huddled together, holding each other. The girls weren't staring at the three white men any longer. Instead, they pressed their foreheads together, their mouths moving in what looked to be silent prayer. The owner's smirk turned into a frown as he watched, which seemed to spur him into action.

With three long strides, he was upon them. He grabbed one of the young women whose back had been partially turned to him and fisted his hand into her hair, yanking her backward. Her long wail broke the low murmurs as her eyes went wide, and she scrambled to grab the outstretched arms of the other women who threw themselves forward, reaching for her too. With a final scowl, the man violently pulled her by her hair and dragged her out of the cabin.

Richard watched, completely oblivious to what was happening before him.

As the field hands went to work, trying to ignore a fellow slave's kidnapping, Richard was stuck wondering what was happening here. Had the woman done something and needed punishment? But then why were Clinton and that other plantation owner there? He hated being out of the loop on the business on his own damn plantation.

Stuck in thought, Richard felt a tug on his shirt. He was also pulled from the group and dragged by James, who smiled at him.

James slapped Richard's shoulder and gave it a firm shake. "No work for you today, boy."

Richard knitted his brows.

"Don't look so surprised. You're being awarded for your actions from yesterday. Follow me."

He did as he was told. The other slaves gave curious looks as Richard followed James, Richard wondering where he was going. The destination became evident the farther they walked, a familiar sound becoming audible. As the two approached the barn, the muffled screams of a woman drew closer and closer with each step. There was a strange sinking feeling, a knowing in his gut before he even took the first step inside. Richard watched as a plantation owner finished with her, climbing off the tied woman—the same one they'd dragged from the cabin—and he was pulling up his pants.

"James! And with a nigger in tow," Clinton chimed.

"James. Parkinson. You two sure Richard won't walk in on us or doesn't have an issue with this?" one of the men asked.

"I assure you, the family is out. We're fine," James said.

"Richard has more things to worry about since he's also missin' now," Parkinson joked.

Clinton let out a satisfied sigh. "Richard doesn't know what he's missin'."

A cold sense of awareness washed over Richard, and he felt that familiar burn of disbelief in his gut at the men's words.

Richard was aware that James loved having his fun. He'd also been aware James and the others must have been doing things like this way before Richard had become a slave, but it was only on other slave owners' plantations as far as he'd known, never his own. He didn't want mulatto bastards running around or to have to go trading in workers who fell pregnant.

Had he been foolish all this time, believing he knew what went on in his fields, shack, and barn? He'd never felt the need to always check in or look at what James and the others were up to regarding plantation affairs because he'd trusted him. James always gave him good results, checking in on his plantation workers and keeping them in line. He'd never known the methods behind it, his preference being to turn the other way and not care what his people did as long as they gave the figures he needed to meet his duties and retain the plantation according to the agreement between his father and Mary's own.

But now, he wasn't so sure anymore.

Richard remembered the girls huddling in the corner earlier that morning, realizing it would indicate this had happened more than once on his own land. And without his knowing, no less.

How long had this been going on? And what about Margret? James already knew she played in the barn, but for him to do this here while knowing that? And what if they had taken Zora instead? What if it was Zora who was going to be taken next? He didn't know anything right at this moment, feeling like a stranger in his own land. If someone had transported him to another country before abandoning him there, things couldn't have felt more alien.

All he knew was that a wave of sudden anger enveloped him.

"Who's the nigger?"

"I promised you a good morning show, didn't I?" James pointed to the woman. "Have some fun," he told Richard.

Richard looked into the woman's puffy, terrified eyes, her cheeks moist with sweat and tears, a ball of fabric in her mouth. Something about that look in her eyes was plaguing his heart, making him unable to move. He'd seen it somewhere before but never paid attention to it. Perhaps it was the memory of Abigail clutching her child to her chest, staring at Richard's father as he cornered them. Or maybe when little Margret snuck out of the house and witnessed her first hanging. Perhaps it was when he'd raised a hand at Mary, threatening to hit her for the first time...

The slaves working in the barn kept their heads down, but he could see the sorrow in their eyes. Then it hit him; the look the woman gave was the same look Zora had.

Richard recalled taking Zora by force that day. Tears cascaded down her temples as she struggled beneath him. Her eyes were pleading, hands desperate to break from his grip. To make him stop. His stomach began to churn, twisting and pulling like a wrung-out towel, and the bitter taste of bile rose in the back of his throat. Maybe he had been wrong.

The sorrowful glances of the other slaves made him realize that the girl wasn't just a commodity but their friend. This feeling of having a burst of sympathy was an abhorrent intrusion. It must have been due to Pico's chirpy comments getting to him.

"Well?"

For a moment, Richard contemplated Zora's hateful glances from when he'd been white, the memories returning to his mind, as well as the memories of how she'd been warm towards him when he was a slave. He didn't want to be hated by her. He wanted to keep seeing her smile at him.

He shook his head no.

James pushed Richard towards the woman. "Don't dawdle," he snapped. "Everyone wants a show. It's what they're here for."

Richard stood tall, his shoulders back and his head up as he shook his head again.

James' face turned red. He moved his jaw in a chewing motion, hands on his hips, and then he slowly nodded. James turned to the others. "Seems like my nigger here doesn't know not to look a gift horse in the mouth," he said. "But I'll tell you what. Y'all came for a good morning show, and I'm on give it to you, I reassure you. You'll have your good morning show."

James looked at Richard. "Hold him down and pull down his britches."

Richard's heart sank, and before he could even take a step back, Parkinson and the other men had him in their grasp. Richard struggled against the men's strength as they pulled him to the ground, pinning his back and arms down into the hay.

James looked at one of the slaves, keeping his head down, moving around the hay bales. James pulled out his gun. "Come join the group," he told the slave.

Nervously, the man approached.

Richard continued to struggle against the men holding him down. With a smug smile, James waved the gun in Richard's direction, never breaking eye contact. "Mount him."

Richard's eyes went wide, filled with overwhelming terror. Upon hearing that, he thrashed harder, picking himself up only to be slammed back down. When the men had Richard pinned down, they punched him twice in the face. Blood flooded his mouth, joining the rivulet of yet more warm blood from his nose, his eyes watering from the punches.

"Get him over!" one said.

Richard tried to fight as they flipped him on his stomach, slamming his face into the ground and pinning his palms flat on the hay. One man reached beneath him, slipping the knot of his pants free before yanking down his breeches until a tearing sound filled the air. As the breeze brushed against his backside, he began to tremble, and it wasn't because it was cold.

The slave held at gunpoint hesitated, but James stuck the barrel of his gun into the man's mouth and repeated his orders.

The anxious slave slowly walked behind Richard and out of sight. There was a brief silence, but then Richard heard the other men jeer, teasing the slave about his lack of performance. The pressure and stress were making it extremely difficult.

"Come on, boy. Get it up!" Clinton said.

"Maybe the bloke should give him a hand," one joked.

Richard tensed, hearing the slave letting out a small sound filled with reluctance.

"Please…" the slave said.

A plantation owner shouted, "Get on with it already."

The slave whimpered.

"Hold on now," James told the others, that smug smile still on his lips. "Can't you all see you're scarin' the poor fella?" he teased.

"You're the one with the pistol to his head," one joked.

He chuckled. "I am, aren't I? All right then." He lifted his hands as though surrendering. Then, he lowered the gun. James inched closer, coaxing the slave as he spoke in calmer tones. "Listen, all you gotta do is close your eyes and enjoy it. Just calm down and concentrate."

There was a moment of tormenting silence for Richard. Suddenly, the men cheered.

"Come on now. We don't got all day."

Richard squirmed, his body tensing.

He needed to get away, but when his efforts were futile, he started to panic. He tried again to force himself up, raising his chest off the ground, but the others slammed him down, one throwing more punches and even a kick to his ribs, telling him to stay still.

"Don't worry, butter cheeks, you're going to enjoy this," said James as the slave approached the man pinned to the earth, half stripped, his ass up in the air. Richard could feel the man kneeling behind him and a sudden, painful pressure within him.

The pressure mounted until it gave. Richard screamed as the slave moved his hips. His screams were deep and low, coming out in short bursts. Richard's nails dug into the earth as his once friends laughed and mocked.

"Look at him enjoying it," one said.

"So this is what he wanted, not a girl," Parkinson mocked.

"Stop being soft," James told the slave. "Put some backbone into it. Go harder, faster."

The man whimpered.

"Harder. Harder!" James pointed the gun to his temple. "I said harder, nigger!"

"Fuck him like the animal you are," Clinton said. "Come on, it's base instinct. Do what we were born to do! Go on, give it to him!"

And he did, tearing inside of Richard, each thrust eliciting a forceful breath from him.

Richard clawed at the dirt, trying to free his wrists from the men's grasp. But he couldn't escape them, couldn't escape the violent and painful thrusts.

Richard smelled the dirt and hay as Parkinson and the others kept him in place. He felt unreal, numb, and slow, painfully slow. His limbs deadened as though needles pricked him all over. The normal bubbling rage always simmering in his chest like a kettle over a fire suddenly doused in ash to smother the flames. He tried to transport himself anywhere in his mind, anywhere but here. Like a dream. Time was still. He wasn't a slave. He was his old self playing with Margret and Henry, singing songs with them, and playing hide and seek. His children would smile, laughing in his arms when he found them under a bed or tucked away in a wardrobe. But the laughter deepened, replaced with cruel laughs. Their laughter, their jeers bound him to this godforsaken place. His body moved, his mind shrouded, trying to grasp onto anything. Instead, it wandered to that night in the shack, wandered to Zora pressed in the dirt as he was now. He pictured himself as Zora, being taken by himself not that long ago, suffering as she did underneath him and unable to feel anything but the pain.

His screams gradually died down into soft sobs as his body fell limp, all power leaving him, his body frozen in place. At that moment, he truly felt like a piece of meat. An animal. He didn't feel white at that moment, more a nothingness, as if everything had been stripped from him.

"See? Ain't that sweet?"

James and the others taunted him. Richard's face heated, a deep flush spreading across his skin as tears steadily streamed down his cheeks. Time was moving too slowly, feeling like an eternity. Soon, Richard felt a wet warmth dripping down him and pressure removed as the other slave stood up, sobbing.

"Well, I'll be damned. Shit really does look like smeared butter. It's like burnt toast." James laughed, "It's like breeding a mare."

Echoes of laughter rang in Richard's ear as he heard a master call them "Dirty niggers." Richard didn't move. Even after they released his wrist, he stayed still, not wishing to see their satisfied, smug expressions. He was used to it, used to seeing them give others those expressions, and now they were looking at him like that. Worse still, he knew he used to give out these expressions too. Now, he hung his head. But he would not admit it was in shame.

James stooped next to Richard, who trembled, breathing hard, ragged breaths, heart still racing. "You should have taken the reward when you had the chance. But you disobeying me, I can't let that slide. See, y'ain't nothin' but property. Best remember that. Now get up. Unless you want another go. I can always organize another little go-around, huh?"

Richard shook his head. *No more, please,* said his expression. *You have broken me.*

Then he rose to his feet slowly, pulling up his pants.

His demeanor was different now, no longer showing the cockiness of before. No longer did he hold the spirit of rebellion anywhere within him. He was, just as his expression showed, fractured inside, right at this moment feeling there was nothing left of him. Which hurt the most, he was unsure. Was it the rape itself? Or was it how James had been going against him all this time?

Maybe it just didn't matter anymore to try and work it all out. He was theirs now, belonged to the plantation, just for this minute—until his indomitable spirit could repair itself and he could return to his rightful position. Problem was, would that day ever come around?

He kept his head down, avoiding eye contact with any of the men, but then he saw the woman in the corner, her fearful eyes hitting harder.

Someone grabbed Richard by the back of the neck. Richard stumbled as they shoved him outside. A chuckle sounded behind him, but he didn't turn to look. Instead, Richard slowly staggered forward on unsteady feet, but he stopped when James' smug voice called out.

"You get out to those fields now, boy. I'd better see a full basket."

Richard didn't respond and didn't look back, but when the barn door closed again, he took it as dismissal. James wasn't even concerned with him following the command. He just knew he would.

The woman's screams started up again, growing louder as he turned to leave, but they grew distant, slowly dying the farther away he got.

With a limp, Richard returned to the fields and saw Zora. Ashamed, he looked down, shivering as he worked in the hot sun, picking cotton. He still felt the vile fluids leaking down his legs, but he didn't dare put his hand back to wipe the content away.

Zora snuck up to him and tried to touch his cheek, but Richard coiled away, still unable to look at her. She froze for a moment, trying to raise Richard's face. Unable to, she gave him a quick hug and a kiss on the cheek before returning to her station.

Richard sat on the floor in the cabin, knees pressed high against his chest, face burning as he looked away from everyone who would surely know what had happened to him. All day, his movements were slow, from picking to moving to turning in his share. Richard was beyond low on quota, but nearly all the field hands rushed to throw cotton into his basket. He didn't understand why, especially after the incident with Jackson, but he didn't care too much to dwell on it. Especially when he reached James. Now, nothing mattered.

The way James looked at him when he turned in his cotton was hideous, stomach-turning. That smug, satisfied smile just mocking him more.

"Barely made quota today from moving too slow, huh, *Butter Cheeks?*" he said. His smile stretched seeing Richard's horrified expression. "Fitting name, don't you think? Fits real nice."

Richard eyed him, angered by the humiliating name, but he kept his composure, moving on.

Back in the cabin, others were tending the woman from the barn. She looked trapped in a daze, holding a slack expression, her hands sliding loosely onto the floor. Richard's eyes quickly scanned the room for the man who had been forced upon him, and when he was nowhere to be found, he let out a small breath of relief. He couldn't bear to see him the entire night, reliving the humiliation.

Zora approached Richard with a folded pair of pants, and he again was unsure why. But he needed them, so there was no room to sit and ponder on it, his hand reaching out to grab them from her the way an ape grabs for a peanut. He changed in a corner with his back to the wall, noticing the others trying to hide sympathetic looks. That's when he noticed them. Red smears and blotches scattered on the seat of his previous pair, one particular large bloodstain sitting like a target, a stain they all would have beheld, and that was why their eyes had followed him.

Dread overcame him. They all knew, and that was even more humiliating. Was this why she had kissed his cheek earlier? Probably. He triple-knotted his new britches, making sure they were nice and tight. Upset, he tossed the filthy pants to the side away from him, extending a leg and kicking them into the dust. Zora quietly swooped in like a ghost and took them away.

Now, Richard sat on the floor in the cabin, knees pressed against his chest, face mottled as he looked away from everyone. Pico sat next to him, patting his hand in comfort but careful not to touch him too much. Zora came over, wiping his face which was still bloody, tender, and swollen from the punches. She pulled the rag away, trading it with a bowl, offering water to Richard while gently stroking his head. "Safe now," Zora whispered.

Pico tried to offer him a bowl of food, but Richard shook his head.

"You don't want to eat?"

Richard shook his head.

"At least drink some water."

He didn't move.

"Please," Zora said softly, the words coming out in a pleading whisper.

Without lifting his head, Richard took a sip of water and lay down, his back turned to the others. It took a moment for them to get up and leave.

Time passed until everyone readied themselves for sleep, lying on their mats. They eased quickly into slumber, but Richard had no such mercy, the memories of the barn plaguing his mind. He couldn't help but compare his couple weeks of cruelty to the lives of his slaves who'd spent years on his plantation. How did they do it? How did they ever survive such humiliation, wickedness, pain, and strife? Was this how Zora had felt after he'd forced himself on her? It must have been, surely. But then again, maybe she would have felt worse. It had to be even more grievous when a person took the treatment for years. By now, it had become a part of them. Richard still had his indignation, his shock, his horror. Most of the slaves were simply used to it, expecting it.

It had become their lot in life.

Richard froze, thinking about another man on top of him. Another man *inside* him. The thought alone made him want to retch. How could he be so weak? And being unable to fight back, no one coming to help... was that how the sweet Zora had felt? Suddenly, Richard realized just how vulnerable and helpless he was. In a flood of emotion, he slowly curled into a tight ball, his body convulsing as he sobbed uncontrollably.

A gentle hand slipped under his neck, a touch he instantly recognized as Zora's—a unique herbal scent from her, not like the dirt and sweat from others. She lifted his head and rested the side of his face on her chest, cradling him like a mother would a child.

With Richard's body curled like an infant, she kissed him on the head and gently rocked him back and forth, one arm wrapped around him, the other tenderly stroking his head. In a soft voice, she began to hum and sing a lovely lullaby in a language Richard couldn't understand.

Slowly, Richard's sobs turned into sniffles, then silence until, finally, he fell asleep.

CHAPTER FOURTEEN

Richard's mind was plagued with the painful memories of yesterday, still able to hear the men who'd once been his friends laughing at his pain, his rape. He wanted to be angry at the man who had mounted him, but all he could see was a helpless slave trying to survive.

Instead, no matter how hard he tried not to and how hard he tried to justify James' actions, he still only got back to the same outcome; James, though not the direct perpetrator, was his rapist.

Richard winced, still sore from the thrusts. Tears threatened to come, but he forced them down. Slowly, he moved in a trance-like state, picking the cotton.

But Zora could see from afar that his basket was not filled enough, same as ever.

Keeping low, Zora helped Richard pick the cotton, slipping her prizes into his basket the same way she always did, no matter if he acknowledged her or not.

Richard turned to look at her briefly. That morning, he had awoken on her bosoms.

She'd held him so soft, like a mother with a fragile child in her arms, nothing he had or had ever experienced with Mary. Not even his own mother, who'd died shortly after giving birth to him, could he recall showing such gentleness and generosity. But what right did he have to be comforted by Zora? Had she had someone to comfort her after he'd had his way with her?

Had she been plagued with the same crippling thoughts he was experiencing now?

Zora looked at him, and Richard quickly veered his gaze away from her, overcome by a tremendous well of guilt.

For once, he couldn't look a slave in the eye.

A sudden gunshot echoed in the air, and Richard feared the worst. Had they noticed Zora was not at her station? James came out of the barn mounted atop Richard's white horse, firing another shot high into the air. The irritated and fractious steed showed the whites of its eyes in annoyance each time the loud noise cracked through the air. Most slaves continued their work while others couldn't, wanting to see what was going on.

"One of the slaves is missing for work in the hay fields," James announced.

Other white workers, including Parkinson and Benji, joined the hunt, searching the different fields and the surrounding areas.

"Doubt that one could escape," Richard overheard one say, and he knew they were right; the slaves wouldn't dare mount an escape bid during the day, especially after what had been done to other runaways over the years. He slipped to the edge of the cotton field and watched the carpenter enter the cabin. "I found her," he announced. "Let's say she has no more worries."

Richard witnessed the same woman he'd seen yesterday now being dragged out of the cabin like a doll, a rope tied around her neck, her hue a purplish tone, mottled like beaten meat before it went into the pan for frying. She was dead all right.

The carpenter pulled her to James, now walking beside Richard's horse. He looked down at the woman, her body limp and pale with dead eyes that stared up as though sending a silent prayer to a god she already knew could not exist. Or could not exist for her kind anyway. Only for whites. The staring eyes were open but looked lifeless as they inspected the sky. Perhaps she was looking to see where she would travel next.

Or perhaps she had fled for it already, nothing holding her here, chained to this sullied earth.

James chuckled. "Well, looks like she couldn't handle us *big* men yesterday," he said.

Parkinson laughed, but Benji rolled his eyes. He wasn't one to participate in those kinds of things, which was why he hadn't been there in the barn. He veered his gaze, trailing over James' shoulder. James followed the gaze, looked behind him, and saw Mary, who wore her immaculate, elaborate, and modest clothes as she always did. Her golden curls were up in plaits and rolls. She showed contentment in her expression.

"Get some niggers out here to dispose of the body," James ordered his men.

As Parkinson and the others scoured the field, pointing to the first able-bodied slave in sight, Henry ran out of the house past Mary, jumping over the porch steps as he hurtled over to James.

"Mr. Walker!" he beamed. "Can I help you and the others find the missing slave?" He bounded on his heels, excited to help. "My father promised me."

His big eyes gazed up with an innocence and wonder that only a child could possess.

James rubbed his hand on Henry's head, messing up his hair. Richard couldn't help but see himself in the action, thinking back fondly, too, to the time his son now spoke of—when he'd promised that when the next slave went missing, the excited boy could help locate him. He could only hope that James would believe the promise and hold to it for him.

He listened, hoping for the slave group in the background to pipe down so the air was quiet and calm enough to carry the pair's voices across the expanse to him.

"Aye, lad," said James. "Well, I suppose if your father made that promise to you, then what harm can come of you helping us find a missing slave?" Then he looked pensive. "But don't you think you'd be better off spending your energy trying to find your old man? We haven't seen hide or hair of him, you know, son."

Son, he called him.

And indeed, James and Henry looked like they'd make a perfect father-son portrait. But his heart sank at the thought. It was as though everyone had forgotten his existence. Even the children who'd adored him so much. They had settled into an easy routine now in his absence, their eyes sparkling at 'uncle' James' kindness.

"I'm sorry though, sport," James continued. "But we already found *this* missing slave. You must've been holding onto old news of the escape, huh?"

He rested his hand on the boy's hair again, fondly.

"Oh…" Henry lowered his head.

James turned the child's jaw with one finger and sighed. "Tell you what, how 'bout I promise to take you with me to find another if one tries to escape? Hm?"

Henry smiled but then frowned. "I wish Papa were here. He'd love to come with us."

Richard softened at the statement. So his children hadn't quite forgotten him. Not yet, anyhow.

James reassured him, "We'll find Richard. I promise. Now, go on back inside."

Henry ran past Mary and into the house.

Richard watched James approach her, his smile brightening with each step, a certain glint in his eye. Richard knew that look well, the same look James had shown years ago when he fancied a neighbor.

Richard had also stood at attention whenever the younger Mary had been smiling that same flirty smile at him. And now, it was James leaning towards her, removing his wide-brimmed hat. Mary's light-brown eyes sparkled. She was glowing.

"Do you think you could send someone to town for me?" she said. "It's just a list of goods and sundries. It's light work."

"It'd be my pleasure."

Soon, Mary handed him what looked like a slip of paper. James grabbed it, holding her hand a beat too long.

"Will you be joining us for dinner again tonight?"

"Of course."

Pico touched Richard's shoulder and reminded him to return to work. "Bosses will get angry," he said. "No one wants Massa's fist."

Richard looked down but couldn't prevent his ears from listening to the two love birds. "Thank God Richard is gone," Mary said to James. "Promise me you won't try too hard to find him. I thank my stars for you every day, James. You are ten times the man Richard was. And then some. Let us all pray to God he never shows up."

"I know. And someday in the not too distant future, the plantation will be mine, and—"

"And it shall be you stoking the hearth fire, and you for whom I bake bread."

"It will," said James with a chuckle. "I hope it's good bread."

"The very best for you."

Richard couldn't see now, but a small pause followed. A pause that he could swear was the right duration for Mary and James to exchange a kiss. His blood boiled in his veins.

Richard bit his lips until he tasted the warm sting of his blood. He didn't care about Mary being tainted by another man. But he did care about the quip regarding James taking over his property. It was something he had never thought of before, but of course, what was to stop it if Mary believed Richard was gone? The property would pass to her, and she could then do as she wished with it. She could also wed again in time. And worse still, it wouldn't be long before someone in a role of authority would be called to say whether they believed Richard should be deemed dead or not, freeing her. James knew plenty of such men who'd be happy to receive a coin or two from him to write the necessary letter if it came to that. He wouldn't have a problem marrying her, and James would own everything for which Richard had worked.

Richard turned in his cotton, the melody of the summer night sounding miles away, making the slave master now turned slave wistful. He remembered taking Henry to his first slave auction, feeling his little son's hand in his when they'd made it to town. He'd been so proud of his son becoming as brutal as him. His mind progressed to recalling that promise to Henry to take him out and find a runaway slave. But now, hearing Henry wanting to hunt a runaway felt wrong. As for James—how long had his supposed friend been smitten with his wife? James was walking Richard's porch as if he owned it, and now it all made sense.

He'd trusted James too much when it came to running the farm, he admitted to himself. There were times James would make his jokes about what he'd do differently if he were in Richard's shoes, but never once had Richard felt threatened by it.

He trusted him, especially since he got things done. But now this? Was he sleeping in his bed too? Was he even using all his power to look for him? Or was James hoping time would just pass till sufficient had gone by for Mary to ask for him to be noted as dead?

Richard's heart stung by James' disloyalty.

And to his surprise, though he tried to tell himself otherwise, it also hurt when it came to Mary. For some reason, he'd assumed that she would always be his.

He had taken her for granted. It wasn't about love, however.

It was about him thinking she wouldn't dare—or maybe wouldn't pull off—having any other man apart from him. Now he saw that even that had been foolish thinking.

All Richard wanted right now was to hold his children again. It was only a matter of time before they weren't his either.

It was the Sabbath, another day of rest and worship for any white man but another day of work for the slaves. Richard knew he was the reason for the continuous labor on the slaves' used-to-be day off to keep up production, but he now hated having made that change.

Everyone in the cabin lined up when the time came, heading to the field at the sound of the horn. They gathered around the cotton shed to retrieve their baskets and bags, but to Richard's and the others' surprise, James, Benji, and Parkinson stood in front.

For a moment, Richard feared one of them might be in trouble. He wanted to look about but was careful to keep his head slightly down instead.

James looked over the crowd, a slow smile forming. "Be grateful," he shouted. "I've decided to give you the day off at Mrs. McLeary's request. But don't get too comfortable. You lot better be ready to work your asses off come daybreak tomorrow. And it goes without saying, none of you steps a single foot off this here plantation. You do, and I'll see that you get shot. So when Mrs. McLeary gives you a gift from the goodness of her heart, you lot better damn well respect it. Any shenanigans, and you'll work twice as hard next week."

Everyone remained still. Silent.

James frowned. "Ain't nobody taught you any manners?"

Pico stepped up. "Thank you, Massa Walker," he said. One by one, the crowd gave scattered low rumblings of "Thank you, Massa," and "Thank you, sir."

James nodded, seemingly satisfied. "Go on now."

Richard glanced at James, assuming he'd allowed the day off since Richard, the slave owner, still wasn't there. The field hands didn't move for just a moment, looking at one another with stares of curiosity and skepticism, fearful that when they moved, they'd be reprimanded and brought back. It wouldn't be the first time someone had made a vile joke like that to set the slaves running so they could be hunted down. But one brave soul turned and headed back to the cabin, and one by one, another turned to follow.

Everyone flooded into the cabin. Richard wasn't sure what he'd do.

Perhaps he would lie down and procure more sleep. Or maybe just wallow in self-pity. It didn't matter to him. All he knew was that a part of him was grateful to have a break from pricking his fingers in the scalding heat.

And he was sure the others felt the same now that they could sit around and do nothing for the remainder of the day.

But to Richard's surprise, they didn't sit about doing nothing. Far from it.

As soon as they stepped into the cabin, they dragged their mats out of the room and began sweeping the dirt floors. Some called to one another, pointing here and there. Men with hammers and nails started mending the huts, and women gathered clothes to be mended, too. They had darning to do and shoes to fix, garments to wash, and floors to scrub. Their day off was just as hard as the toil outside in the plantation fields. They chose no rest for themselves on this day.

Richard stared in awe, not quite sure what he'd imagined when it came to a slave's day off; in fact, he'd never taken the time *to* imagine, but there they were, still busy as bees mending their huts, their clothes, and cleaning. Richard stood around, slowly stroking his arm as it hung loosely at his side, unsure of what to do. His eyes went from person to person as they moved about, taking on tasks. He felt lost in a sense, even though he was surrounded by so many, and a knot began to form in his chest.

A hand was placed on his shoulder.

He gasped and turned to see Pico. "Come to the stream with me. We wash," he said.

Richard nodded heartily.

Down at the stream, Richard stood in the moist soil surrounded by trees, watching as both men and women crouched and threw water on themselves. And a bit farther upstream, he saw others washing their clothes. It dawned on him that he had never washed his own clothes before, neither the clothes resting in the main house nor the rags now worn on his back. Most seemed to focus on scrubbing in the regions most prone to sweat. Richard looked down at his own clothing and frowned. He'd stopped noticing the smell days ago, but now he took in the stains, likely there forever, but he thought that perhaps having something clean on his body would feel nice.

Some slaves washed their clothing items after working all day in the field, but that was only if they had the energy and the time to do so. Stepping close to the stream, Richard froze when he saw Zora some ways down. Her skin was smooth, her whole glorious shining body exposed. The lashes on her back that he had created were in plain view like a hideous branding on her skin. How could he have done this to her, someone so kind to him now?

His own guilt bit at his conscience. Richard tried to look away, but the scar on her right thigh fixed his eyes now, too. How had she gotten it? There were many men and women there with scars, others spared from them, but hers stood out. Somehow, he knew they told a deeper story. Feeling a little uncomfortable and knowing he shouldn't be staring, he turned away.

After this, Pico got his attention, waving for him to come and wash up too.

Pico washed himself, his body lean and muscular. Richard couldn't help but look at the scars on his back, just as prominent as Zora's own.

Richard stripped his clothes, feeling somewhat exposed for both the fraud and the heinous slave master that he was at heart. He felt, in short, vulnerable.

He could not even maintain personal hygiene as a slave. Clothes went unwashed, baths were infrequent. The scrub down at the dirty river was truly the best he could hope for. And it still was far from being enough. Richard washed himself, too, as best he could, knowing he'd stunk all this time. It wasn't only about being clean, either. It was about hygiene. The mites, ticks, and lice could bite at his skin and introduce infections and diseases. His genitals were sore and chafed with blistering wounds from never cleaning his private parts these days. Now submerged in water, he scratched them religiously, flakes of his dry skin patches catching under his fingernails. Even from such a distance, the pungent smell reached his nostrils, the scent close to the musk of the mold growing in the barn on the hottest summer days.

He missed his clean bed too, the one he had now permanently stained with the dirt and dust he carried in from the fields.

He missed warm baths, washing soap, and a toothbrush. But especially when he started remembering that day in the barn, he furiously rubbed his skin, desperate to get rid of the grime and every minute bit of filth that might still be clinging to him.

Upon dressing, he remembered the pants Zora had given him, appearing at just the right moment to save him from how he had felt like a helpless piece of meat. Even now, he was about to cry until he caught Zora watching sympathetically as he put his pants on.

Back at camp, they built a fire to dry their clothes. A man called to Pico, beckoning him over to help with the hut. And again, Richard stood among the chaos, unsure what to do. On his typical day off when he was white, he'd go out shooting with James, drink in town, catch up with documents, or play with Henry and Margret. Now, he just stood around like an unknowing child.

In the distance, Richard noticed a woman in a plaid dress going up to any man she could, but they waved her off after a short conversation.

"You. Hey, you over there."

Richard turned. A plump woman with a red head wrap and striped, brown dress with mismatched buttons waved him over as she fixed a pot dangling over the fire pit.

It was Olivia. She used to work in the house until he'd found a better cook. Olivia's cooking wasn't bad per se, but she talked too much. He and James used to joke; she could talk a coon right out of a tree.

"Cut me some more wood for the fire, would ya?"

She pointed to a wooden block with an axe in it and a pile of logs beside it.

Richard wasn't sure how to feel. He'd never been told to do anything by a slave before. But with nothing else to do, he went to the block and picked up the axe. As a young boy, he'd tried to chop wood, but his father had scolded him for all his efforts. Lining up the wood, Richard swung the axe, but the log wouldn't budge. Instead, the axe got lodged inside. Richard had to put his foot on the log to pry it out. He tried again, only to get the same results.

"Come on now, put your back into it. You can do better than that."

Richard glared at Olivia before letting out a frustrated sigh.

He took a deep breath and swung the axe in the air, bringing it down on the log with all his might, splitting the wood with a deafening *crack*.

"There you go!"

Richard let out a prideful sound and moved on to the next one.

And the next, each a little easier.

"Hol' on now. That's enough. That's enough," the woman said, smiling. "Got into the swing of things and almost couldn't stop." She grabbed the wood. "Thank you, kindly. You did good."

The lady tossed the wood under the pot. Richard watched from the side, catching his breath.

"Do you want to help?"

Richard shook his head. He'd never cooked before. Never had to.

"Sure you do. Come over here and make yourself useful instead of standing there like a lost child. Lord knows you could learn a thing or two."

Richard paused, not sure what to make of her words. After some hesitation, he did as he was told, taking tentative steps towards the pot until he stood beside her.

Olivia stirred their breakfast in the pot, showing him how to boil cornmeal. She dumped three giant ladles of the grainy cornmeal using a scoop hand-carved from wood. As she topped it off with water, particles of dust flew into Richard's nose, and he tried not to react to the way it tickled. She kindled the fire and began to stir, and after a few moments, the water began to bubble. At one point, she slapped the ladle in his hands and told him, "Have at it!" His eyes widened, and he stared down at the cornmeal like it might jump out and burn him. He took a step back when the bubbling turned violent.

Richard slowly lowered the ladle into the pot and kept stirring, only looking up when a man approached, holding something in his hands. The man smiled at Olivia and then nodded at Richard. It took a moment for Richard to realize the slave was carrying meat. Richard's eyes focused on the man. He thought he would feel angry knowing the food was taken, but instead, his stomach only grumbled. He was sure it must have come from the house's leftover dinner.

He considered ratting the slave out, like he essentially had done to the man who approached Margret, but what stopped him was the thought of another 'reward' from James, not any regard for another slave's feelings.

Then he thought, *What's the point anyway? Why report someone to the men who keep me whipped and sodomized?*

When the time came, Richard ate the meat with everyone else, with great gusto, too.

A few slaves sat around the pot to eat their meals while others wrapped up some of their tasks. Some ate with utensils, others with their bare hands, forming the food into little pinches in their fingers and dropping it into their mouths. As Richard sat outside eating, he watched the camp, some slaves still moving about like the tiny insects skittering through the dry grass.

He was still fascinated that they spent their non-forced working time mending their huts, clothes, and making pots and pans. He saw how they lived, how they interacted with one another.

Seeing this brought him a small sense of normalcy, reminding him of how he'd walk the halls of his manor and occasionally spot a house slave sweeping or clearing the tables. Now, they persistently cleaned their cabins with what Richard could only note as garnering a sense of pride in their work. This was in their blood. Every slave was clean.

As the day progressed, they grew less and less busy, some finally taking the time to relax, some children playing in the background. Mats returned to the cabins, reed brushes put away against the wall. Richard sat on a log, now watching a few making clay bowls and pots. Micel was seated across from him. Richard looked up from his pot and gazed at Micel's unpleasant scar before touching his own. But Richard's attention was drawn elsewhere. Now, the same woman in plaid was going around to more men, asking about the female slave recently buried. She asked the men to do something for her, but they all declined her request.

"What is Sylvie on about now?" one man asked.

"She wants one of us to go to Amelie's grave site."

"Why?"

He simply shrugged.

Amelie. That was the girl's name? Richard thought.

He looked to the oak tree, watching Isaac's and Solomon's bodies swinging from the branches, remembering the girl's lifeless eyes.

But his thoughts were interrupted when Zora sat with him. The way she looked at him now, with wonder and curiosity, stirred up worry in his gut. He wanted to squirm at the feeling of her eyes on him. He felt unsure and awkward around her, guilty. Could she see through him and know?

Richard tried to keep his head down, burying himself in his work. He shifted from side to side, careful not to look her in the eyes. He couldn't bear having her know who he was or what he did, even if it was unlikely that she would because of his appearance. Despite all that, he loved having her near him, even if he felt unworthy.

But he looked up when he heard her chuckle.

"Never make bowl?" she asked him.

Richard looked down at his work. It was supposed to be a pot.

"Lumpy," she teased. She took the pot from him, her hands gliding along the curves and arcs as she showed him how to mold it before handing it back. Richard tried mimicking her instructions but still couldn't get it. She molded the bowl with ease as if it was nothing. Zora placed her hands over his and guided him. Her hands were his hands, and they pulled and stretched the outer rim of the pot, shaping it into a perfectly rounded shape. Her fingers pinched his when the pressure needed to be added, and she used his larger ones to smooth the bumps and marks as though he were a paintbrush.

Richard tensed from how close she was but found a little comfort in her not knowing who he really was. He stole quick glances, wanting to learn more about her, wanting to ask her where she went at night but wasn't sure how to do this, being mute and all.

"Do you have family?"

The question surprised him. He looked up at her when she released his hands. Richard nodded and put up two fingers.

"Two children? They were sold?"

He shook his head.

"They are alive?"

Richard nodded, and she smiled.

"You were separated?"

Richard paused and looked toward the house, but his thoughts were interrupted by the sound of horses neighing in the distance. He turned his attention towards the sound, watching his family coming back from church, seeing young, finely dressed Henry climb from the coach and small Margret—wearing her favorite dress and pink ribbon—skipping with her teddy bear before going into the house with Mary.

He turned to Zora and nodded. After a pause, Richard pointed to her.

"Do *I* have family?"

He nodded.

Zora's shoulders slumped. "I did. We were separated too. Sold to different masters."

A lump formed in Richard's throat. He was used to seeing slaves separated from their families. He'd even done it himself, but hearing it now saddened him for some reason. Maybe it was just Zora. Maybe he just didn't want to see her sad. At the same time, he reproached himself for caring. *These are slaves,* he reminded himself. *They are born to serve, be that in whatever way suits us. If that means splitting us up…*

Us. Splitting us up. Us?

How had the word "us" worked its way into his thoughts?

I mean, if that means splitting them up… them, the slaves. They're born for us, so we, the slave masters, can get the best from them.

He tried desperately to correct himself.

But even as he thought it, he knew that he felt more the slave now, far less the master.

Richard pointed to Zora's scarred leg, hoping to change the subject.

"My leg?" Zora slightly lifted her skirt and grabbed her thigh. "Got this when taken. Men attacked. Tried to run and—" She balled her fist and dragged it up her leg.

Zora pointed to Richard's neck. "Can you tell me?"

Richard simply shook his head. Zora didn't move. For a moment, she just stared with an expression he couldn't interpret. Then, she gently touched the burn on his neck before gently sliding it up to the scar on his cheek. And for a moment, he tensed but gradually relaxed, letting himself sink into her warm hand.

"Master, he named you?"

Richard went to shake his head but stopped. "Butter Cheeks" was far from a name.

"No good name?" She stared as Richard shook his head. "Then I'll think of one."

As dusk settled in, the once lively birds waned, making way for the incessant chirruping of insects. Richard sat alone against the interior cabin wall, his ankles crossed, knees pulled to his chest as others ate their small meals for dinner. He paid attention when he heard one of the slaves—the woman in the plaid dress, Sylvie—pacing around the room, speaking to anyone who would listen.

"Please," Sylvie asked the others. "Someone, please be fearless and go collect my dear friend's necklace."

It took Richard a moment to realize Sylvie was speaking about the young woman who couldn't take life anymore. How would the girl have even come into possession of such an item? Perhaps it was made on his plantation like some created dolls from corn shucks and sticks. No slave was allowed a possession, at least not on his plantation, so it must have remained hidden.

"Please," she continued. "It's important. We carved it together some time ago. Please."

Others were silent, fearing such a dangerous task.

But she persisted in her request.

"Stop this nonsense!"

Richard turned his head to see an older man with matted hair who interrupted Sylvie. All eyes were on him.

"Who in their right mind would dare to be caught outside past the massa's curfew only to deface an already made grave? Don't disturb the dead. Amelie's in a better place now, so just let it go."

Tears filled Sylvie's eyes as she stood helpless in the middle of the room. "Please…"

Others remained silent. Richard kept his eyes locked on the ground. Why was the necklace so significant to this woman? It was just that: a necklace. An object. He thought for a moment what it would be like to lose something significant and how that might feel. But then, with a sinking feeling, he realized he *had* lost something. His home, his children, life, and identity. In all ways but in his own mind, he wasn't even Richard anymore. If he had the chance to hold on to something from his life, he wouldn't hesitate to take it.

The room remained silent. Feeling numb, Richard volunteered by raising his hand, knowing what path to take to where the slaves' bodies were buried in unmarked graves.

No one said a word. They just watched as Richard slowly stood and walked to the door.

Richard snuck out of the cabin, moving with stealth and all too warily through the shadows, careful to avoid lit areas. It would have been dangerous for him to light a lantern, so he waited until he was far enough away. After stumbling in the dark, he finally made it to the slaves' communal burial grounds in a wayward location in the forest, separate from the main cemetery.

Plantation owners didn't want to use more valuable arable land for a slaves' cemetery, and Richard's father hadn't been any kind of an exception when he'd chosen this site years ago.

But now, Richard compared the cleanly white grave site to this barren one. He paused a moment, gazing out at all the rows and rows of unmarked graves—nothing but sticks tied into crosses—unsure if the allotted plot he was viewing contained only Amelie's grave.

How many bodies had been buried there? How many suffered and died at his hands?

Seeing the vast number before him was shocking, even to white Richard.

Richard's heart grew heavy with each step until he came upon freshly tilled soil. He held up the lantern and stared at it, his heart troubled and aching, though he was unsure why. But he shook the thoughts from his mind and placed the lantern on the ground, grabbing the shovel that had been left behind from the day's burials. Then, he proceeded to dig.

Some ways in, his hands began to blister. Richard stopped to catch his breath, his chest heaving as he sucked in the cool night air. Wiping his brow, he continued to dig ever so slowly until he felt soft material.

Wrapped in a shroud, her head facing west, Richard carefully uncovered the mound and stared at the lifeless body, unable to help imagining himself lying in that sorry pauper's grave.

He and Amelie had both been brutally raped that day, but one was in the ground, and the other felt like the walking dead. Zora had helped him through it, but who had assisted poor Amelie?

What if I end it? he thought. *What is this life worth to me now? It tortures me daily.*

He contemplated if he should do the deed like she did. But he stopped himself, thinking of his children. What if Zora was the woman those men dragged out that day? What if something like that happened to Margret? At that moment of tranquility, it occurred to him that he must have been so cruel to his slaves. The food, shelter, and how they were overworked struck his core, a feeling he couldn't explain or describe other than searing, unrelenting guilt.

Perhaps now he understood why the maid Abigail had also slit her tiny child's throat, not wanting to subject her beloved children to this life. Better dead than be put through this.

A tear trickled down his cheek, his heart troubled. He covered his eyes with his hand.

A firm palm gently settled on his shoulder. Richard jumped, snatching his hand from his face as he sucked in a sharp breath and whipped his head around. But he immediately released all panic when he saw Pico holding a rusty shovel.

"It's unfortunate," Pico said. "She was so young. The cruelties are put upon us daily, even when we toil to the very bones of our bodies. But we must push on."

Richard turned, trying to hide his tears, but as he thought of those words, he searched the body and checked Amelie's skirt pockets. All he found was a snapped piece of string as though it'd been yanked free.

What could have happened to it? Richard briefly recalled that day in the barn. Had she worn it then? He hadn't paid attention to it, but perhaps she had. Perhaps one of the men had damaged it then.

Richard paused, unsure what to do. He could close up the grave now, but an aching in his chest—the thought of Sylvie's helpless face—wouldn't let him leave empty-handed. He peered at Amelie's face, dirt in the crevices of her discolored face and eyes. Richard leaned in. He grabbed a section of her curls and paused. Richard's other hand held her head with gentle care, securing it in place. He then silently apologized to her in thought before turning his head. It seemed harsh, defiling her body, but he didn't have a knife or scissors to make the task any easier. What else could he do? With a tug, he pulled a lock of her hair from the roots before tying it with the string. Pocketing the memento.

Richard stood tall now, beginning to shovel back the earth upon Amelie. He was taken aback when Pico stayed to help him rebury the woman, too.

Why would he do this for me? Why risk punishment when I wouldn't for him? Richard hung his head low again.

He carried the lock of hair in his hands and returned to the cabin with Pico at his side. Once safe in its walls, Sylvie sprang to her feet and quickly approached Richard; her eyebrows raised as if to question if he was successful. Richard held out his hand to show her the lock of hair.

Tears welled in her eyes. She ran forward as if he clutched a great gift of enormous worth, but she paused when looking closely at the lock of hair in his hands. As she studied it, her brows furrowed, a frown forming. She looked up at Richard. Richard pursed his lips and lightly shook his head. Her gaze and shoulders slowly lowered, but she nodded, seeming to understand.

"May I?" she asked, holding out her hands, her voice shaking.

Richard handed it over. Another man brought a lantern across and placed it on the floor. Richard stepped back, unsure of what was happening. But then he understood. He watched with much intrigue, witnessing their funeral, watching them bury the lock of hair in the dirt with such love.

Pain furrowed their faces as Sylvie tenderly buried the object, and soon, all the men and women chanted as some held back their tears, even those who had been reticent to help.

Richard stood silently, unsure how to be during such a tradition. It was different from the white man's tradition of a pleasant cemetery with an opulent headstone that would endure through a century or more. Instead, this poor woman would be lost to Earth's soil. Would his fellow slaves even remember where she'd been buried in a few years' time?

Thelma must have also wished to give Solomon the same respect, this being the means of comfort and closure. How it must have cut her deeply not to be able to say her simple goodbye.

Zora walked up to Richard, taking his hand. He gazed at her, and Zora kissed him gently on the cheek, startling him. She pointed at the turned dirt and whispered, "I thank you."

CHAPTER FIFTEEN

Richard woke up with the comforting feel of Zora tucked deep into his arms, her head nuzzled into his neck. Surprise rippled through him like a shudder, freezing him in place. For a moment, he was afraid to move, afraid to rile her or break contact. His hand hovered over her arm. With a gentle touch, he pushed on her shoulder, waking her from a deep slumber.

Zora's eyes slowly opened, only to see Richard sitting up, writing something in the dirt. Richard now pointed to Thelma's name, jabbing a finger.

Zora looked bewildered at Richard, who pointed again at the ground.

She was doing her best to avoid looking at the word, refusing to acknowledge it, even scuffing at it with her naked heel in the dirt. She commenced looking around to see if anyone else had noticed. Or perhaps she simply could not read it?

That was when he remembered; slaves couldn't read or write, at least they were not supposed to. Doing so could earn them one hundred lashes or worse. Richard wanted to slap himself for forgetting something so important. For being so sleep-addled-minded that he scrawled in the dirt, desperate for someone to see what he couldn't say. What if Zora reported him?

But then, he noticed her studying the word before looking about, cowering again.

Is she making sure no one's coming? Richard thought. He placed a hand on her shoulder, bringing her attention back to him, and slowly mouthed, *Thel-ma.* "*Thel-ma!*" Zora looked at the word, then his mouth, whispering her own attempts to sound out the syllables. After a few passing moments, Zora could say Thelma's name, the word rolling freely off her tongue, causing Richard to nod in earnest. Zora leaned in.

"Taken back to evil place with evil master," she whispered in broken English.

Richard's hopeful expression slowly morphed as the news sank in. Tears stung his eyes, welling up before he could gain composure. He started to cry, feeling that his only chance to return to his normal life was finally gone. He'd hoped no one would buy her so soon, that he would obtain the chance to see her again. He scuffed his hair in frustration, wanting to know where she was.

Who took her? Maybe then he could find his way to them.

Though confused, Zora comforted him by stroking his arm. The horn sounded, signaling it was time for the workday to start. Before getting up, Zora erased the name in the dirt, shook her head, and told Richard, "Won't tell."

And somehow, that brought him the most comfort of all.

Richard was disturbed by the news of Thelma. How would he ever find her so she could reverse the curse on him now? For slaves, going to certain places was restricted without a written note of permission from the masters. So, it would be next to impossible to find her. If he had to do this, he would first need to escape the plantation, and that was a suicide mission in itself. Having administered them, Richard knew the punishments meted out to runaway slaves.

So he couldn't be careless, or he'd end up crippled, or worse. Whatever the case may be, he decided that he would rather die trying than do nothing and remain the way he was. After all, was death so bad? Why so? It would give him everlasting peace and rest, and freedom.

Freedom in more ways than one. Yes, freedom from the toil of each day as he was living it now, but also freedom from terrible sins, freedom from his own self and all its hidden secrets.

Even if he was somehow restored to his former self as white Richard, could he ever take up life as it had been? Would he die a thousand deaths in the jailhouse of his memory if he once more became slave master, knowing the good the slaves had done for him?

As Richard worked in the fields, he saw his youngest, Margret, entering the barn, holding her beloved teddy bear. He shook his head, recalling the many times he had bitterly scolded his daughter for entering the barn. Richard couldn't fathom what would have happened if Margret had walked in to see the rape or anything that had gone on in that barn on that terrible day.

He shuddered at the thought. But then, an idea came to mind.

Richard looked about. There was one driver in his section, another atop a horse in another square section across the way. James had arranged it so there were at least two on duty at a time, but he'd place an extra for unruly sections. When the drivers turned their heads and sauntered farther away from him, Richard crouched low. He slowly inched his way through the field to the edge, picking along the way, occasionally stopping when a driver turned. Soon, he reached the edge of the field adjacent to the barn. When the coast was clear, Richard snuck inside.

Within seconds of seeing Margret, a wave of memories of his rape flooded his mind, freezing him in place. It clung to him like a shroud, the weight of that day pressing down on his chest. He couldn't breathe. Standing there felt like stepping back into the past, reliving every bit of it. But this opportunity to see his daughter outweighed everything, even the heavy emotion. He let the bright pastel colors of her dress guide him out of the darkness of his thoughts and further into the barn.

On entering, he briefly met eyes with the slave who had been ordered to mount him. But Richard knew it wasn't by choice; he also was a victim and had been forced.

They quickly veered their gazes, Richard forcing himself to breathe.

Other black men working in the hay noticed Richard's presence. Some eyed him curiously, but others ignored him as he tried to get Margret's attention. He had to tread lightly; if she screamed, he was done for.

When she turned to see him approach, she took in a sharp gasp. Margret stepped back away from Richard, hiding behind her teddy bear. Holding up calming hands, Richard quickly took some hay from the ground and made bunny ears and a goofy face.

If anything would help her to know him, it would be this shared silliness between daddy and daughter. And she did. Kind of. She gasped again, slowly lowering her teddy bear. "Do you know my daddy? Did my daddy teach you that silly face?"

Richard shook his head and pointed to himself, but she simply gave a bewildered expression. He waved her over.

Margret hugged her teddy bear tight and took a step back. "My daddy said I'm not supposed to talk to slaves in the barn. The slaves are unclean and not as educated as we are."

Did the girl—*his* girl—have a clue what she was talking about? And had he really hurled such appalling and unforgivable insults? Richard, at a loss, thought for a moment. Then, he looked around, deciding to take the risk of writing on the ground even with others present.

Margret cautiously walked towards him.

"You can—"

Richard quickly held a finger to his mouth to get her to lower her voice.

She lowered it. "You can write?"

He nodded.

"You're not supposed to write. Daddy doesn't like that. You could get in trouble. Only men like Daddy get to write. *And* read," she added.

Richard nodded again but pointed to the ground. Margret, still hesitant, took another step forward and looked, reading the words on the dusty earth.

'I am Richard.'

"That's Daddy's name. Do you know where he is? I miss him, and he was going to tell me a story. But I haven't seen him. Not for ages."

Richard nodded and pointed to himself. Then he jabbed his finger back at the name and at himself again. When Margret looked confused, he added, *'I'm your papa'*, in the dirt.

"You're… You're Daddy? But you can't be."

He nodded.

She jerked her head. "No, you're not."

Richard pointed to his scar. Then he wrote, *'I touched something hot, remember?'*

Margret wiggled her lips to one side, thinking. "I don't know… If you are Daddy, then when is my birthday?"

'August 21, 1826.'

"Hmm… what is my favorite dress?"

'The yellow one with pink flowers.'

Margret's eyes widened. "How did you know that?"

Richard pointed back to what he had written: *'I am Richard.'*

She stared at Richard for a solid minute. "What's our secret spot?"

Richard smiled, erased all his entries, and wrote, *'The first broken step on the porch. I left you lemon drops.'* As a finishing touch, he tapped the side of his nose.

She gasped, looking at him, *really* looking. "D-Daddy?"

He nodded.

"Daddy! You are Daddy!" Excited, Margret ran and embraced her father. "I knew you'd never run away. I just knew it!" she admitted.

Richard just melted, savoring the feeling of his daughter in his arms. He had missed her so much. Meanwhile, the slaves in the barn exchange confused glances, wondering why a white child was calling a black man her father.

Margret hopped down and cocked her head to the side as she eyed him, touching his coily hair and looking him over. "Why are you negro? Did you eat too much chocolate? Henry says if you eat too much of it, you can turn into one."

Richard gave a breathy laugh and shook his head. *That boy*, he thought.

Then Margret stunned him in the next sentence. "Daddy, you used to say the negros' color was because they were filthy. And that I mustn't play with them in case it rubbed off on me."

Really? Did I? he asked himself, aware of the answer.

He hung his head. It was easier to change the subject.

Quickly writing Thelma's name in the dirt, he pointed at it. Underneath, he wrote, *'Witch'*.

"I *knew* it," Margret said. "Daddy, I knew she was."

When Richard wrote, *'Where?'* Margret said, "Mr. Walker told Mama he'd returned her to the market a few days ago and sold her to a Mr. Bennett."

Days? A few days ago? Richard thought. Zora was right; Thelma had been successfully sold. But only days ago? Richard sank at the news. If he hadn't been wallowing in self-pity and fear and actually gone back to look, he might have been able to end this.

Shaking his head, his mind wandered elsewhere.

Mr. Bennett. Why does that name seem so familiar? Wasn't that the name of the man who sold Thelma to me? Could it be the same man? But why?

"Daddy, I have to tell Mama." Her eyes were alight with glee, but he knew Mary's wouldn't be. Not that his wife would accept it was him anyway.

The words had quickly brought Richard out of his thoughts, however. Margret was already tucking her bear under one arm and hiking up her dress with the other, ready to take off, but Richard took a sharp breath and quickly grabbed her by the arm before she could rush off.

No! No! he thought, quickly shaking his head while frantically waving his hands. *'Secret'*, he wrote in the dirt.

"Why?"

'They'll be mean to Daddy.'

Margret paused for a moment after that. What was she thinking?

Maybe she was musing on Henry about the times he'd been mean to her. Or perhaps something else. But then she stared at his scar. Her eyes softened as she gently stroked his cheek.

"How'd you get that scar?"

Richard gave a soft smile and shook his head.

"Why don't you speak, Daddy? Is it because of this?" She touched the burn mark on his neck.

He nodded.

"Do you need a doctor?"

He shook his head. *No.*

"Does it hurt?"

Richard smiled but shook his head.

Rapid footsteps approached, and Richard quickly erased his words from the dirt. One of the slaves rushed to him. "One of the white men comin'," he said before shuffling away as quickly as he came. Richard didn't understand why he chose to warn him, but he was grateful for it, nonetheless. With little time left, Richard signaled to Margret, holding a hand in the air and using the other to feign scribbling on it.

He repeated it. Then he pointed to the last step of the porch in the distance before tapping the side of his nose.

Richard wanted Margret to bring some paper and ink, instructing her to hide it away where they both could find it. She nodded quickly, her eyes showing comprehension. It wasn't difficult; father and daughter had been hiding things here for so long.

"Secret spot? Today?"

He nodded.

"But you don't like me going into your office on my own. Is it all right?"

Truth be told, he would have been fine with a crayon and drawing book from her room, but he didn't have time to explain that right now.

He quickly nodded, knowing an overseer was coming.

Margret agreed, and Richard hurried her out of the barn before James could see her.

He then slipped out of the barn and back into the field just before James could see him.

Richard took a moment to rest his hands on his knees, blowing out a slow breath and throwing himself back into work before a driver saw him slacking. He moved quickly, driven by new motivation. Richard could only hope that Margret would be able to slip the paper and ink under the deck by tonight without anyone noticing.

CHAPTER SIXTEEN

Richard snuck out of the cabin in the middle of the night after staying awake, waiting for all to fall asleep, especially Zora, who still lay next to him. If he had woken her, she might have tried to stop him or ask questions, which would have been understandable.

Tiptoeing out of the cabin, he headed straight for the house through the pathway in the cotton field, eventually hiding himself in the shrubbery across from it. Richard waited patiently, observing the drunken workers making their last rounds before going home. When the chatter ebbed, doors closed, and candlelight from the house was blown out, he took a deep breath and proceeded to inch towards the house.

I'm so close, he thought. *Please don't let them catch me.*

There was rustling in the bushes.

Richard instantly ducked down. Had he been found? He pressed himself down into the shrubbery as small as he could, hoping whoever was there couldn't see him. But alas, it was only a bush rat, the little chitter scurrying far out into the shrubs.

Richard heaved a sigh of relief, waiting a few moments to regain his composure. Then, he fixed his eyes on the porch. He hoped his daughter understood his gestures and had been able to put the supplies under the step.

But what if she hadn't?

This night would have been for naught.

And there was no telling when he'd see her by chance in the barn again or if he'd be lucky enough to sneak into the barn once more without being caught. But there was no time to think about it, and only one way to determine if Margret had succeeded. Richard positioned himself. Just as he prepared to sprint to the main house, his body flew, slammed to the ground, tackled from the side.

Panic flooded over him, thinking, *I've been caught!* He thrashed about, trying to break free from his attacker's grasp, but the man was strong. One of Richard's hand slipped free, ready to swing, but it stopped when he saw those familiar small eyes and the burn scar on his nose.

Pico.

"What in God's name are you doing, man? This will get you killed," Pico demanded, giving Richard's shoulders a firm shake. "Are you wanting to revolt against the massas? Don't be foolish! You've seen what happens. Haven't you taken enough of that treatment?"

Richard, still pinned to the ground, pushed Pico off him and furiously waved his arms, pointing to the deck, but Pico simply scrunched up his brows, not understanding.

Richard straightened himself, moving into a fit of charades. He felt silly doing it; he'd never had to gesture this much before. But after Richard exaggerated a writing gesture and motioned pen and paper and the step, Pico understood.

"Ah," he said. "You need to put something in a box? But why?"

Or maybe he didn't understand at all.

Finding it exhausting to explain as a mute, he pointed to Pico, then the cabin, repeating the motion when Pico remained still.

"No," Pico said, shaking his head. "I will not leave."

Richard let out a frustrated sigh. This was a waste of time, but instead of trying to argue, Richard gestured for him to stay low in the bushes. Then, he pointed to the ground before putting a finger to his lips. *Stay here. Keep quiet.* Pico nodded.

Richard slowly inched forward closer to the edge of the bush. He looked both ways before sprinting to the porch, skidding to a stop by the stairs. With a move here and a tug there, he slipped the slab open, grinning with relief when he found the paper, ink, and pen hidden under the wooden step. Richard held back a chuckle, but a wide smile spread across his face at the half-bitten tea cakes, and small pieces of sorghum drops that lay there as well. He snatched them up, shoving them into his pockets, knowing Margret would be sad if he left them.

He placed the pen between his teeth, pressed the stack of paper to his chest, and clutched the ink tight in his fist so it wouldn't spill. He closed the lid of the step and turned, ready to race back to the bushes.

Voices boomed with laughter as stumbling footsteps approached.

Richard quickly shuffled back and ducked, pinning himself to the side of the steps. His heart pounded, quickening as each heavy step grew louder and louder. He curled his body as small as he could, straining to remain unseen. But the shadow on the ground was closing in.

Just before the workers walked past him, a loud *thud* sounded. The workers, suddenly alert, stopped to listen. "Aye, you hear that?" Richard was curious, too. He looked about. It was then that Richard saw Pico cock his hand back to throw another rock at the stables opposite them. Diverted by the noise, the workers scuffled toward the stables, giving Richard time to escape back into the bushes, striving not to spill the ink or fumble the paper and pen.

Richard and Pico raced through the fields and barged through the entrance of the cabin, collapsing with relief. A few others at rest propped themselves up to stare at the cause of the disturbance, including Zora.

Breathing heavily, Pico said, "You are completely out of your mind!" Still trying to catch his breath, he turned to Richard and continued, "With all the bold, lunatic stunts you pull, you act like you have the reckless spirit of a white man."

Richard paused a moment, forgetting the need to catch his breath.

Then, gradually, he began to laugh.

Pico stared at him, confused. "Well, now I know you've really lost your mind," he said.

Richard laughed harder at that, not caring about the weird breathy noises coming from his lips. *If only he knew.*

A gradual smile braced Pico's lips. Eventually, Pico joined in.

A few slaves smiled along with the two, but most looked confused, Zora among them. Others seemed annoyed by their disturbance.

To Richard, it almost felt wrong to laugh, but he couldn't help it.

"It's nice to see you show some other emotion for once," Pico said. He leaned in and spoke softly. "It was worth you taking the paper. Though, I can't imagine what you'd need it for."

Taken aback, Richard stared at Pico.

He never thought he'd find himself laughing in that dreary place.

Richard patted Pico's shoulder to get his attention, then put his hand to his own chest before giving a brief head bow. *Thank you.*

"You are thanking me? What for?" Pico asked.

Richard thought for a moment.

For taking me under your wing? For finding a way to make me laugh in a depressing situation? For having my back? Trying to stop me from doing something foolish? So many things, almost countless.

Before Richard could respond, Pico said, "You are a crazy friend."

Then it hit him. Richard firmly grabbed Pico's shoulder, pointed to Pico's chest, then placed his own hand to his, repeating the gesture. *Friend.*

And this time around, he had no hesitation in saying it.

Richard took the paper, ink, and pen outside with a lantern to write a letter to his neighbor, Samantha—who was rumored to be an abolitionist sympathizer—begging for her help to free him. The idea had crossed his mind when he spotted Margret going into that barn that afternoon. But whoever would have thought he'd ask *her?* Now, he went outside behind the cabin to keep it secret from the other slaves. From past experiences, he knew that some slaves were not great at keeping secrets. Also, this way, the light from the lantern wouldn't be seen from the main house.

Richard stared at the blank paper, pen ready, but what would he write? That he was Richard and needed help freeing himself and wanted to meet with her?

That a witch had wickedly cursed him to live this cruel life?

No. No way she would believe him. Then again, Samantha probably wouldn't believe anything coming from Richard.

He needed to say something in the letter to convince her to meet with him.

When Richard was young, a slave had fled from the plantation, but he was found in less than an hour hiding in a white man's house. His dad had turned in that activist and shunned him.

"These nigger lovers are thieves in their own right," he'd said. "Harboring them is no different than harboring a monkey from a zoo." Now Richard was seeking one's help and could only imagine what his father would think of him.

Richard centered his focus. What if he mentioned he'd had a change of heart? No. He didn't expect her to believe him. *What would Richard say?* Maybe he could lie and say he'd harbored a slave, not his own, and was facing financial discrimination because of it.

He needed the man gone and wanted her to send him north.

No, that wouldn't make sense, and she'd hate him all the more for it.

Richard scratched his head, frustrated, unable to come up with a way to convince Samantha.

Then it hit him. He wouldn't be able to convince Samantha. But a slave just might. He wouldn't write as Richard, but as a slave because, as painful as it was to say, he *was* one. Here he was, living with them.

His pen began to move, scratching words on the page as fast as he could:

> *Dear Ma'am,*
>
> *Please do not be alarmed to receive this letter from Richard McLeary's daughter, Margret. She has trust in me, and I trust her too.*
>
> *And please do not be alarmed to hear that I am a learned slave captive on Master McLeary's plantation. He does not know I am able to read and write, so I know I am putting you and myself in danger for writing this script. But I beg you, trust this is neither deceit nor ploy.*
>
> *My master has vanished to a place no one knows for some time now, and I feel the time is opportune as a slave who could write the injustices going on and to give you insights you need to help free other slaves. In return, I ask that you help free me.*
>
> *Yours ever,*

He hid the note on his person before burying the other materials.

Once inside, he lay next to Zora, her back facing him.

As he prepared for sleep, she turned and faced him.

"Sneaking out, bad," she lightly scolded. Richard gave her a *don't be hypocritical* look. Then she smiled. "Just be careful."

She looked him deep in the eyes, a smile gracing her lips.

Richard didn't move, wishing he could ask what was on her mind. But he didn't have to wait long.

"Smiled, first time," she said, her voice still low. In broken English, she said, "It's first time I see you laugh. Sometimes, seems impossible here, but a moment like this, it gives hope to me."

She leaned her head in ever so slightly. "Promise me, when times hard, you remember this moment. You fight for it."

Richard nodded. She smiled and touched his cheek. "Kamau," she said, burying herself in his arms and falling asleep. It took him a moment to realize what had just happened, that she had just given him a name as she'd promised. Richard smiled and held her tight.

CHAPTER SEVENTEEN

Another grueling workday arrived. Though tired from his late night, Richard was on a high with anticipation, wondering if he'd be able to deliver his letter to Margret. For now, it was a waiting game.

Outside in the fields, Richard heard a slave blacksmith call out to "Massa" as he emerged from the barn, presenting the halves of a broken hand hammer.

"How the hell did it break?" James said.

The worker explained how he had been using it, and the way he described it showed tremendous ignorance.

"Well I, I's preparing to shoe the horses, but the backdoor of the forge, it stuck, so I use a hand hammer to open it."

"You dim-wit. You ain't supposed to be usin' it like that. Can't even complete a simple task. I swear y'all niggers worse than children. Damn!"

James threw his head back and let out a long, exasperated growl at the inconvenience. "Wonderful. Now the task of creating new horseshoes I had planned is delayed because your incompetence damaged our equipment."

"Forgive me, sir."

James sighed, chewing the side of his cheek. "Hold off on the horseshoes until we get another hammer. Until then, go"—James waved his hand to think—"go help feed the horse or somethin'."

The man nodded and hurried away.

As he did, Richard asked himself how such a sturdy tool could possibly have broken. It would have taken an insurmountable amount of force. Then, he noticed a few slaves, including Pico, in the field with subtle grins on their faces. When he caught Pico's eye, Richard shook his head, giving a quick one-shouldered shrug. His friend slowly worked his way over to him while still picking. "The tool broken," Pico whispered as soon as he reached Richard, still keeping his head down. "Small act of rebellion."

Richard didn't understand and shook his head.

Pico looked over his shoulder to see if they were being watched, then ducked back down.

"We... We are stupid to white men, inferior," he said. "Show them their beliefs."

Finally, Richard understood. This way of resisting the masters played into the white man's own inherent bias. In fact, doing so was the furthest thing from ignorant.

Richard couldn't help but laugh to himself. And he was surprised that the deception didn't even anger him. The man's action showed intelligence, but it left Richard to wonder. How many silent acts of rebellion did the slaves express or execute all this time, right under his nose?

Like the sharing of the cotton, for example. He thought about Zora. Something told him her pretending to be mute was yet another act of rebellion, another form of defiance from her. She would never just lie down and be acquiescent; every act was to push back.

Richard smiled to himself. *These sneaky niggers indeed.*

He paused at the thought. *Niggers.* It didn't feel right on his tongue. No. He chuckled to himself. *Hm. These are some sneaky people. And the whites... not so intelligent sometimes.*

As the others worked, Richard waited until noon when James and a few others would go eat lunch, leaving one white and one black slave driver—whom James recently appointed—to manage his fellow peers. Another display of James' act as 'master'.

Minutes seemed like hours as Richard watched James sit in *his* once-favorite rocking chair, looking out into the cotton fields. As soon as James finally went inside, Richard snuck off to the barn to see if Margret was there. He sure hoped so. When he saw her brown hair, relief flooded over him. He started towards her, but his strides quickly slowed, then halted. There, standing beside her, was Henry. Richard quickly backed away.

"No, I don't want to play with you," she said to Henry. "I'm doing something important."

"What in here is important? You're trying to listen to their stories again, aren't you?"

"No, I'm not."

"Then what?"

"I can't tell you. It's a secret."

"Then tell me the secret, and I promise I'll leave you alone."

"I can't tell you though. I told him I wouldn't. It's my secret. Could you please just go? I want to play by myself. It's girls' stuff, that's all."

"No, you don't want to play by yourself, Margret. I know what you're doing because you're a bad liar! You just want to listen to their stories again. *Papa says* we're not supposed to be in here. We're *never* supposed to be here because… Well, because we might meet the slaves by accident. And like he says, who knows what they might do to us if they catch hold of us?"

"But *you* come in here, so that's just stupid! If you're so keen on doing what Papa said, what are you doing in here? So, *you* come here too."

"Not as much as you."

"It's not a competition for who can be baddest, Henry," she said, putting her small hands on her hips and sounding like her mother; this was a thing Mary sometimes said when the children argued. Margret attempted again to shoo Henry away, but that just made Henry all the more stubborn. He sat cross-legged on the floor, making clear how he wasn't for moving.

She got up and slapped him on the head. "Henry, just go!"

He leaped up, shoving Margret to the floor.

Richard's fatherly instincts kicked in when Henry pushed her to the ground so hard, and without thinking, he rushed forward, knocking over a pail. Of course, it had been Margret who started the fight, but his blood was already boiling because he, too, hated how Henry was being stubborn. Richard's head was mixed up, too. Henry was correct and following his own orders.

There was no world in which all this mess would make sense. Anyway, now Richard had knocked over the pail and created a terrible racket, his and Margret's secret might be revealed.

However, Margret was crying loudly by now, and because of this, it seemed his son had not heard the noise outside. Richard slowly backed away, attempting to sneak out himself.

Then, a shiver ran down his spine. Someone from behind grabbed a firm hold of Richard's shoulders and then his upper arms, grappling with him, clutching tightly onto him, and refusing to let go. Richard backed up and tried to spin around to see who it was. He couldn't. In the very next moment, he was on the floor, flung to the stony ground just outside the barn.

Now, he looked up. It was Benji standing over him. What was wrong with Benji that he had to be so rough? Then he recalled that he, white Richard, was the one who'd taught Benji and the others to behave that way with the slaves. He was the one who had insisted, "If you find a dirty nigger doin' what he's not supposed to, or you find a dirty nigger somewhere he shouldn't be, messin' or interfering with the land or the property or my children or wife, you hurt him well and good, right?"

Everything he had ever said, and everything he'd ever told to his men, was coming to hurt him now.

To the left, Richard heard footsteps now approaching. "Well, well, well. I come out here to find the children to bring them in for lunch, and here I am, finding you lurking about yet again. You never learn, do you? You're a nigger in desperate need of a good beating. I'll see if I can get that organized for you since you're obviously gagging for one."

Richard said nothing. There was never any sense in arguing; it just made things worse. Like all slaves, it had taken him a bit of time to learn it. But he knew it by now.

Stay quiet. Head down.

James joined Benji's side, hovering over Richard. "It would be in your best interest to tell me why you're in the barn gawking at the master's children yet again and not at your post in the cotton field, but you can't do that now, can you? Because you ain't up to it."

James delivered a swift kick to Richard's ribs.

Curled up in pain, Richard glanced beyond James and into the background. James saw him looking and swiftly turned to do the same. The children were there and staring at them, both engrossed in the ugly event unfolding before their eyes. James looked at Benji.

"Mr. Cohen, would you kindly escort the children back to the house."

It was an order, not a question.

Benji gave a brisk nod.

As he directed the children to the manor, Margret asked, "Is he going to hurt him?"

"Don't worry, sweetheart. You don't have to be scared. He won't hurt *you*. Mr. Walker will make sure of that."

Margret called out in a panicked screech, "Please, don't hurt him!"

It gave the men pause, but her words faded as she disappeared inside the house.

James looked down and gave Richard a puzzled look.

"Now why would the master's child go 'n say a thing like that?"

James took one slow step toward Richard. Forcing himself upright, Richard frantically scooted himself backward in the loosened dirt, unsure what to do. He turned to the field. Some of the field hands looked over in horror, while a majority continued their work, too scared and fearful for themselves to look at what was going on.

Pico was there, holding Zora back tighter by the arm, and when he noticed James pulling out his gun, Richard stopped pushing along the floor.

James crouched to Richard's level and waved his pistol. "I'm gon' get to the bottom of this nasty business, mark my words. Now, what were you eyein' them kids for, hmm? I see you skulking around and oglin' the master's children a lot these days, dirty damn nigger. What you got in mind? Not gon' rape 'em, are ya?"

James toyed with Richard as he traced the gun along his body, dragging out his words. "Now… Where should I shoot first?" He paused. "It seems another lesson's in order, don't ya think, Butter Cheeks? Ya wantin' more of the same, are ya?"

A vile grin slithered onto his lips as he slid the tip of the pistol close to Richard's mouth. "You calmed down for a while after that session in the barn. So perhaps I should get another one of these niggers to fuck you in your sorry asshole since you ain't had enough. What say you?"

Richard trembled at the words, remembering *that* day, the one day he had tried so hard to forget and put behind him. But how could he ever forget that? It was heinous, biting into his psyche every day. He would never be free of it. Then came another equally hideous thought. *Never be free…* Perhaps this was how his slaves felt when they, too, had been abused.

And in any case, they would never be free of their chains. Never free of their terrifying recollections. Never free of their past. Most of all, never free of their color that caused all this suffering for them in the first place. He'd been a critical part of their torment. Maybe a small part of him now believed he deserved everything he got, everything James issued to him for doing all that to the slaves. But that thought didn't stop the overwhelming trepidation running through him—his once dear friend, now a master he absolutely feared and resented. The very person whose chilling eyes promised nothing but pain and torment.

At that point, Richard was ready to do anything to make James leave him alone, including praying. Perhaps that would right his wrongs. God was a master who might understand when another asked for His mercy.

But this was God's own way of punishing him, wasn't it?

James sneered before pointing the gun at Richard's head, taking a warped joy in pulling back the hammer. Richard was still as he stared down the barrel.

But Richard saw something else too. He saw Pico, unable to hold himself back anymore—at least, that's how it appeared to Richard.

Maybe Pico needed to save him so he wouldn't die like his brother. Maybe he was just a better man than Richard could ever be. Whatever the reasons, Pico rushed up and tackled James, the bullet hitting the bark of the oak tree instead of its intended target. Richard struggled to his feet as Pico wrestled with James.

Noticing James grabbing his other pistol, Richard snapped himself out of the shock, grasping at James' arm when he pointed the gun at his friend Pico.

It forced James to throw the gun into the bushes. Gun lost and losing against Pico, James called for assistance. Pico landed a punch, hitting James' face before two white men restrained both Richard and Pico, twisting their arms tight behind their backs. Pico hissed out in pain, and Richard gritted his teeth: any harder, and their shoulders were sure to dislocate. James rose to his feet, wiping the blood from his lip. "Bring him to the oak tree," he ordered the other men as he jabbed a finger Pico's way.

"What do we do with the mute?" Parkinson asked.

James stared at Richard with cold, bitter eyes. "Make Butter Cheeks watch the hanging. Then we might think of something real *special* for him."

Richard's blood went cold.

Parkinson and a group of others struggled to restrain Richard as he tried to grab Pico's arm to pull him away from the angry men. Putting up this struggle was pointless. Soon, the whites had a cruel hold on his arms, doubly ensuring Richard wasn't successful.

Bringing both men to the oak tree, the white men held Richard back as he watched Pico fight, the man to be hung somehow managing to muster all his fighting strength in his final hour. His body writhing and kicking, Pico was even throwing some men off. Others, however, clung on, tightening the rope around his neck. It was noticeable that now, the men were not especially rough with Pico, particularly given how he was trying to fight back. They did only what they needed to, to restrain him and get their job done. The job of executing a nigger.

It was surreal to witness since it almost appeared the men were allowing Pico some small amount of humanity as his days drew to an end.

It was a false humanity: these men surely were in possession of none.

With great difficulty, one of the men made sure the rope was secured tight and immovable around the thickest branch of the tree where Solomon and Isaac's bodies had been hung.

Richard tried to break free as he watched the plantation workers lifting Pico to his feet, even trying to scream, to beg them not to take his friend.

Pico looked at Richard with desperation. His look said, *Help me.*

"Friend. Family. Brother—"

The men yanked on the rope, pulling Pico into the air where he moved wildly, thrashing like a fish on a line, his arms desperately trying to claw the rope away from his neck. Deep gurgles and choking noises escaped from his throat as his legs viciously kicked at the empty space beneath him. Slowly, the jostling waned, weakening to a feeble twitch until all movement stopped. His shoulders slowly dropped to hang limply at his sides. His eyes, blood-filled, stared down at Richard as though he could see into his soul. A warning. Now, poor Pico remained perfectly still. The remaining life was pulled from his body. There was a wetness dripping onto the ground from between his legs. Pico had pissed himself in the strangulation, not uncommon but especially undignified to see happening to a friend.

Richard's knees buckled as his body went limp. The moment his skin changed color, he was cast into an abyss. And for a while, he'd been walking and feeling his way through the dark until that one light, that one hand—Pico's hand—guided him out. But now, that light was snuffed out.

Richard collapsed, burying his face into the dirt as tears poured from his eyes. And he still had his own punishment to look forward to. Surely, it would be coming next.

"Search for my pistol," James ordered the white drivers. "And make sure them slaves don't walk around that area until it's been found."

Richard continued to cry as he heard footsteps approach, then they halted as James crouched beside him. "What? You really think this is over, boy? You think you two can attack me and put it into all of your heads that you can—what—revolt?" James said. "Much as I'd love to spare you because you kind of remind me of someone, I can't do it, see? Because one day, one nigger revolts, and the next thing you know, half the plantation's following their example.

"That just won't do, Butter Cheeks, and I'm sure you can see why. Maybe we need to make another example of our own. The thing about overseers is we see everything. And I see you've gotten acquainted with some *friends*, haven't you, Butter Cheeks? Friends like Nini. And there was me thinkin' you only had an eye for men. But it seems you don't mind either way."

Richard stopped breathing. He cursed himself, knowing James saw right through his antics with Zora lately. "I should go into that field right now, drag Nini out here, and have her burned at the stakes. Or maybe let someone have a little fun with her beforehand. Teach you never to try something so stupid again. Understand?"

Richard's sadness quickly turned to rage. He looked James dead in his eyes.

It achieved nothing. With a wide grin, James headed towards the field.

"Guess I'll burn that bitch myself," he said as he went. But Richard grabbed his leg, then threw up pleading hands, the employed drivers watching with smug smiles.

James smirked. "Take him to the forge."

Richard blinked, taking a moment to register what James had said. He wasn't being taken back to the barn. A tiny ounce of relief made his hands tremble. Still, his heart sank.

'To the forge' conveyed only one thing. Something hideous. Something abhorrent.

Four of the group grabbed Richard, dragging him to the forge near the barn and stringing him up by his arms. The rope pulled against his skin, burning and cutting into the already dry, cracked places. He gritted his teeth and tried not to give them a reaction as they continued to yank and pull the ropes, only satisfied when a pop or two could be heard. Once he was secured, one of the workers tore open his shirt so his back lay bare. James taunted as he heated a branding iron with the initials R.M. in the fiery forge.

"I'll make sure to make another branding iron with my own initials," James said.

Richard trembled, gripped with fear and anticipation as his eyes tracked the movement of the red-hot iron that would sear him deep.

Parkinson gagged him with a dirty rag on James' order so he wouldn't bite his tongue.

Moving forward, James held the glowing iron, eyeing it with an amused look as he slowly turned it in his hand, visibly examining it like he would a new blade. The letters R and M were prominent now, burning brightly like a heated stove.

Richard trailed him with his eyes as James walked behind, out of sight.

Then, there was silence. And Richard waited in tormenting anticipation, his breath quickening. Then everything seared, a sharp *hiss* sound filling the room. He screamed as the scorching reddish-orange metal plate was promptly applied on a long pole to the quivering flesh of his upper right shoulder blade, imprinting upon it Richard's initials. A slave, now the property of himself, the slave owner.

As the iron peeled away, taking a layer of his flesh with it, he let out a broken, muffled scream. He felt faint, finding it difficult to breathe, and nearly passed out from the excruciating pain. There was the faintest sound of sizzling skin and then a flash of severe pain that accelerated above anything he could imagine.

After a few seconds, the intensity leveled off, but at that point, it felt like fire. Richard's body was in shock by now, every limb shaking and juddering, also freezing cold except for where the skin had been seared. He went limp, his head bobbing as he drifted in and out of consciousness.

"Guess this makes you mine now."

After a while, James ordered the others to throw Richard into the shack.

They dragged him mercilessly by his arms and tossed him inside into the rough, weathered planks that formed the small structure. It felt surreal, as if this just couldn't happen. How could James, of all people, treat him this way? Yet he did, and with a slam, Richard was left there in the dark, alone. Unable to move. Unable to bear the wretched loss of a man he called *friend*. Unwilling to accept this had all been meted out by that same man, Richard curled himself into a ball, buried his face in his hands, and cried uncontrollably.

Richard felt beyond weak in every way conceivable. Physically, mentally, and emotionally, his mind was in a whirl of confusion, something probably akin to the final hours of a dying man. Lost in a whirl of agony, his mind was playing vicious tricks on him, projecting scenes over and over. Scenes of the past. Scenes of the future. Scenes of something hovering in between the two. In some scenes, he was white Richard, the man who had it all. A pair of beautiful and well-behaved, perfect children. A large house on a plantation. A job that made him the envy of many.

He had money to spend and fresh running water, hot and cold, and plenty of food in the larder.

In other scenes, he was black Richard, the slave, the no-good one, the worthless one who deserved nothing but a damn good kicking and thrashing every minute of every day for something he had done or something he had failed to do. Richard who could never get it right. Richard who could never please his bosses because they simply chose never to be satisfied.

He envisaged himself wetting his britches as a reminder of seeing poor Pico's last minutes. Each time he shut his eyes even to blink, he saw Zora being flogged, Pico being hung, a huge barn rat being drowned in Henry's own little hands, Margret lost in a world of tears.

And he saw countless men being shot and whipped and beaten and dragged and burned. He heard their deathly screams of persecution and anguish, of loss and loneliness and hate.

He saw women being made to strip and put their brown asses high in the air to take what the men would be giving to them, over and over and again if they didn't take it well.

And worse still, he saw himself pinning kind, sweet Zora to the hard ground, raping her, hearing her cry and moan, devoid of any words because there was nothing worth saying.

His reality was a kind of make-believe, a never-ending series of the most tormenting nightmares. He imagined Pico sitting in the corner saying "friend," just like on that first day he had seen him in the shack. His mind replayed every scene in which Pico had helped him too.

Richard didn't bother trying to figure out how long he had been locked in the shack, listening to the world turn. This was like jail, the cruelest form of mind games and control. Sure, he hated being outside doing the hard labor. But being shut inside was far worse, losing the sense of belonging.

And then it came to him that he did, with the slaves, have that. Belonging. It was something he had never truly had as white Richard. Now, he could hear his former world happening outside—the thunderous cracking of whips, the yell of a driver echoing through the fields, the occasional cry of agony—and he abhorred it. Maybe it was only because of his own injuries that he had feelings for the slaves now, feelings for them and feelings about them. But one thing was for certain: right now, with his wounds so fresh and all the insults so raw, he understood in which world he lived his better life. And to his horror, he discovered it was the harder one, the black one. They gave him a community. They treated him well.

From here inside the shack, just occasionally, he'd hear James shouting orders at the other white drivers to find his damned gun before everything spilled over and spiraled out of control. "Find it, find it, find it!" A missing pistol wasn't good, and it told in his tone.

"We have to find it, or some nigger's gonna get funny ideas. C'mon, find it!"

"It couldn't have gotten far."

"Maybe one of the niggers already took it."

"Well, there'll be hell to pay if they did."

Thankfully, at some point after, someone was sent in to check and tend to Richard's branding wound, which had swollen beyond belief. The skin would have split if they hadn't taken a clean blade and sliced a long, thin nick at the side, allowing it to swell more, which was vital for healing. But now, they'd have to dress that wound as well, not just the burn. But it was still better that way.

An infected burn could cause him to not perform as well, and of course, James didn't want that any more than Richard did.

Outside the shack, Richard heard Parkinson stating how everyone was tired of James and his ways. The way he'd stepped into Richard's shoes, it just didn't sit right with him.

He reckoned there was some sort of funny business going on.

"And he thinks I'm gonna go tearin' around all over hell's half acre, strainin' heart, and lungs to go huntin' down his goddamn gun? There's plenty new ones to be had, but no, he has to have his own, the bastard."

"I know. He thinks he's turned into somebody now that he's sleepin' with Mrs. Mary."

Richard could barely believe his ears. But the shock of that news didn't last long. After all, it was what he'd been expecting for quite some time. He'd seen how the two looked at each other, and it was obvious how they all assumed white Richard, the slave owner, would never be back. Of course, he didn't give a rat's ass what happened to Mary. She could open her legs for anyone she chose, and he wouldn't care except to be angry she was behaving like some common whore and was still his wife, at least until such time as the authorities deemed him dead…

But he very much cared about the implications of what that meant. The ramifications… that James would be free to formally acquire the plantation and the children.

Then there was the unhappy matter of Benji and Parkinson talking about "the mute".

"Why does James keep him around?" Parkinson said. "He hasn't given any clues about Richard's whereabouts even if James keeps the pressure on him, like. It's like he don't even know where the master is, so he couldn't tell even if he wants to. Reckon it wasn't nothin' to do with him, jus' a coincidence he was messin' with Mrs. Mary on the day Richard took off. And have ya noticed, no one seems to be lookin' for the master no more neither?"

"I think James just likes toying with him," Benji said.

"Humph. If he were my nigger, I'd kill him. In fact, I woulda had him strung up from day one. I mean, he was in Mary's room, for Christ's sake. If anything, I thought that'd be reason enough for James, the way he be lookin' and fawning over at her all the time. There's no reason James should insist on keepin' that nigger alive!"

"Well, he's not our property," Benji said. "Reckon he's waiting fer the nigger's true owner to want to claim him, then James can put a pretty price on his head."

"Yeah, but that dangling one over there wasn't our property either, but Richard's. And if that were true, why'd he just go and brand the boy with Richard's initials? Hm? Shit…"

"It's not lost on me, Parkinson," Benji said. "There's no consequence to James since he used Richard's initials. He could still get the money. But brandings can be removed, cut out. And he could still collect the reward."

Parkinson grumbled. "Well, I'd say we forget the owner's reward for returning him and just sell him. The longer we keep him, the lower the value because no one can say he appreciates in value because of gettin' fitter or learning more skills and what have you. That nigger's just a liability if you ask me."

"Well, it's customary to wait for a master to claim his slave. If you have an issue with that, bring it up with James. He's acting master. He calls the shots."

Parkinson scoffed. "Hell, yeah. Ya think I don't know all that? But I think we both know James is tryin' to do more than just call the shots. If I didn't know no better, I'd say James was gettin' too tall for his britches. That mute son of a bitch is more trouble than he's worth. No sense in holdin' back whippin' him now since James is already claimin' him as his own."

Dread clawed at Richard's chest. He was scared to hear those statements, afraid they would take everything from him, afraid that he'd be forgotten. And above all, he was afraid this would be his permanent life.

Sometime later, Richard was released from the shack and thrown right back into the cotton field. The next morning, the sun had yet to rise as Richard snuck out into the yard. It went without saying, but James had made it clear for the slaves not to touch Pico's body and not to bury it.

But Richard wanted to take him down so badly he was willing to risk another punishment. After all, it wasn't as though he valued his own life these days. What was another thrashing?

He turned to Solomon's body and Isaac's body next to his.

Richard stood underneath Pico and tore off a piece of his piss-stained cotton pants as tears streamed down his cheeks. Once upon a time, Richard had thought he knew what true friendship was. But now he knew that had never been so. Once he'd met Pico, he realized a true friendship, what it looked like and stood for. And now, his man Pico was gone.

Richard brought the torn piece of Pico's clothing into the cabin where the others had been eagerly waiting for him as if looking forward to a long-lost son returning from a bitter war.

Olivia took the piece from Richard, touching his hands.

"I promise you," she said, "Your friend lives on. We'll see that he does."

Richard dug a hole in the ground with his hands, placing the material inside before covering it over with the dirt. He wished he could do so much more. He wished he could rise high, lift the bruised body from the gallows of the tree, and lower him, cradle him in his arms. He wished he could look into poor Pico's opaque eyes and say how sad and sorry he was.

"Come. You have done what you can," Olivia said, leading Richard to the center of the cabin.

The slaves sang songs of farewell to Pico.

I know moonlight, I know starlight,
  I lay dis body down.
I walk in de moonlight, I walk in de starlight,
  I lay dis body down.
I know de graveyard, I know de graveyard,
  When I lay dis body down.
I walk in de graveyard, I walk through de graveyard,
  To lay dis body down.
I lay in de grave an' stretch out my arms;
  I lay dis body down.
I go to de judgment in de evenin' of de day,
  When I lay dis body down;
And my soul an' your soul will meet in de day,
  When I lay dis body down.

As they sang, each of them walked past and stooped low to touch the loose dirt with bony fingertips before placing their hands to their chests. Some paused to whisper words, letting their hands linger for a while longer. Others wept, unable to do more than mumble broken goodbyes. Richard looked among the slaves, admiring their deep care for one another, how these *people* showed so much love. How they soaked up so much pain with immense dignity. As he stood there, he posed himself a question. Why did people like him and his father always treat *these* people like dirt, like shit, in fact, torturing them at the slightest provocation—or more commonly, at no provocation at all?

And how had he ever seen them as being different from himself? So inferior to himself, to be exact? He paused at the thought, the accidental word again, the one that'd flitted through his mind. These people. Yes, they *were* people. People like he was.

They laughed like him, hurt like him, loved like him, bled like him...

Your blood is the same color as that of your property. You're no better.

Mary's words rang in his ear. And he saw the words in a different light now.

As much as he hated to admit that he respected anything his wife said, this time, she had been right. But Richard no longer saw them as property. Everything had changed.

Zora stood next to Richard. As the slaves sang, Richard said a prayer in his head, something he never did, apologizing to Pico for failing to help him. He expressed that feeling of helplessness again, also expressing gratitude that Pico had risked his life to save him.

Richard apologized for any way he'd mistreated him as a slaver, explaining that it was only happening right now because he had come to see he hated himself and the world. That he was a terrible person. He hated himself for ever being a part of such brutality and humiliation being meted on these people. These fine people who would do anything to allay another's suffering, their pain, their loss, or public humiliation. These people who would give their last mouthful of food to another man and who would stand in the way of any of their friends being tortured.

He took an oath that he would make James pay for Pico's death and would never own another slave if this affliction were ever to be lifted. Zora's fingers laced into Richard's hand.

Without looking at her, he squeezed her fingers and interlaced his own with hers, steady tears falling down his cheeks. A strangled sob escaped his lips. The lips that still refused to speak because, like all men with the background of a slaver, his god felt him undeserving of speech.

For now, Richard could only hope that Margret would be in the barn today. There was no other reason to wish to go on. No other reason to claim that he deserved to breathe or feel.

CHAPTER EIGHTEEN

For the rest of the day—in his spare shirt—Richard peeked into the barn from afar, hoping to see Margret playing inside. But for the entire day, she still didn't show up. His heart was bereft, and his skin chilled with fear that perhaps something might have befallen the dear girl.

Wouldn't that be just his luck, for something terrible to happen to one of the children while he was in no situation to help them? But it was silly to worry now. Not so soon.

There would be an explanation, he was sure. But then again, *was* he sure? His logic told him one thing, but his instincts wanted to lead him in another direction.

After a terrible, nightmare-filled night in which he could not sleep for turning from one side of his body to the other, thinking about where Margret may have gone to, he returned the next day.

Even now, he didn't spot her either, almost weeping as he hid out in his secret place.

As Richard lined up to give away his cotton, he was left telling himself that tomorrow was another day and that he had to cling to the hope of his daughter being alive and well.

He had to think that perhaps she had been kept inside for bad manners or poor behavior, or perhaps she was sickened with something. *Nothing has happened to my girl. She is fine. It is all going to be fine,* he told himself.

Richard looked two men ahead of him, spotting the young man, Micel, standing tensely, gripping his basket tight. Richard eyed it, seeing it was short on cotton. He picked some out of his own basket and nudged the man before him, telling him and the other slaves to pass it up. One by one, the cotton moved up steadily until it was dropped into the young man's basket.

Micel looked back, and Richard gave him a nod. Micel nodded back. When Richard watched his good deed help save the slave from a sure beating, that was when he saw Margret running into the barn.

Worse luck, James had noticed her too, and he shook his head.

But thankfully, he was more concerned about collecting the day's bounty.

As the slaves were sent back to the cabin, Richard slipped out of the pack and hid in the cotton field until James returned inside the house. When the coast was clear, he slipped into the barn as usual, casting his eyes around eagerly, his heart still dancing with happiness that he had seen his little girl looking so fit and well after the worry he had faced.

At first, he didn't spot her, but then Richard found her hiding in a corner.

She was seated quietly on the hay, doing nothing but making bunny ears. He startled her for a second, but she calmed upon seeing him, moving the bundle of hay out of the way.

He froze upon hearing her sobs. But again, he told himself it was nothing, couldn't possibly be anything! He thought back to when he had caught her looking just as upset as this, and the reason. It was not so long ago, before everything changed. This was when Henry had drowned the rat in the barn, holding it by its long tail and pressing its head into the water.

But he was taking no chances in case these tears were something more serious.

He rushed over and saw Margret's face buried in her teddy bear's chest as she cried. Richard gently placed his hand on her shoulder, and when she looked up, his heart dropped into his stomach. Her face was covered in bruises, along with her arm.

Richard frantically pointed as tears of anguish and fury welled in his eyes. Her own were red from crying.

Looking up at him with her beautiful brown eyes, Margret said, "I'm hiding from Henry, Daddy. He hurt me because I told him it was a secret, but he wanted me to tell him. And I"—she sniffed—"I tried to tell him that you'd been cursed by the witch. But he slapped me and said it was such nonsense." She cried harder. "And he called me a nigger lover."

Richard's gaze lingered on Margret, regret pooling in his eyes. He tightened his jaw, allowing the thick silence of culpability to flood over him. The inescapable truth was there, clinging to him like a shadow, and he despised himself for it, despised himself for raising Henry to be that way. And now, he had made his little girl, his pride and joy, suffer so much. Pity welled deep in his gut, not just for his young son for not knowing any better, but also for his little daughter for having to grow up in an atmosphere of prejudice and hatred that he fostered himself.

Henry was growing up to be everything Richard had always said he hoped for.

She cried. "Daddy, where were you for the past few days?" she asked, wiping her tears. "After they hurt you, they wouldn't let us outside to play, but when they did, you weren't there. I thought you would become a scarecrow on the tree. Henry said you'd become one. I don't want Daddy to turn into a scarecrow," she cried. And his heart nearly broke.

Both Henry and Margret knew that the lynched slaves were punished because they were "bad." Margret viewed them more like scarecrows, while Henry was more in touch with reality. But to hear the fear in his daughter's heart shattered his own.

Thinking of Pico and being locked in the shack, Richard simply wrote, *'I'm sorry.'*

A tear ran down Margret's cheek as Richard wiped it away with his thumb. "I wish you could come back home. *When* can you come back home?"

He shook his head, and her voice cracked.

Richard wrapped his arms tightly around her and quickly made bunny ears of hay. It took a moment, but her sobs quieted, and her expression gradually softened until a subtle smile tugged at her lips. And soon, she was back to showing her usual cheery grin.

Once he heard Margret's cheerful giggle, Richard handed her the paper and pointed to the name on the letter before pointing to Samantha's yellow house in the far distance. Then he brought out a separate paper on which he wrote instructions:

> *When you go to town with Mama, ask her to look at the woman's hydrangeas, then place the letter in the flowers, or hand it to the lady if she is present.*

Margret pointed to the word "hydrangeas."

"What's that?" she said.

He pointed to the word "flowers."

Richard wrote in the dirt, *'Don't show anyone.'*

Margret nodded and smiled. She gave Richard one strong embrace before skipping back into the house. Richard rushed and slipped back into the line.

In the slaves' cabin, few questioned where Richard had gone; they were worried. "Thought Massa got hold o' you again," one said. They were just happy to see that he was all right, especially Zora. Upon his entering, she'd been pacing along the dirt floor, but as soon as she spotted Richard, she rushed over, embraced him, and delivered a quick, unexpected kiss. Their eyes widened. It surprised them both, along with the other gaping men and women gathered around. Zora stepped back. She touched her lips, pausing for a moment, then walked the other way.

Richard could have sworn he caught her blushing.

Unable to sleep, Richard thought about the kiss. It felt nice. Warm. Tender. But he was conflicted, certain Zora wouldn't have done that—or any of her other kind and affectionate gestures, for that matter—if she'd known who he really was.

Suddenly, a gentle hand tapped his shoulder.

Richard turned to see Zora with a finger to her lips. She waved for him to follow. Richard sat up, watching her skillfully maneuver around the others, no doubt well-practiced from her many ventures out. When she noticed he hadn't moved, she stopped and waved him over again.

He got up and tiptoed over the other sleeping bodies, quietly following Zora outside as she carried a lantern. She went behind the cabin, out of sight from the main house, and Richard watched as she dug something up with her hands. To his disbelief, she brought out a small drawing book, leather-bound, that was tattered and shredded at the ends as though rats had nibbled on it.

It was one of the many books he had purchased for Margret. Why would Zora have it?

How had she come to have it in her possession?

Slaves weren't allowed personal possessions on his plantation, let alone journals.

Zora dragged him down to sit beside her. Then, she began to talk in calm tones. "Please read," she said. She patted the journal.

What? Does she want me to read it to her? He was unable to do it. Didn't she know that? But Zora clarified, "For you. Practice."

A warmth filled Richard's heart as he realized Zora's intentions; she assumed he had not seen words in a while and wanted him to have the opportunity. He smiled at the kind gesture. And it wasn't until now that he realized how much he'd missed seeing and reading words.

Richard took it from her hands, opened the journal, and read through the first page.

The writing was bad and barely decipherable, filled with many errors, but with each entry, the writing gradually improved:

> It is cold out tonite as I writ this. I admit I am scared to do so. It fels strange writing in a childs drawing book and dificult with charcol crayon. But it was all Djenabou could give me. I am gratful, and happy that we are reunited again.

Richard furrowed his brows. *Djenabou? Reunited? What is this?* There came a break in the page. Richard assumed it was a new entry.

> I don't like wurking in the house. Only good thing is being close to Djenabou.
>
> White men lok at me. I fel safest in the kichen away from there stares. But I have been beaten and put outside to wurk the gardens today for refusing to bath. Sometimes I wonder if it was best wurking the filds.
>
> This family wasts so much food. I saw one of the slaves take some from the trash pile but said nothing. Hopefuly the others eat good tonite.
>
> Djenabou keep talking to litle white girl. I

fear won day shel be in trouble.

I was almost caught tonite trying to see Saikou in the fild wurkers cabins. I hate they put him in the filds away from me and Djenabou. But he was happy to see me and I him.

The master beat me agin today. My boddy sore and brused and mite cry. I did not met him in his room when call me yesterday. That lok in his eye it scar me. I hate when he calls upon me, but better Nini than Zora.

Richard froze. *Nini?* He looked at her, realizing what he held in his hands. All of this, it was Zora's own writing. There was no doubt it was hers. To think he'd had an educated slave on his plantation this entire time. She was full of secrets. But it made no sense; how could Zora have come to learn writing? The slaves were ignorant. Everyone knew they received no education. Their brains held nothing more than the brains of the monkeys in the trees, back where they'd come from. At least, that's what he'd always been told.

He looked at Zora, pointed to the journal, then to her.

She nodded. "My life," she said.

Richard felt a lump in his throat, anxious over what he might read next. Overcoming his shock, he continued to read.

Master Micleery keep watching me, he follows like shadow. Why dos he favor me? I don't like him to pick on me, hit me when angry. He always angry.

My wrists are bruised from the chains. Djenabou broke the mistres vase. A white man wanted to beat her, but I put my body over her. They beat me insted. I took the blame. I don't want to see her hurt.

My back stings from floging. I almost hit the white man from the pain. It was a mistake, and I was scared. I ran outside to climb tree, angered them more.

Richard figured she must have written the entry recently because they matched the parallels of his memories of her life on his plantation. How many entries had she managed to write during her time here? Richard scanned the next page. Zora's following entry was smudged as though she penned it in tears.

I writ as though ill sufocate. My body is stained by master's touch. My burden for his crulties upon my family. I am alone. I feel I should die.

Richard quickly closed the journal, catching his breath. To have his atrocities thrown back in his face was unbearable.

Zora offered him a soft smile.

"I come out to read writing, to practice," she said. "But I've not practiced for a while. No more charcoal to write since no longer working in house."

Richard opened the drawing book and pointed to Djenabou's name, and she nodded, explaining her story.

"Djenabou, she is Fulani woman stolen off coast of Guinea near where my parents lived. She and her son Saikou are uh…" She searched for the word. "…wanderers. They encamped near the missionary fort recently build. White men, Christian. They taught English and French to locals to spread their God's word. I did not understand it. The Christian make me afraid of Djenabou because she was indigenous, you understand? Medicine woman, they say dark enchantress using magic. Others feared her as well. As a wanderer, she helped heal sick in travels. I did not understand why helping woman doing good was bad and became curious.

"I gathered courage and we work together while in missionary fort and wanderer camp. She taught me plants. Uh… medicine. My parents did not like me sneaking to the fort, so I kept my relations with Djenabou secret. She was wise woman, blessed with great power. But there was something different about her. I grew to trust and care for her until Djenabou was like a mother to me, her son, Saikou, my brother." She let out a little sigh and looked off as though lost in her memories. With sad eyes, she turned back and continued.

"So, a warring tribe raided the area, killed all missionaries and my parents, put place to the torch. Djenabou and Saikou were only few survivors after our tribe slaughtered. Djenabou took me when white men gathered us…" A tear fell. "They sold us to Americas."

Richard slumped his shoulders. He glanced at Zora, then at the page again. She had been illegally sold. Richard had always known that her English was sloppy, but he'd naturally assumed she was originally from a slave-owning state. He swallowed, his heart heavy.

"Coming here… All I see are white faces free, happy. Black faces, they in chains. We are ignored and silenced. The three of us, they bring us to the market. And they sell me to horrible man, separated from them. They take my name, call me Nini. I promise I would not answer to it. So, they call me mute. So be it."

Richard smiled at that.

"But also, I stopped speaking because people who sold me might noticed I was learned. I did not want to be in trouble with masters. Never told slaves because I not want to tell my past and what I gone through. Don't want others to feel… less.

"On Master Hemings' plantation, I heard of slave healer who had a son, and hoped it was Djenabou and Saikou. Sold to a Mr. Bennett."

That name again, Richard thought.

He remembered the old man who'd sold Thelma and Solomon to him.

"I was desperate to see my only family and left to find them. It was hard, but I did. I escaped from master's to go to Mr. Bennett's field so I can talk with slaves there. But his men caught me and locked me in chains until my master was found."

Zora paused to think a moment but smiled softly. "A woman came to me. I don't know how, but she knew why I was there. She told me Djenabou and Saikou were sold. I find that their new master named them Thelma and Solomon."

Richard paused. His heart sank.

"That woman spoke to me, saw I was there. She was an angel, but Mr. Bennett evil man, said Djenabou was wicked. My own master heard rumors of Mr. Bennett's slave being a witch and wanted to sell me. He said I was um… ill or… infected—yes, infected by her, did not want her wickedness around. So, he sold me.

"On that market day, fate. Djenabou and Saikou, they were there. I thought I would never see them again, but they were in chains with a slaver. I stared at him. Challenged him so that he buy me too and we be reunited. And he did. We all went with Master McLeary."

Zora frowned, lost in thought. She turned to Richard.

"Kamau, are you a runaway?" she asked.

Richard hesitated. He wanted to come clean and almost wrote it for her, but Zora gave a gentle smile. "You don't have to tell." She paused. "But you were in master's room, yes? Was he there?"

Richard shook his head.

"I wonder where he is," she thought aloud. Her eyes began to water. "Perhaps it is good he is gone. Master McLeary is a cruel man, worse than my old master. He…" Her lips quivered. "He took my family. I feel it is my fault for Saikou's death. If not for my defiance against master, Saikou would live, and Djenabou would be here."

She cried, her tears glistening on her cheeks.

Richard wanted to comfort her but felt it was wrong to. He was the cause of her distress.

"No one knows where master is, but you are lucky you come here when you did. Would be much worse if master here." She paused to gather herself. "I was surprised you knew of Djenabou when you ask me. She took this... this journal from master's daughter's new stuff and she never realized it. This journal, it is all I have of her." She gripped the drawing book tightly. "I hope she is safe."

Richard was still. He thought back to Thelma's time on the plantation—the way she cared for Zora, expressing concern; the way she defended her, refusing to leave her side. Thelma had been like a mother to Zora, and Solomon, who'd been killed under Richard's instruction, was like her brother.

And he'd stripped that all away.

Zora cried. "I pity Master McLeary, wherever he is. He took so much from me. Please, I don't want him take you too."

The words sent a chill up his body. Everyone was feeling the loss of Pico, and her telling all this to Richard now was because she didn't want to lose him too.

Richard bit back the tears that wanted to escape. He bit down on his lip hard enough to draw blood as he looked away from her own tear-filled eyes. How could he have been that disgusting to anyone, let alone to one so beautiful inside and out, one so warm and kind and giving? He masked his thoughts, encasing them in a blank expression. Should he excuse himself from her?

But she only pushed herself closer to him.

"Please," she asked. "You stay longer?" She rested her head on his chest, and he held her, knowing it wouldn't last once she found out the truth.

CHAPTER NINETEEN

Four days had passed, and Richard kept checking the barn for a small sign of hope that Samantha had written back. What if he missed her letter? What if Margret couldn't get it to Samantha? Perhaps it would have been better if he'd asked her to put the letter in their secret spot. No. If he did that, he would have to check it every night, and that was more dangerous than what he was doing now. He was already in James' bad graces and fully belonged to him now, which meant his punishments would be nothing short of severe and potentially life-altering. Still, the thoughts grew his worry and impatience.

He was restless. Not even Zora could keep him from risking his life two days ago.

He remembered her grabbing his wrist, and shaking her head for him not to go, remembering Pico's death. Richard reassured her he'd be all right with a light nod and left, returning safely back to the field. But today, that restlessness came back, hitting him again.

Richard waited for the perfect moment to take action, and it came when Parkinson put all his attention on a slow picker. James and Benji looked in their direction. Perfect. Richard scanned his surroundings, searching for Zora, who was busy picking. Good.

He wouldn't have to reassure her again. He kept low as he slowly snuck to the barn once more. He scanned the area quickly, his hopes diminishing when he saw nothing there.

Richard turned to leave but stopped in his tracks, surprised and panicked when he saw Zora standing over him. He found Zora's bravery and guts kind of impressive but wished she wouldn't be so stubborn just for once. Richard quickly took her hands and pulled her into hiding as she questioned him in broken English.

"What are you doing?" she whispered. "You could get in trouble like last time."

Richard pointed to the road just past the willow tree. But Zora gave a puzzled look. With his finger, he wrote *'Escape'* in the dirt.

She shook her head. "Not leaving."

Richard shook his head. He pointed to the word, then himself.

Zora's brows raised. "*You* escape?"

He nodded.

Richard heard whistling approaching the barn, the other slaves signaling to him.

"One of the men comin'."

The worst was running through Richard's head.

He imagined the skin peeling off Zora's back, and the image ripped at his heart. Unable to get Zora out safely, Richard pushed her into a pile of hay, quickly covering her in it, hiding her from James, now standing in the doorway of the barn.

"Butter Cheeks," James called Richard again as the other drivers joined him. "Skipping work again, hm? How many times do I have to catch your ass lazin' around in here? You really love this place. For the life of me, I can't fathom why. Somethin' to do with seeking out children, I suspect."

He grabbed Richard by his neck and brought him outside. "Apparently, you haven't learned your lesson. Guess I've been going too soft on you."

Richard did his best not to look at the hay pile, fearing that James and the others might look and find Zora.

Sparing no time, the men swooped upon Richard, grabbing him

by the arms and dragging him outside. Fear rushed through him for the pain to come, pain the likes of which he'd never experienced. They tied Richard to a whipping post, his back bare as James snapped the whip, watching the blade-like edge cut deep into Richard's skin. The blade seemed to stick upon its landing, digging into Richard's open flesh deeper each time. The sound of his flesh splitting open made him want to vomit, and the sweat pouring off him was burning the wounds. Richard had only experienced light lashings until now, and he found this pain unbearable as tears threatened to pool in his eyes. Over and over, James moved his arm with ferocity as he lashed at Richard's back. Benji, as he always did, kept a stolid, business-like expression on his face, showing neither displeasure nor enjoyment. Richard heard the others laugh, but their laughter sounded distant as Richard watched Zora sneak out of the barn and return to the cotton fields.

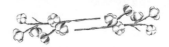

Warm blood dried in the summer air as Richard was left tied to the post, forced to endure the full strength of the noon sun beating down on his butchered skin. He passed out from time to time, dizzy from all the pain. He was happy that Zora hadn't been caught, and to his surprise, he wasn't thinking about his bleak future but instead focusing on protecting her.

His legs were weak from all the standing, and the sun's heat on his back added to the pain. He involuntarily flexed his back as he repositioned himself to stand up straighter, and that was when the pain shot anew, and he almost fainted. It wasn't until the sun had turned bright orange and the crickets started to sing that Richard was cut down and brought back to the slave cabin. Two men laid him down on a mat on his stomach. Others quickly gathered rags to tend to his back. Each press to one of the gashes worked a pained grunt from his mouth as his back arched to get away from the feeling.

Zora quickly got Richard some water as others cleaned his wounds.

Without hesitation, Richard grabbed the bowl of water and drank copiously, soothing his dry mouth. As soon as he lowered it, Zora took his face into her hands.

"Can't lose friend," she said, her eyes puffy and red.

Richard smiled, placing her hand on his chest, right over his heart. Rather than a quick kiss, their lips met for a few seconds, parting softly, slowly. Zora looked deep into Richard's eyes.

"Kamau, you my Kamau, my quiet warrior," Zora said, keeping her hand on his chest.

CHAPTER TWENTY

After the brutal whipping, Richard missed a day to go into the barn, too hesitant and frankly too weak. Then, another day passed, and another. But it wasn't just fear of another beating keeping him, but also his injury. It was impossible to move; every lift of his arms pulled at the swollen wounds trying to heal on his back. Each time he'd tried to rise, they would open again, and he'd go faint from the throbbing that seemed to go bone deep. On the fourth day of waiting, risking his life to steal a simple glance into the barn, he finally felt that his efforts were not in vain. There, sitting on a pile of hay, was Margret's beloved teddy bear wearing hay bunny ears on its head.

He sucked in a breath when he saw Parkinson enter the barn to check on the workers, pausing his movement right where the letter was hidden.

Footsteps quickly approached, clunking loudly in the dirt.

Richard kept his head up, eyes fixed on the barn when a soft *tap-tap* on his arm snatched his attention. He turned to see Zora, her eyes darting urgently to the side. Richard followed her gaze, turning just in time to spot a driver heading his way, noticing him not at work, no doubt. His heart pounded. With a quick glance downward, Richard refocused on picking the cotton. The driver's footsteps stopped, then switched directions.

It was a close call, a situation that could have soured had it not been for Zora alerting him. Still, he desperately wanted to race into the barn but knew he couldn't.

He'd have to wait until the sun went down.

As soon as it did, Richard rushed to the stuffed animal, not even looking to see if James or other drivers were nearby. He lifted the bear—and froze. Nothing was there.

He looked around and then across to the floor by the hay bundle. Nothing. Breath quickening, Richard panicked, pacing as he ruffled his hair. Had Parkinson or James found it, perhaps?

Or worse, what if James had caught Margret delivering the letter to the barn?

Richard slipped back into the cabin, devastated. All of his planning, and for what? What would he do if this didn't work? He paced the cabin, stopping to gather himself when others gave him questioning looks. He was lost in thought on what next step to take until Micel approached, discretely removing an envelope from his pocket as he did.

"I took this before the white man could see it," he said. "Seemed important."

Richard was at a loss. Dumbstruck by the shock of the moment. Gazing up at Micel, who returned his stare, Richard's eyes wandered to the healed scar on the boy's cheek. A pang of emotion tugged at his heart, realizing that Micel had just spoken to him, or rather, spoken at all since the day he'd given him the mark.

As the gravity of the situation finally dawned on him, Richard couldn't hold back any longer. He moved forward, pulling Micel into a quick, powerful embrace. The boy stiffened with surprise, taken aback by the sudden gesture. Still, Richard took the envelope from him, his attention drawn to a note in handwriting he didn't recognize.

Richard quickly went outside behind the cabin to read the note away from the others. The sun was setting, casting a soft glow over the surroundings, just enough light for him to read clearly.

July 30th, 1833

My Dear Sir,

I admit I was alarmed when the young girl approached me and left a letter in my garden, and even more so when I discovered you are a literate slave. I know it must not have been easy, even dangerous, for you to write this letter and arrange a way to get it to me.

It is no secret how Mr. McLeary, known to be the slave breaker, rules his plantation with an iron fist. The accusations of mistreatment at Richard's farm have been rumored. And so has Mr. McLeary's disappearance.

I must admit, a part of me wished to toss out your letter, thinking this be a trick upon me, especially since you claim to be a servant of Richard's. But the Christian in me won't allow me to ignore a blatant cry for help. That's why I ask you to please give me a few days to make some arrangements and meet me at midnight in two days by the willow tree to go over plans and details. I commend your bravery and offer *you encouragement. I ask, please keep fighting.*

Please excuse my lack of closing as I do not want to reveal myself in case something were to happen to this letter.

Truly Yours,

With joy in his heart, Richard hid the letter on his person like a man hides gold. In a way, the letter *was* gold to him.

Today, he moved faster in the cotton field; this nightmare was almost over, and soon, he'd be able to find Thelma and return to his old life. Pick after pick, Richard took the cotton from the plant, happily putting his findings into his basket.

A scream cut through the air, startling him from his work. Looking up, he peeked over the plants, trying to see what was happening. When he heard one of the fieldworkers call Nini's name in a frantic gasp, he abandoned his basket with a *thunk* and broke into a sprint. He rushed over, pushing past the others, ignoring the shouts. All he cared about was getting to her.

But James and the other white workers beat him to her.

James stood over Zora and nudged her with his foot. "Wake up," he said. When she didn't respond, he kicked her with the tip of his boot with some force, causing her to roll over onto her back. Without thought, Richard jumped and pushed James away from her, grunting and yelling, still unable to speak at this most frustrating of times. In the corner of his eye, he could see Parkinson swing, but Richard couldn't move fast enough to miss the powerful hit to his jaw.

James ordered two slaves to bring Nini to the cabin, then called to

Benji and Parkinson. "Tie him to the post. Whip him until his skin peels off, and be sure to expose his back to the sunlight."

Parkinson yanked Richard away from Zora, and Benji soon followed.

They dragged Richard to the post as instructed, tearing his shirt from his back, which had barely had any time to heal from the last time. Lash after lash, Richard endured, his thoughts solely focused on making it through the beating to get to Zora.

After Parkinson received his fill of amusement from Richard's punishment, Richard was allowed to return to the cabin. It had taken him a long time to shuffle over, constantly having to stop and blink away the stars dancing across his vision. He'd vomited once from the pain, leaving the bitter taste of bile in his mouth that seemed to match the metallic smell of blood. Once he'd finally made it, the others tried to tend to him, but he pushed them away and found Zora lying on the floor with a cloth on her head. Richard fell in a heap beside her, the pain more than he could bear. His back was peeled, the metallic stench of the blood and rawness invading his nostrils. Every movement felt like daggers piercing his flesh.

But despite his own wounds, Richard partially lifted himself off the ground and tried to tend to Zora's bruised sides and bleeding head from the fall. He looked around for something to wipe away the thickened blood. He had no idea what he was doing, so Sylvie, who stood nearby with a cloth in a bowl of water, helped him. Richard tended to Zora with as much gentleness as he could muster, hoping that it almost didn't hurt at all for her since she barely moved.

He cleaned her wounds with a gentle hand, letting the rag just barely brush her skin. He'd fed her sips of water and stroked her hair, just as she had done for him only nights before.

His surrounding peers stood watching in respectful silence.

When Richard moved to the wound on Zora's shoulder, he saw the stripes on her back from when he had whipped her himself. Now, he deeply regretted the sight of them.

"Kamau…"

Zora's eyes opened as she called out to him, extending her hand.

Richard propped himself up on his knees and took it, intertwining his fingers gently with hers. He gestured to Sylvie and pointed to Zora, asking what happened. The helping woman exchanged wary looks with another helper. They turned to him. "Zora is with child."

Richard was too shocked to move.

He only turned when Zora placed his hand on her belly. "Master's child," she said.

A wave of nausea swept over him as bile rose in his throat. Richard swallowed, not wanting to believe what she had said. He checked over his shoulder to make sure no one was watching before writing *'James?'* in the dirt. Zora shook her head and said, "Master McLeary."

Richard was still. He wasn't sure how to feel, too conflicted with so many emotions. And though not worthy of the feeling, there somehow came a brief happiness upon hearing Zora was pregnant with his child. It flooded his heart and soul as if a ray shone directly from the sun.

He loved the fact that Zora was carrying his child.

And he hated it.

He hated the fact that Zora was carrying his child, one he forced upon her. And he hated that they wouldn't rejoice in the creation together. Because it hadn't been him in the form she had come to care for. No, this would always be the master's child, her rapist's child. And he hated it. He hated that his child would grow up in the twisted world that he had created for himself.

Richard's mind was in turmoil.

However, he knew one thing for sure. He had to protect Zora and his child at all costs.

CHAPTER TWENTY-ONE

Come night, more determined than ever, Richard snuck out of the slaves' cabin and headed to the willow tree. He stepped on something going through the bush, nearly twisting his ankle as he tripped in the dirt. When he looked down, he saw it was James' pistol, well and truly snagged right between a shrub entangled in a cotton bush.

Richard picked up the gun. He felt the weight of it, nearly forgetting what it was like to hold one, how it felt to have it around his waist. The gun was loaded. He thought quickly. There was no sense in abandoning the weapon, was there? Who knew when this could be of use? Richard hid it by placing it further in the bush and burying it in the dirt, tying a small torn piece of his shirt to a stem to mark it. It could be useful someday.

The sudden sound of quick footsteps approached. Richard turned, envisaging one of the drivers about to interfere, but he was relieved when he saw Micel.

Richard pointed to him with a curious expression. Micel pointed back.

"It's dangerous," he said. Richard put a finger to his lips and pointed to the willow tree, doing his best to tell Micel what he was doing. It took the young man a moment to figure out the complicated puzzle. But when Micel did, he said, "I want freedom too."

Richard's brows raised. He was surprised and a little impressed. He hadn't expected Micel to understand so quickly. Not only was this young man observant, but he was also sharp-witted.

Richard agreed with a nod as he tried to convince the young man to return to the cabin; it would be too difficult to sneak himself and another to the willow tree at the end of the winding driveway.

When Micel tried to go with him, Richard held up his hand, pointed to Micel, and then to the ground. *Stay here.* When Micel shook his head, Richard jabbed a finger at his chest and indicated toward the ground more forcefully. He thought of Pico as he did, not wanting another dead man on his conscience.

"Will you return?" Micel asked, looking slightly hurt.

Richard nodded and pointed to the cabin.

After some convincing—more pointing and holding his hands in prayer—Micel slowly stepped back, wavering on his feet. Finally, he turned and headed towards the cabins, occasionally looking back as though checking to make sure Richard was still there. Once Micel returned to the cabin, Richard continued to the end of the driveway.

Looking past the cascade of drooping branches and leaves, Richard arrived and saw a dark figure standing among the shadows, holding a simple dimly lit lantern. As the figure peered sideways, the faint glow illuminated the face hidden beneath a black hood. It was Samantha. Richard cautiously approached her, hoping she hadn't come to trap him and turn him into James. Her back was turned to him as he gently placed his hand on her shoulder. Samantha jumped and turned.

She looked him over, her expression turning from surprise to anger.

"You must surely be mistaken, sir," she told him. "I'm not ready to sneak any slaves out yet."

Her words confused him. It wasn't until she looked over his shoulder that Richard understood. Micel was seen in the distance, not having left yet. As soon as the young man noticed he had been spotted, he turned and rushed back down towards the cabins.

Samantha fumed.

"I cannot say I understand your desperation for freedom, but anyway, the impatience of a man is foolish. You have my deepest apologies, but this is not the time for escape," she offered.

Richard frantically shook his head, trying to resolve the misunderstanding.

She turned to leave, but Richard grabbed her arm to stop her.

Richard took a sheet of paper out of his pocket; already written was his name. *'I am Richard McCleary.'* Of course, he hadn't written this in the letter before because he knew she would have dismissed it as some stupid prank or a waste of her time.

Now, with her standing right there in front of him, she'd have no option but to believe him.

At first, Samantha stood still, not understanding. Richard pointed to his name on the paper, then at himself.

"Why don't you speak?" she said.

Richard shook his head.

"You are unable? Is this how you've come to be learned?"

Not wanting to waste time on the subject, Richard again pointed to the paper. This time, Samantha looked at it closely, raising her lantern. But she doubted. "I'm very sorry, but I'm afraid you must be confused," she said.

Richard picked up a stick and wrote a reminder to Samantha that over a month ago, he had approached her while she'd been outside, tending to her hydrangeas.

"Forgive me if I'm not convinced. It's quite common for others to spot me in my garden."

Richard thought for a moment, then tried again. *'You wore a blue dress.'*

"Perhaps, or perhaps not. It was so long ago, I'm not sure I recall myself."

He huffed. After a pause, he wrote in the dirt once again. *'You moved into a yellow house no more than three months ago.'*

"Again, sir, that is common knowledge among my neighbors."

Richard ruffled his hair. He thought those would be foolproof assertions to convince her, but Samantha didn't seem to get it. Frustrated, he jerked his hands. Richard stared at her for a second, trying to think of other ways to sway her, trying to grasp onto anything in his memory that would scream *I am Richard!* But none came. Then he slapped his hands on his hip, lowered, and turned his head as he let out a unique scoffing sound. He turned, turned to her, then turned back towards the tree.

"Honestly," Samantha said. "I don't understand why you would call yourself such and claim to be that grotesque man. Truly, sir, it is not a name any man should aspire to."

That sparked an idea. Richard took the stick and wrote in the dirt.

'Even dogs have names.'

Samantha jumped, stepping back in disbelief. "No," she said, shaking her head. "I believe no such magic is possible."

Richard was happy to see a reaction from her, but now he scrambled to come up with a way to convince her of how he'd been cursed. He wrote in the dirt the first thing that came to mind.

'A witch named Thelma put a curse—'

"Thelma?"

Richard looked up. Samantha's bright, wide eyes narrowed. *"You know Thelma? The medicine woman?"*

Though confused by her change of tone, he nodded.

She swallowed, lowering her hood. "Did Richard—" she paused. "Did you happen to purchase her from a man named William Bennett?"

He nodded, this time intrigued.

Samantha sucked in a deep breath. "Mr. Bennett is my father. A few months ago, my father originally purchased Thelma. She burned down our home because of him."

Richard's jaw nearly dropped to the floor.

"The first day I saw her, Thelma was coupled with a young boy and a young woman," Samantha said. Richard realized she was talking about Solomon and Zora. "Thelma and the boy were obviously related, but the woman... All three of them seemed so close, like family. But Mr. Hemings came and purchased the young woman."

Richard thought about writing Nini's name in the dirt but chose not to. If he did, Samantha might be appalled to hear she had landed on his plantation and back down from helping him, and he didn't want to take any chances.

"I remember Thelma's anguish as I watched them drag her away. A family had been separated, and it was going to happen again with her son.

"My father wanted to purchase Solomon, and only him. I'd never heard a mother cry so fierce, so I begged Daddy to keep them together. I didn't want them to be split up further. At first, my father seemed adamant about his purchase, but then he obliged. Called her a wedding gift to me.

"At first, all seemed well. My father grew intrigued by her knowledge of plants and medicines. Said he'd never seen someone of her kind with such knowledge. But the longer Thelma resided on the plantation, performing healing acts, the more my superstitious father saw her as a witch.

"Eventually, Thelma clashed with Daddy, and strange accidents happened around him and the plantation. He wanted to sell her off because of it, against my protest, but he would keep Solomon. After Thelma found out, the plantation mysteriously caught aflame. Even though my father had no proof that it was Thelma's doing, he figured it was her way of retaliating. Upon my request, he sold her with her son to not incur more of her wrath.

"I am ashamed of myself for not being able to convince him not to sell them at all. But I will be honest to say a part of me feared her wrath as well. Blessed with a mother against such ideals but cursed with a slaver as a father, made to take on his family plantation. Perhaps it was a blessing it burned. Oh, that dreadful man. My husband is further from his temperament, and I thank God for that. He left me here to help Father and tend to the plantation to sort out the disaster. I'd call it a blessing." Samantha caught herself. "Sorry, I digress."

Richard pointed to Thelma's name on the ground. Underneath, he wrote, *'Where?'*

She pursed her lips, a frown taking place. "There's been talk around town about you, Mr. McLeary. How you disappeared. It was one of the reasons I responded to your letter. People were looking for you, and when I'd heard you disappeared, I wanted to see if my father's suspicions of Thelma were true. I never imagined I'd find you like this."

Richard furrowed his brows. *'What suspicions?'*

She paused. "Only a few weeks after your disappearance, my father caught word that Thelma was being sold again. After hearing about Mr. McLeary's—*your* disappearance, Daddy figured Thelma had something to do with it. I thought my father was mad when he declared to claim her as his own again," Samantha said. "But he did. He found her at the market and…"

She paused again, looking at Richard sympathetically. "My daddy had her killed, refusing to let her witchcraft harm anyone ever again."

Richard's body didn't know how to react; it just shut down, frozen to a point where he was hardly breathing. His head hung low. He threw a hand to it as he paced, frustrated tears swelling in his eyes. *No, no, no. This can't be.* His only hope, gone.

Samantha wrapped her arms around him, comforting him. "You long for freedom? So you finally understand such cruelties?"

Taking in her words, he nodded.

Samantha was silent for a moment. "Fine," she said. "I'll help you. But only because there is a different air about you."

She paused. "My friend is a clerk of the court, somebody who runs the administration side of the court's business, what cases get seen, documentation issued pursuant from them, et cetera. He works at the county court where the certificates of freedom are issued, so I can reassure you, Mr. McCleary, I will help save you from the cotton fields, and together, we'll find a way to save you and turn you back to normal."

As tears flowed down his cheeks, Richard raised three fingers and pointed into the road.

Samantha quickly understood. "You want to free yourself and two others? That's very noble. It shall be arranged."

Richard nodded, truly grateful. Zora was right. She was an angel.

Still, Richard stared, full of curiosity, a question gnawing at him ever since the day he'd seen her in her garden.

"What troubles you? Pray tell, what's on your mind?"

'Your father's a slaver. Why do you help slaves?' he wrote.

Samantha stared at his question for a moment. A tight-lipped smile replaced her sadness, but no twinkle presented in her eyes. "When I was young, my father always taught me never to be alone with a black man because they were animals with bad intentions. I feared them, saw them as evil. One day, I got separated from my father, and men—drunk white men—pursued me. It was a slave who saved me. He hid me, fighting and leading the men away, but was killed because of it. That man saved my life. It got me wondering who really was the bad man."

Richard's tears began to dry as he stared at Samantha, *really* looked at her.

She cleared her throat and raised her hood, securing it back into place.

"My friend will be arriving at my father's plantation in a few days, so please wait a while so I can discuss this with him. Until then, don't lose faith. I will send a letter to Margret, and it will tell you when I have the freedom papers and am ready to sneak the three of you out."

CHAPTER TWENTY-TWO

The days seemed to drag as Richard anxiously awaited Samantha's letter. Things seemed to grow ever harder, and the work more demanding. But Richard stayed diligent, determined to stay out of James' bad graces. Zora had returned to the field but was moving slower, taking a few moments to sit down, hiding among the cotton plants. Richard made sure to help her, ensuring she had more than enough cotton to hand in at the end of the day. And she kept on dropping that same sweet smile at him.

Three days after seeing Samantha, Micel bumped into Richard.

"That young girl left somethin'," he said to him.

Richard peeked into the barn the first chance he got and finally saw Margret's teddy bear standing upright. He glanced around to ensure that no one was near and quickly slipped inside, as quietly on his feet as possible. Folded neatly and looking out of place among the hay was the letter. In a beautiful script, ink staining the paper, Richard read the words he'd been hoping for.

Meet me at the end of the driveway by the willow tree at 1 a.m. in two days. My friend and I will take you and two others to get the paperwork for freedom.

Richard beamed. After so long, he was finally going to be free.

"Daddy?"

Richard turned, shocked to see Margret hiding behind the hay bale again. He approached her with a smile but stopped when he saw the sad look in her eyes.

He gave her a concerned look, frowning as he ran his thumb over her cheek, meeting her eyes. Her lip quivered.

"Are you leaving?"

Richard sighed. She must have read the letter. He nodded.

"I want to go with you."

Richard shook his head, his expression softening. *'Dangerous'*, he wrote. *'Promise you won't go to willow tree.'*

Margret sulked but nodded. "Promise."

She gripped her teddy bear to her chest, her head down. Richard gently lifted her chin. He took hay from the bale and made bunny ears. She gave a soft giggle.

'I'll be back.'

"Promise?"

He nodded.

Richard gave Margret a tight embrace before turning to leave.

"Wait!" Margret held up her teddy bear. "Take him. He'll keep you safe."

Richard smiled. *'Leave it here for me,'* he wrote.

She nodded, her eyes searching his for a moment longer. "Daddy, when you can talk again, can you tell me a story?"

He smiled, nodded, and left the barn.

As the sun set and the slaves returned to the cabin, Richard instructed Zora and Micel to follow him the night after tomorrow, and they would walk out of there like free men. Zora looked down at the ground. Richard lifted her face and smiled.

"Scared," she said, a tear rolling down her cheek. Richard kissed the tear away and placed her hand on his chest. Her fingers curled into his, and she smiled.

Zora touched her belly, then held Richard's hand over it. "Live with me. Us, family," she said proudly. "Kamau, my family."

Richard smiled, touched by her words, but as he saw his hand to her belly, hearing her call him "Kamau," he felt something unsettling. An uneasiness tugged at his heart as he thought about how seriously Zora was asking him to live with her and, in essence, asking him to be a part of her life. He knew she wanted to stay with Kamau, not Richard.

A whirlwind of quarreling emotions raged within him. He found himself caught up in a tangle of doubts and wavering thoughts, torn between the yearning to embrace Zora's kindness and the weight of truth on his shoulders. But no matter how many notions danced in his mind, longing to stay by Zora's side, the guilt screamed within him, haunting him like a banshee's wail in the night. At that moment, he decided she ought to know the truth about him.

Zora was about to retire for the night after a long day's work when Richard waved a hand, signaling her to meet with him. They walked a little ways behind the cabin for privacy.

"Why are we out here?" she asked. "Why bring me here?"

With so much heaviness in his heart, Richard pulled and unfolded the paper from his pocket, the same one he had shown Samantha. He lifted it up, showing her what it said.

'I am Richard McCleary.'

Zora squinted her eyes, lifting the lantern. "Your name is Richard?"

He nodded. Pointing to his surname. Richard *McCleary*.

Zora's smile dimmed. "I don't understand."

Richard pointed to the paper, then to himself. But Zora stared, confused. Trying to get his point across, Richard repocketed the paper and went to where he had buried his supplies. After digging up the pen and ink he had hidden, he took out the paper and wrote on the back.

'You believe Thelma is a witch?'

"Others believe. She is but woman."

Richard shook his head. *'You believe she has power?'*

Zora nodded.

Richard continued to scribble, explaining the night he'd heard the whispers, then all about Thelma's curse and how he had woken as a black man. But with each word, Zora seemed more perplexed.

'I tried looking for Thelma but got the news of her death instead,' he wrote before showing her.

Now, Zora wasn't smiling. "Kamau, what are you saying?" she asked. At first, it seemed Zora couldn't understand or believe the implications of his words. That he was her master or *any* words coming out of his mouth. And it only worsened when he brought up Thelma's death, so Richard took a different approach. He grabbed the pen again, using his leg as a table.

'The day I purchased you, I spent $2,500 on you.'

She read. "Master did, yes."

He shook his head, pointing to himself again. But she just shook her head. *'I told you that you were just property. I said this.'*

She gave him a quizzical look.

Frustrated, he pointed to his neck. *'Burns from Solomon. Chicken blood.'*

"No, no, you not him. Why say this? Why say this?" She looked at the words again. "Diary? You have read in my diary?" Her words were hopeful.

But he shook his head.

Richard sifted through his memories, trying to find something that would make her believe without a doubt that he was Richard. He needed to share some information about something that only the both of them could have known, something that wouldn't be in her diary. And he did, but he shook at the memory. He tried again to search for another, but his mind kept returning to this one. Richard lifted the pen again, his hand shaking.

'That night I threw you in the shack, I'—he stopped his pen from moving, finding it hard to continue, a throb in his chest—*'I had my way with you. Forced myself on you.'*

With an ache in his heart, he wrote how, before leaving the shack that night, she whispered to him, "I hope you get everything you deserve."

After the words left his pen, he regretted it. It was stupid of him to remind her of her foes.

Richard held the paper and folded it, unable to accept his own words.

He stood, gripping the paper tight, hesitant to give it to her. But he did, extending his hand towards her. Zora slowly took it.

She unfolded the paper and read it. He watched her expression fall, fingers twitching before slowly crumpling the paper, her teary eyes distant as it fell from her trembling hands.

"You... Master?"

Richard slowly nodded, and he could tell by the sudden anguish on her face that Zora finally believed. She cocked her hand back and slapped Richard so heavy-handedly he stumbled to the side, dazed, ear ringing. He had no time to gather himself because Zora lunged forward and threw wild fists at him, and he let her.

Then she pulled back, crying until she sank to the floor in tears. Richard approached to calm her, but she pushed him off. "Every night, I cry. Never the same."

Richard remembered when he'd catch her crying at night, seeing her curled, whimpering silently to herself.

"I cared for you, kissed you, and I, I carry your child!" She covered her mouth, realizing what she had just said. She turned to Richard with rapid tears rolling down her cheeks. "But you are same man that took *everything*."

Richard tried to reach for her, but she screamed at him, "Stay away from me! Leave me alone!" A few people in the cabin came to check the commotion, some telling them to keep their voices down, but Richard paid them no attention.

He fell to his knees to beg for forgiveness, but she pushed him away. And again, he crawled forward, placing himself at her feet, but again, Zora gave him a hard shove. Richard reached for her one last time, but as his hand extended, she flinched, making a pained noise that pierced straight through his heart. He lowered his hand.

Unable to calm her, Richard slowly stood, leaving her outside to cry as he walked past the other slaves. He went back inside, sat with his back against the wall, and silently cried.

CHAPTER TWENTY-THREE

The next day, Zora ignored Richard, avoiding him at all costs. On the other hand, Richard had decided to give Zora time, even though he doubted she would ever forgive him. Then he thought, *What if she doesn't run away with me? What would I do?*

Zora paused for the briefest moment, doubling over and holding her stomach and mouth before picking again. But James noticed.

"First fainting, now holdin' back the mornin' sickness? Seems like someone bit the serpent."

Richard was going about picking cotton when he heard James call out for "Nini" as she worked the field. James started laughing upon seeing her. "Bitch, you've been knocked up already? Who's the daddy?" he asked Zora.

She didn't respond but kept her head down.

When James turned to see Richard staring, he laughed again and signaled Richard to join them. "So you *do* know how to mount?" James cajoled him. "I guess you did learn something from that lesson."

Richard bit his tongue, forcing his head to stay down.

James simply chuckled before turning back to Zora.

"Usually nigger gals like you slow production when you begin to show, but you're not a usual nigger, are ya? You get more things done. Be a waste to trade you." James hovered over her as he leaned in, contemplating the situation. "Nini, I'm happy you'll be increasing the number of my slaves by one. I even promise to be at the delivery to receive the baby."

Richard fumed, clenching his fists as James spoke those words. He looked him dead in the eyes.

"You got something to say, Butter Cheeks?" James said, but for the sake of Zora and his unborn child, Richard swallowed his rage. He shook his head and lowered his eyes to the ground. "Then I suggest you keep your head down and get back to pickin'."

As James ambled away, Richard and Zora exchanged lingering glances. They both turned away, keeping their heads down as they picked the cotton.

Come the night to run away, Richard met with Micel at their planned meeting spot near the cotton fields. He found the torn shirt he tied around the bush, then dug up and retrieved the gun he'd kept hidden in the bushes.

He tucked it into his waistband, tying the strings tight.

For a while, the men anxiously waited for Zora to appear, and for a moment, he feared she would even tell of their escape. *No,* he thought, gaining control of his irrational thoughts. *She'd never do that.* But that didn't stop more thoughts from bombarding his already anxious mind. Richard promised if she didn't show, he'd help Micel be free, but then return and continue to suffer alongside Zora until another opportunity appeared.

Rustling filled the air. Micel and Richard ducked, holding each other's shoulders. The movement neared, and Micel held his breath. Richard felt for him; he was undoubtedly afraid of being hanged, and it would be all his fault if they were caught.

As the cotton plants before them parted, Richard grabbed a rock near his feet and readied himself. He raised his hand, only for Micel to stop him. Zora's slim frame came into view, and Richard's heartbeat slowed down. He stared at her, wide-eyed. *She came.*

A cloth was tied around her back, hanging heavy, and it occurred to him she had fashioned a makeshift pack. It only carried a few items, judging from the lack of bulge and weight.

"Not here for you," she said, interrupting his thoughts. "Here for me and child."

Richard swallowed. He couldn't help but feel hurt, but he nodded. He needed to give her time.

He tried to take Zora's hand, but she yanked it away. Richard stared at her longingly, but knowing he needed to hurry, he let her go and turned to lead the way. Now, he took his pistol that had been pressed against his hip as the three hid in the shadows and headed to the willow tree. As the three made their way, they made sure to avoid lights on the plantation given off by torches and lanterns.

Almost there, Richard thought. But his thoughts were shattered when he heard a gunshot from behind. How did they find them? And so quickly? How did they know, especially when he had hidden all the letters? But Richard didn't have time to think about that.

He grabbed Zora's hand again and ran. If she protested, he did not notice.

The light of a torch glowed in the distance, quickly becoming closer with every passing second. Richard paused for a moment, unsure what to do.

If we keep running this way, we'll lead them straight to Samantha, he thought.

With one driver nearly upon them, Micel turned to Richard and Zora. "You two run. I'll lead them the other way and meet you," he said.

Richard hesitated. Why would he make such a sacrifice for people he barely knew?

With the torch getting closer, Richard reminded himself that he was not just saving Zora. He was saving their child, too. He gave Micel a brisk nod, then pulled on Zora, and the two ran to the tree. He didn't look back to see what would become of the younger man and pushed his legs to move faster, never letting go of Zora's hand.

Another shot rang out.

Richard tried to ignore Micel's scream in the distance and how it gripped his heart. But he had to focus on saving Zora. He couldn't let his sacrifice be for nothing. So close to the tree, he could see Samantha in her black cloak.

Zora gasped at the sight of her. Samantha, too, appeared wide-eyed, shocked.

"Miss Bennett?"

"Nini?"

Zora slipped from Richard's grasp, and the two women embraced. After exchanging quick hugs, Samantha said, "You'll have to explain everything to me later. For now, we must hurry. My friend awaits us farther down with a wagon. Don't worry, as he has done this before. I will help guide you there, and he will transport you to a safer place. Where is the third?"

Richard shook his head.

He suddenly felt a bullet fly past him, hitting the bark of the tree.

Samantha was trying to hide behind the tree's thick trunk, but the driver, Parkinson, who emerged from the shadows, recognized her immediately.

"So the rumors were right about you," he said. "You're nothin' but a nigger-lovin' harlot!"

Richard pulled the gun from his waistband and pointed it at the man. He had seen them, seen Samantha's face. If he lived, and they let him go, she would be prosecuted for the aiding of slaves. Her life would also be at risk. To protect Zora and Samantha, Parkinson had to die. No matter what.

Richard tucked Zora behind him, her fingers grasping at his shirt, pulling his collar against his neck.

A twig snapped.

Parkinson suddenly turned and fired a round, shooting at a shadow. Richard gasped, and his heart snapped when he saw the familiar brown curls. There in the shadows before him stood his daughter, a crimson-red patch spreading outward from the hole in the center of her nightgown.

The innocent little girl stood there for a moment with her teddy bear in her arms, looking at the blood on her hand.

"Daddy?"

Her voice was a whisper. The blood-splattered bear fell from her fingers and tumbled to her feet. It seemed to unfold gradually, the way her little legs gave out as she fell to the ground.

Richard let out a barbaric scream, his voice cracking through the empty night air as he shot Parkinson in the head. His body swayed, then tumbled to the ground with a loud thud. Then, everything went still. Silent.

Richard immediately dropped the gun. As the firearm fell, he heard Zora scream.

"Didn't want to believe," she said with a trembling hand to her lips.

Richard turned and saw her with terror in her eyes. Samantha ran up and placed a hand on Richard's shoulder.

"Richard, you're—"

But he was too preoccupied with his daughter to care what she might be saying. He threw her hand off him and waved frantically, beckoning them to hurry and go, telling Samantha to save Zora. Whether the words were aloud or in his head, he didn't know. He motioned for Zora to leave, but she was fixed in place, only to be pried away by Samantha.

Richard rushed to Margret, falling to his knees as he took her in his arms, her small body limp and weightless as he cradled her close. Her fallen teddy bear was drenched in blood like her nightgown. But she was not dead. Her eyes were still open as she gasped for air, her tiny chest wheezing and expanding in an unnatural rhythm as if the lungs could not inflate enough. His hand trembled, and he didn't know where to press. He needed to stop the bleeding. He *had* to stop the bleeding. But there was so much now, the warmth sinking into his pants as his daughter paled before him. *No, no, no, no. Margret, look at me. Look at Daddy.*

Margret coughed up blood.

She blinked slowly, tears in her eyes. "Daddy..." The words were weak, barely a whisper.

Something soft nudged his hand. He looked down at his daughter, weakly pushing the teddy bear his way. "You forgot..."

Richard began to cry, a broken wail clawing its way from his chest. He pressed his face into her hair and breathed in her grassy smell.

"Did I help you, Daddy?"

He nodded repeatedly, trying to muster a smile as tears soaked his cheeks. But now, they came harder, like raindrops in a storm, each one heavier than the last. He wished he could talk. Wished he could tell her, "Yes, sweetie, you helped me."

He kissed her hand. "You helped me."

Margret raised her hand and slowly placed them on her head, forming bunny ears. Seeing that only deepened his anguish. Her small hand slowly fell to her sides as she took a long, ragged breath. A faint gasp escaped from her pale lips. Her eyes became distant, void, the gleam fading out until there was nothing reflecting his daughter back at him. With a shaking hand, Richard brushed her hair from her face, caressing her cheek before losing himself in a deluge of grief. It ate away his insides like parasites on a carcass, and the bile built up in his throat as he could do nothing but watch. He wanted to vomit, to let all the pain out, but he just sat there, empty. He opened his puffy eyes again before fully drowning in sorrow. His wails were like a siren, calling out into the night for someone, anyone, to come and save his little girl.

Her body lay limp in his arms, warm but floppy like her own ragdoll, her arms out to the sides, hands curling into gradual soft fists. Her eyes stared.

As he cried, he shut her eyes with the lightest touch of his fingertips. Then, he held her close and closed his eyes too.

Richard thought back to everything that had led to this moment and everything he could have done to prevent it, hearing the same chants of the night he'd been cursed, the last words uttered by Thelma: "Feel what I feel."

The click of a gun sounded. Richard opened his eyes and looked up, staring down a gun barrel with James at the other end. And right behind him was his son, Henry, who stared in horror. This was his last time. He was sure he was dead. The way Margret's body lay lifeless in his arms, he was sure of it. He closed his eyes, anticipating the inevitable.

"Richard?"

His breath caught, shocked.

Richard looked up, his mind churning as James lowered the gun. *Richard.* He was sure he'd just heard him say that. How had James known it was him?

He moved his mouth, trying to find words. "You see me?" he finally said. Richard heard his voice crack as he spoke, shocked that words came out at all.

He barely even recognized his own voice anymore. It had been so painfully long.

"The hell kind of question is that?"

A mix of confusion and disbelief etched across Richard's face. When he looked down, he gasped. His once-black skin was now white as the moonlight. Richard remembered Zora's expression when he'd spotted her in the distance, being pulled away from the scene by Samantha and the clerk. She was shocked, eyes wide and mouth open. So he really was white again.

Richard didn't question it. He picked up his daughter, sprang to his feet, and shot past James and Henry. He ran to the plantation faster than he knew he could move, yelling for help.

The only two to arrive were Mary and Benji, who stood still when they saw Richard holding his daughter's lifeless body.

CHAPTER TWENTY-FOUR

Richard sat on the porch steps of his house, still donning his blood-stained clothes as James rocked on the edge of the chair, taking a sip of brandy from his glass and sitting back. He'd heard James barking orders a few minutes ago to Benji and any other nearby white worker. "Find Nini and that damned nigger Butter Cheeks!" he said. He was furious, threatening, "I'm gon' skin 'em alive if I ever find them."

Richard already knew Zora was long gone, and deep down in his heart, he knew his daughter was, too. Thelma's words, "Feel what I feel," echoed through Richard's head.

"You were right, Zora," he said to himself. "I got what I deserved."

James leaned to look at Richard, but Richard quickly turned away.

He fixed his gaze on the ground.

James cleared his throat. "Henry's up in his room if you want to go see him, though I'd imagine you'd want to change first," James said, trying to break the silence. But Richard said nothing.

James now told him Parkinson and Benji had spotted the first runaway slave and shouted for people to help. They were having yet another smoke outside before heading to bed, which was unusual for them. They heard and spotted movement from afar. James had rushed inside the mansion to wake Henry, letting him come along.

"Didn't see the harm," he said. "Henry's always wanted to see how they'd be punished, so I figured he could go in the field to witness everything. But I don't"—he sighed—"I don't know how young Margret got it in her head to follow."

James shifted in his seat, Richard's silence clearly eating at him.

"Richard, where in high heavens have you been all this time? Came out of the woods like a ghost, damn near givin' me a heart attack." James scratched his head, "I'm still tryin' to figure out why you're wearin' them baggy nigger clothes. And that scar? You get that in the woods too?"

Richard looked at James sideways, contemplating what to say to him. Should he be honest?

But when Richard heard Mary's anguished scream from inside the house, he turned and looked James dead in the eye. The man who used to be his loyal friend not so long ago slowly straightened himself, a startled, shaken look in his eye. A fearful, cautious look Richard had almost forgotten, a look he was used to seeing on the slaves he'd intimidated.

And it wasn't until then that he remembered the color of his skin.

"Why don't you ask the slave, the one you call Butter Cheeks?" Richard said.

The bewilderment that took hold of James was evident. Shaken up, James rose from his seat and went into the house. Richard stayed seated on the porch, tears cascading down his face as he listened to Mary wail in agony. He covered his nose and mouth and bawled into his hands.

The doctor, covered in Margret's blood, proclaimed that the girl had passed away at 2:23 a.m.

Mary didn't want to prolong the wait for a funeral and tried to keep it small. As people cloaked in black gathered to lament their late daughter,

Mary wrapped her arm around Richard's, but he pushed it away.

Richard approached Henry, who sat on the porch, playing with Margret's teddy bear. His eyes were bright red and puffy, his cheeks wet from the steady stream of tears. Richard sat next to him. At first, he didn't know what to say, so he just asked, "What's on your mind, son?"

Henry bit his tongue and rested the teddy bear on his thighs, some of the speckles of blood still staining the fur. A painful reminder of how Richard held his daughter's body. "It's my fault, isn't it… Maggie's death? What if she overheard me talking to Mr. Walker? She's always trying to do things I want to do." The tears started to flow again as he tried to catch his breath between his cries.

Richard wrapped his arm around his boy and held him tightly. This was a moment he'd never believed would come. It was surreal and should have been momentous. Instead, it was the most horrible time. Both of them united again, joined in grief.

"Nothing that happened is your fault," Richard said firmly, blaming himself.

Henry shook his head, pulling back to look Richard in the eyes. "No," he said. "It's not. It's the runaways' fault. If them niggers would have just stayed out of trouble, none of this would have happened. They deserve a death far worse than Margret's."

Richard was aghast, blatantly reminded of how he'd been raising Henry all wrong. And in the end, he came back to the same point and blamed himself. Richard tried to explain to Henry, to tell him that it wasn't their fault either, but Henry merely looked confused.

"Why do you defend them?" he said, sounding exasperated with his father.

Richard pursed his lips, trying to find the right words. Indeed, why did he defend them?

Was it because they were kind and filled with heart, love, and generosity? Was it because they were loyal and family-minded, gracious and selfless?

Or was it because they were warm, sincere, and truthful?

He could not think of many reasons. Only those few. Richard burst into tears, crying like a baby. Meanwhile, his small, bewildered son stroked his hair, the gesture reminding him of Zora and Pico.

"The slaves... the slaves are people too," he barely whispered. "They're no different, son."

He settled on the simplest form of words he could think of when, although he had found his voice again, the right words wouldn't come.

"None of this is anyone's fault," Richard said. "If anything, it was mine."

Richard released Henry from his grasp. "I plan on going into town after the ceremony. Wanna come?"

Henry shook his head, declining the offer. Richard understood and kissed Henry on his head.

When the funeral began, Mary and Richard watched their daughter's body lowered into the six-foot hole. All Richard could think of was wishing he could turn back time and shoot at Parkinson before Margret had fallen victim to him. Richard wished he hadn't stalled.

He wished Margret were still here so he could teach her differently, and he could better see the world through her curious eyes. Mary tried to hold onto Richard's hand, interrupting his train of thought, but he swatted it away, not caring about who may have noticed it.

He turned to her and whispered in her ear, "Hold onto James, not me."

Mary stilled, her mouth agape as she stared at Richard with wide eyes. Her lips moved, but no words were spoken.

After the ceremony, James approached Richard, offering his condolences. "We failed to find the two runaways yet," he said, "but we at least caught one of the bastards."

Richard turned, panicked for a moment, wondering if they'd captured Zora. But then he remembered the cacophony of gunshots that night, along with the screams.

Micel.

Richard brightened at the news, glad Micel hadn't met a gruesome demise. He fought back a smile and sigh of relief. Instead, he shakily inhaled and stood up taller.

"Where is Micel?" Richard asked.

James furrowed his brow. "How'd you know it was him? Did Benji—"

"Where?"

"In the shack. But don't worry, he's gon' get his."

James followed as Richard strode to the shack and swung the door open.

Micel, beaten and bruised, one of his eyes swollen shut, shed tears as he cowered in the farthest corner. He especially exuded fear upon seeing Richard, lip quivering as he tried to bury himself deeper in the corner.

James joined Richard in the doorway. "Caught that son of a bitch close to the willow tree. We slit his feet and removed some of his teeth so he could tell us where the others were headed. But he won't speak of where Nini and Butter Cheeks are going. Not yet, anyway."

Richard glowered at James, who cocked his head.

"What?"

"Put him back with the others."

"*What?* He tried to run—"

"Put. Him. Back… with the others."

Richard said it slowly, his voice as hard as a whip.

James took a small step back and swallowed. But then straightened.

"Now, Richard, I know you're grieving, but don't let that cloud your judgment. He needs to be punished. He was there that night… he played a part in all this." James cautiously stepped forward, placing a light hand on Richard's arm. Richard glowered at it. "Why don't you go and rest?" James said. "I'll deal with him."

But Richard's eyes narrowed. "You must have gotten too comfortable in my absence, James. Hosting your little entertainment shows in the barn with men like Clinton, casually flirting with my wife." James' eyes widened. He stared for a moment before clearing his throat and retracting his hand from Richard. "Seems like you've forgotten your place. But I remind you, this is *my* plantation. And I call the shots. Now put him back with the others," Richard repeated. "Like I said, I'll deal with him myself."

James simply stared at Richard with bewilderment. Finally, he went inside and yanked Micel onto his feet, ordering a few men to bring him to the slave quarters.

As Micel was released, James stood in the dirt as he watched Richard walk to the barn log stump and pick up an ax. Slaves quickly coiled back, but Richard paid them no attention.

Richard stepped up to the shack, raised the axe high, and swung like a madman. Hit after hit, the shack crumbled and splintered. The blade of the ax, in combination with Richard's rage, cut through the aged wood as though it was made from hay. Guests watched in bewilderment but remained silent, merely seeing Richard's action as a terrible expression of his grief.

The soil was still being packed down as Richard quickly washed his face and threw on his finest clothes. Mary walked into the room, her black dress swaying. She stopped in her tracks upon seeing him.

"Where are you going?" she asked. "After all, we still have guests to entertain."

"Why don't you entertain them with a story of you sleeping with James behind my back?" he said sarcastically. "Everyone will surely love to hear about the cheating wife."

"You're no better," she spat.

Richard stopped fixing his collar and stared at her. But not with malice. As he took a moment to realize his hypocrisy, he calmed himself, his expression softening.

In the calmest, gentlest way he could muster, he nodded and said, "No... No, I'm not."

Mary was taken aback. She stood still as Richard pushed past her, heading to town. He had some fixing to do.

CHAPTER TWENTY-FIVE

The sun was setting as Richard returned to his plantation on his white horse, a large stack of papers bundled in his hand. It was the middle of September, six weeks since Margret's funeral, more time than Richard would like to have passed with things still the way they were on his plantation. But in his time of wait, he had been changing things around there. After he'd become white again, he had given the slaves Sundays off.

He also had Solomon's, Isaac's, and Pico's bodies taken down from the oak tree. Richard was also more lenient these days, never raising a fist to anyone or giving a slur. He even sacked some of his white workers. The workers left thinking he'd sacked them in grieving.

They reckoned grief was responsible for a whole lot of perplexing changes about the place.

James questioned the sudden amendments, and so did Benji in his own silent way. Richard wasn't sure why he'd kept James for so long. Perhaps because he was still knowledgeable about the crops and finances.

Apparently, external changes weren't the only things different. At some point, Mary pointed out that Richard woke very early nowadays and that other slave tendencies seemed to have laid claim to him of late.

He cleaned after himself now, too, made his side of the bed, and picked up his clothes.

Richard shocked Benji and James when he'd joined them in the fields, watching his workers and making sure his overseer wasn't harming them. The two often exchanged questioning glances.

"Where is your horse?" James asked.

"The walk isn't long," Richard said.

"You hate walkin' to the fields."

"I managed just fine."

He also never spoke about where he'd been for that month. Many saw him in grief. Others saw him losing his mind. But he was completely sane.

But those changes still weren't enough.

Richard brought his horse to a halt a few feet from the brown barn, the stack of papers in hand. Slaves were still at work. On cue, a few stable workers took the reins of his horse. James approached as Richard dismounted, stiffly greeting him.

"Coming from town?" he asked. "What kept you?"

"Business," Richard simply said, walking past him to his office.

For an entire day, he locked himself in, stamping his seal on each sheet of paper and signing his name. He knew his field workers would be busy turning in their pickings soon, looking forward to some food and a little rest. But no, today, all their lives were going to change.

Richard started for the fields, remembering the long walks every morning when he'd been a slave. He was used to walking and enduring the heat now. Slaves were lined up outside the cotton shed. When he spotted Benji, the driver gave him a curious look.

Richard walked to the cotton shed, seeing that James was collecting the cotton from the field hands. As Richard approached, all the slaves coiled, all but one. She was a recent trade James had done before Richard could say otherwise. She had met his gaze as he approached, warily and unmoving, blocking his path for a moment too long. James marched forward, snatched the young woman from the line, and raised his fist, but before James could swing at her, Richard grabbed hold of his arm and threw him back. The young woman stumbled and fell backward. Richard turned to her, extending his hand for her to take. She froze for a moment. After looking into his eyes, she slowly took Richard's hand. He lifted her before yelling for everyone.

"All of you, leave your baskets and follow me."

After some hesitation, all of his slaves, including the domestic ones he'd gathered before heading into the fields, were standing in front of Richard's house. James and Benji stood to the side.

Richard went into the property, only to return with a wooden lap desk. After scanning the wary group, he grabbed a man by his shirt and led him to the step before sitting down, bringing out the stack of papers.

Richard analyzed the trembling man standing in front of him, taking in his features: a scar on his lip, dark complexion, roughly six feet. He wrote the characteristics on the paper and handed it to him. Unable to read, the man looked at Richard, confused.

Richard pointed at the paper and said, "Your freedom."

The man repeated his words as if bewildered. Richard nodded.

Next, he pointed to all the slaves and yelled the same word. "Freedom!"

The papers waved in his hand, yet still, the slaves were confused and too afraid to move.

James remained in the dirt, dumbfounded, as he watched Richard write out free papers. He called to Richard as he wrote the next paper. "Richard, what the hell is this? What the hell do you think you're doin'?" But Richard ignored him. This ought to have been done long ago.

Richard looked at the slaves again. "Freedom!" he yelled. He lifted the papers over his head and pointed to the willow tree at the end of the driveway.

A few brave souls walked up to Richard and, soon enough, held their freedom in their hands. One, in their native language, translated to his fellow captives, and all rushed over.

But a sudden gunshot in the air made them all freeze. Richard immediately stood, pushing past the slaves, giving the stack of papers to the young woman James had nearly beaten. Richard placed his hand on his gun as James waved his around, questioning Richard's sanity.

"Have you gone mad?" he said. "What is this some, some kind of joke? Think of the numbers!" James calmed himself. "Now I know you are grieving, and I have been patient in your sorrow, but you still have a family to look after, and this manumission won't solve it."

"You're right, James. *My* family. I think I know best how to care for them. Don't you? Or did you have some other method in mind? I suspect we have different ideas."

James pursed his lips. "Do you know how quickly this plantation will run into the ground without these niggers? Think of the profits, the expenses—"

"I don't care about any of that! Who gives a shit about *any* of that?"

The words began to spill from his mouth like a fountain. Once the first one had been uttered, he couldn't stop. Richard told James about his time as a slave, vividly recounting the horrible things done to him, and what he witnessed happening to others. James' face twisted in confusion at what he was saying.

"What in God's name are you babbling about?! Why are you spouting this nonsense? Have you gone mad?" James paused, shaking his head. "You're starting to sound like Margret, spewin' these fairytale stories."

Richard caught himself. "You wouldn't understand… They're human, just like we are, and deserve to be free. No," he corrected himself. "Not like we are. Not to me. To me, they're better."

The slaves looked among themselves in shock and then began to murmur.

James glowered at him. "Maybe the others were right. Maybe you have lost your mind. Hell, I was running this place better when you were gone!" James was disgruntled about being dethroned; Richard could see. He saw that bloodthirsty look in his overseer's eye.

One freed man, paper in hand, turned to leave and was heading to the willow tree, but James shot the man in the leg. He fell to the ground, clutching at his calf, letting out a guttural scream of pain. A few slaves rushed to help him. The rest recoiled. Richard quickly stood in front of the others and pointed his gun at James.

James was already pointing his at Richard.

"They're just property," he said, reminding Richard of his own words. Then he cocked his gun again and shot a woman in the chest. Richard reacted with no hesitation and shot James squarely in his.

The sound of the gunshot lingered, reverberating through the air. James stumbled back, gripping his chest. For a moment, he stilled. He looked down at his bloodied hand before looking at Richard, a shocked, deeply pained look in his eyes. Words were difficult to speak as he stumbled again, his feet slipping from under him as he landed on the ground with a deafening thud. A thunderous cry erupted from behind, one he knew too well. Richard looked back at the woman, who died in the arms of an anguished man. Then, another blistering scream sounded from the mansion.

"James!"

Mary rushed out, falling to her knees, uncaring of the dirt smearing her dress as she took James into her arms, the man struggling for breath as he choked on his own blood. Richard turned to the other freed men and women. "Take your papers and run. A woman's waiting at the end of the road. She'll help you. If you have your papers, take them and go."

They did. The men quickly bolted, women hitching up their dresses as they took off, but some with papers in hand remained where they stood, most of them being house workers.

Mary yelled, "No! No, stop them!"

Richard walked up to Mary and James, watching as James gasped for air. His eyes were fading embers dimming with each desperate breath, but his gaze remained on Mary's, clinging to them until his breath ceased entirely. Finally, he moved no more. Mary wailed, pulling James' head to her chest. Richard simply stared. Everything—the assault, the beatings, punishments from his so-called friend—could finally be put behind him. Or so he thought. But as Richard stood there, watching James lie in the dirt, he felt only a small relief but also a loss for someone he once considered a friend.

With tears flowing freely, Mary turned her bitter gaze to Richard. "Are you going to shoot me as well?"

"I won't shoot the mother of my children," he said, returning his gun to its holster. "I sent word to your folks, telling them our relationship has been redefined."

"In what way? You tell them I am an adulteress? It will go the same as you."

"No, I told them no such thing."

She looked surprised, but her glare never left. "You'll lose everything and more. You know that, don't you? You remember the deal with my father and yours."

"I am no longer afraid of losing the other half of this property. And I am no longer going along with my father's ideals. As soon as your folks come, I just want you off my damn property. See that it happens."

Mary fumed, her nostrils flaring. She reached for James' spare gun, ready to aim, but a hand swooped in and snatched it from her. Richard stared, shocked.

"It's apparent how people follow mindless impulses in grief."

Richard turned to see that Benji was still there. He looked at the pistol in his hand.

"Do you also have a gripe with me, Mr. Cohen?"

Benji looked at James' motionless body. "The way I see it, I saw an owner protecting his property, and it's not my right to tell a man what to do with said property. However, I also saw a slaver who's lost his mind siding with niggers. I'll save you the trouble of ending my employment. I hereby resign. I shall leave on my own accord since there's no good to be had in working with someone sure to run himself into the ground." Benji sighed, giving Richard a look that almost seemed sympathetic. Or perhaps he was sorry for him.

Benji walked over and handed Richard the pistol. "I don't know what's changed you so drastically, sir, but whatever it was, I don't see it as a good thing. I hope you find your way someday, Mr. McLeary."

Richard politely nodded. "I already have."

Benji turned to Mary. "Sorry for your loss, madam." He tipped his hat to her and then to Richard again. Then, he left.

Richard turned to the woman James had shot. A man was cradling her dead body. Richard, with tears in his eyes, went up to them. The crowd around them cowered when he came near. This was surely a time when he would beat them terribly, or he would take the body and do something wicked and base with it. But he did not.

Instead, he said that he was sorry.

He approached the man who unflinchingly held his ground, gripping the body in his arms tighter. Then, Richard handed him two free papers and said, "I'm sorry." Everyone there was stunned.

As he turned back to his porch, he wiped the tears from his eyes. And all the slaves stood staring, startled by the man's impossible show of compassion and emotion. Although he was back to his proper color, nobody could recognize him now.

Richard put away his gun and sat back on his porch steps, thanking the female field hand for holding his papers. But he was surprised to see some of the others had followed him, less afraid.

One by one, they lined up. Richard went through every single one, analyzing their faces, heights, skin tones, scars, and names. He documented each person's features before handing them the papers. The sun gradually hid behind the trees as Richard wrote nonstop. His hands cramped, but he pushed through it.

Finally, Micel timidly approached. Richard paused upon seeing the scar on his cheek.

"I'm sorry, Micel," Richard said as he handed him the paper. Micel looked up from his paper with confusion and a little disbelief. After a moment, he swallowed roughly and gave a sharp nod. He took a few slow steps back, watching Richard with bewildered eyes before turning and heading to the willow tree, never looking back. Finally, no more slaves remained.

In a way, Richard was free, too.

Richard felt a tug on his jacket and turned. The freed woman—now known to be Sary—who Richard had spared from James was holding one last paper.

But there were no more slaves for Richard to give it to.

Richard offered a gentle smile with a nod and took the paper from her. Unsure what to do, she gave an unbalanced curtsy and made her way down the road, leaving him standing with the paper.

Richard knew one paper would remain, but he had not already filled it out; he didn't need her in front of him to know her height or scars. He wrote all of her features right then, picturing her face, remembering her eyes, her skin, her scars—the scar on her thigh from when she had been stolen.

Perhaps it was pointless, maybe even wishful thinking. Samantha's clerk friend would have provided forged papers by now, ensuring her safe passage. And yet, he considered this final paper, endowed with his own signature and seal, as a way to make it official, ensuring her freedom was not only recognized in the eyes of the law, but in his heart as well.

Richard could only hope Zora would return here to receive her paper.

Someday.

CHAPTER TWENTY-SIX

———————— ONE YEAR LATER

Richard got dressed and stood by the tall mirror, looking at the scars on his face, his neck, and his back. He often thought it was all a dream but then was reminded it wasn't by those very marks. Even they had been useful, the whole experience having taught him many things. The cabins that once housed the slaves had been torn down, the shacks' wood burned, and their ashes drowned. The cotton fields that had been worked all day were now burned and replaced with tobacco, vegetables, and corn.

Sugar cane fields were productive, now occupied by workers Richard paid.

Having lived the life of a slave, being reminded of those grueling days in the field, he had vowed never to own one again. After handing out freedom papers, most of the men and women had left, many never looking back or acknowledging the kindness of the unexpected gift.

But he never expected any form of acknowledgment or thanks. Why *would* they thank him? After all he'd done... he was hated by so many. Some, however, had returned.

Whether this was out of fear of Richard or fear of the outside world,

Richard didn't know. However, he never kept them back as slaves held against their will. He paid them duly and treated them nicely, just like the good human beings they were.

And with their help, he still managed to keep profits up, though not as much as before.

Now, Richard lived a more fulfilling life. He stood over Margret's grave, leaving her favorite flowers by it like he did every morning. He'd even had headstones made for Pico, Solomon, Isaac, Amelie, and the woman James had shot, leaving flowers for them as well, including some for Charles. Richard had asked for the location of his grave, which wasn't far from Amelie's, and there he solemnly placed a headstone.

There were headstones for all, in fact, even though he didn't have their names.

The people in town thought he was insane for such a massive order of headstones. They thought he must have lost his mind for most of his recent actions, tongues gossiping in hushed whispers whenever he passed. There were many rumors in town. Some thought he'd gone bankrupt and sold his slaves to pay off debts. Others thought the death of his daughter must've led him to do so, driving him mad and even leading him to kill his loyal friend. But having Benji as a witness, he was not punished for James' death. He said this aloud to Margret's grave, explaining the rumors going around like a conversation with her as though she was alive.

"I hope you're proud of Daddy, Maggie."

Richard worked the farm, tending the fields alongside the many black workers he paid or anyone willing to work regardless of color. It was rewarding but demanding work, but dear Samantha stopped by once a day, bringing cookies for Henry and lemonade for Richard.

It took Henry some time to adjust to all the different faces around, but Richard was determined to raise his son the right way from now on.

It would take steady progress to undo all the bad things he had done, all the lessons he had taught his young son—lessons in how to be hateful, callous, and cruel.

As he worked, Richard thought of Zora, wondering how she was.

Samantha had told him Zora had fled up North. Months later, she contacted Samantha through a letter, explaining that she was doing well there and was due to give birth soon. But Samantha hadn't heard from her since. Still, Samantha would often write letters to her, giving them to her clerk friend to send to her, even if the letters were never replied to. She encouraged Richard to write to her, too, but he was afraid to. What if she didn't want to hear from him? There was no reason why she should.

Richard thought about sending Zora's journal, but when the cabins were being torn down, he'd searched for it, finding it wasn't there.

He made several attempts at writing a letter to her afterwards, but each time he failed miserably. At one point, he even asked Samantha to write one for him.

"No," she said plainly. "I won't close this door for you. This is all your own doing."

It took months before Richard worked up the courage to write to Zora. He sat at his desk and stared at the blank paper. Even with pen in hand, he struggled to find the right words. What should he write? What should he say? He lost count of the many times the ink on his paper curdled in his hesitation. The way it thickened like his chest when he attempted to declare his love for her. His mind was a shroud, trying to think of how he might tell her he missed her. That he was sorrier than he could ever begin to explain with mere words. That he wanted to spend his days showing her instead. But every time he touched ink to paper, he was filled with the bitter, gnawing guilt that reminded him he had no right. Who was he to love her as he did? The one man who only took from her. Why would she want his love? He wanted to ask about her, about their child, wanted to write all that he wished to say, to write for mercy, pleading for her forgiveness. But nothing felt appropriate. What right did he have to ask for anything? No, his written words couldn't take shape—could never measure up, for his suffering was less than hers and always would be. No amount of words could fix the damage already done.

Now, working in the barn, Richard felt a pang of sadness, wishing so much as a single sight of her and his new child. Not being able to set eyes on the baby felt far worse since Margret was no more. Richard cried and prayed for forgiveness every second of every day. He was sorry for everything he had done, but being sorry wasn't enough.

He had even paid the price for being such an oppressor, but that wasn't enough either. He still suffered all the same—slave or no slave.

Richard was having flashbacks in his memory when Henry's giddy laughter interrupted his thoughts. As Richard moved the hay around in the barn, Henry played hopscotch alone just outside the barn doors. Richard could hear the boy singing a song with so much gusto, and he decided to join in, purposely getting the words wrong. Henry laughed and gave his dad a big hug. When he turned, Henry froze.

"Pa, I can see people comin' to the house," he said.

Richard always worried that those who despised him for giving his slaves freedom would come and hassle him. Seemed like today was likely to be the day.

"Stay in the barn," Richard said to Henry as he went outside. He placed his hand firmly on his gun, ready to draw it as he marched down the road.

But the one who was coming wasn't to be feared.

When he saw Zora's beautiful face, his heart fluttered.

Walking next to Zora was a tall man and, in his arms, a baby. Richard jogged up to them, smiling as he wiped the sweat off his brow and dabbed at his face with a dirty rag. Zora smiled, that sweet smile she used to give him back when he was a slave.

"Hello," Richard said, taking a moment to find his words. "And who might this be?" Richard looked at the man behind her, noticing the cautious, nervous look in his eyes.

Maybe he was just frightened to see how Zora approached a white man so casually.

"This, husband," Zora said. She paused and again said, "This is *my* husband."

Richard's heart skipped a beat. "Zora, your English sounds excellent," he said. His stomach turned and cramped as he forced a fake smile for her. Zora had moved on, finding her happiness. What else had he expected?

Zora looked around, noticing the workers. "The fields are gone," she said. She spoke more eloquently. "Samantha told me they would be."

Richard was surprised. "She wrote about me? About the plantation?"

Zora nodded. "In the letter, it mentioned a crazed ex-slave owner who claimed to have been a slave himself before. That he went mad and made several big changes to his plantation because he could not live with his own demons. Hard to believe, but I trust Mrs. Sterling." She gave a soft smile. "I'm happy to know the changes are true. The air here feels so different. Heartening."

Now it made sense to Richard. It explained why she'd had no fear of coming back.

If she hadn't known all this, she couldn't have been assured that he would not claim her back as his slave and throw her new family into the mix. He didn't know why she was here, but he didn't care either. Right now, he was just glad she was an arm's length away from him.

"You really have changed, haven't you?" she said.

Richard called on Henry to get the paper lying on the table right by the front door. Henry slipped into the house and rushed to his dad, handing him the paper and stepping back to hide behind his father's leg. He looked at Zora and gave a timid smile. She returned a bright one.

Richard handed her the paper. "You're free now, Zora," he said with a grin. Zora's eyes widened as she looked at the paper in disbelief, stroking the official seal at the bottom of the page that gave her freedom. After a moment, Richard took a deep breath and asked about the baby boy.

Zora smiled. "His name is Solomon," she said, taking the child from her husband. "Me and my husband, we help free slaves, helping them reach the North. I hoped that you could watch my son. I fear he'd be in danger otherwise."

Before Zora could even beg for Richard's help, he happily took the baby boy into his arms, remembering what it was like to hold little Margret and wishing he could be the one able to hold Zora in his arms every night. The man was a lucky fellow to receive such a privilege.

"Why me?" he asked.

Zora frowned as though confused herself.

"I don't know," she said. "Something in you has changed. But something inside *me* feels this Richard will protect him. That this Richard is a good man. Very good man."

He didn't know what to say.

Zora kissed her son goodbye before kissing Richard on the cheek, tears in her eyes. "Please take care of Solomon," she told Richard.

"I will," he said. "I'll treat him as my own son, no different than Henry." Henry looked up, wide-eyed. "And Henry here will be his brother, in name and in deeds, till you return for your baby."

She smiled. "Thank you for everything, Kamau."

Richard blinked, taken aback. It had been so long since he'd heard that name. And for her to use it now... Had she forgiven him? He teared up, his voice catching as he nodded. "But I should be saying that to you," he said.

Zora turned to leave. Before she could, Richard said, "I'm sorry... for everything." Richard knew those might as well have been empty words. No amount of *sorry* could erase everything, every cruelty he had ever committed. But what else could he do? What else could he say?

Zora stared at him for a moment with an expression he couldn't understand. Then, with a smile, she nodded and departed with her husband, leaving Solomon with Richard.

The days quickly became months. Little Solomon was growing up so fast, his skin now a delicate honey, his hair in dark, tight coils. Shortly after Zora had left, he had to get Solomon registered. In cases like this, as rare as they were, the white owner would have acquired a grant of manumission to free the mulatto child, and Richard did just that.

To anyone brave enough to ask, he told everyone that it was his child, and he was proud. People gave him judgmental stares and remarks, and some men he once did business with grew distant, appalled that the "nigger breaker" was now a "nigger lover". But Richard wasn't ashamed of his black son in the slightest, no longer worried about maintaining appearances.

Solomon was a reminder of Richard's cruelty towards Zora, but also a reminder of his determination to keep her safe.

Richard read a storybook aloud to both of his sons in the library. Even though Henry claimed to be too old for such things, he stayed to listen regardless.

There was a knock at the door. Richard rose, removing Solomon from his lap.

"Henry, keep an eye on your brother, will you?"

Richard placed Solomon down and went to answer the door, surprised to see a man who was dressed in a black frock coat, a horse and a wagon idling behind him.

"Good evening, sir. You are Richard McLeary, yes?"

"I am. And you are?"

"A postmaster of sorts." The man pulled a package and a letter from his leather bag. "For you on behalf of Samantha Sterling."

Richard looked surprised. He took the mail in hand, wanting to ask the man more questions, but he tipped his hat and left on his wagon just as swiftly as he'd appeared.

Perplexed, Richard looked at his items to find a package with no sender listed on it. Richard thanked the postman and returned to the house, flipping the package over in his hands. He walked back into the library and watched the two children playing together.

Henry was gentle with Solomon, a stark contrast to how he behaved with Margret. He often helped him eat his meals, carefully cutting up the meats. Whenever Solomon cried, Henry comforted him with hugs until he grew quiet. If Solomon had a nightmare and Richard couldn't reach him in time, Henry made sure to tuck him into bed. Oftentimes, Henry just watched Solomon with a sense of wonder, as if his baby brother were a second chance.

Richard opened his mail, his mouth falling agape. It was Zora's journal and a letter addressed to him. He traced his hand over the name. *Kamau.*

He quickly opened the letter.

Dear Kamau,

I hope these items find you well. I send my love to Solomon and can't help but wonder what he looks like now or how he acts. I admit, sometimes I wonder if I've made the right choice of leaving him. Please hug him for me.

I have paired this letter with my journal, the one I showed you the night I took you behind the cabin. The journal is for Solomon when he is older so that he may understand why I am not in his life anymore. I hope to see my son again one day. And you too, of course.

I encourage you to read as well, Kamau. There are many things hard for me to express, many thoughts captive in my mind that long to be freed. It is my hope to share these with you as I did that night.

Yours Truly,
Zora

The journal. Richard had searched for it but could never find it. Zora had taken it all along.

Richard opened it and skimmed through. The book was nearly filled, and the writing greatly improved, but his eyes focused on one entry she had made months ago.

> Some nights like this one, I find that I can't sleep. I remember those nights in the cabin, the cold nights, the smell of must, and the fear of death and pain waiting on the new day.
>
> Richard was an awful slaver, a feared man I wish I could say I was unafraid of. But that would be a lie.
>
> But then, I'd think of my time next with Kamau.

Richard's lips slightly parted in surprise. She wrote about him? About Kamau? He sat up more in his seat, his eyes hungry for her words.

> I was happy with him, happy that this rough, quiet man bloomed kindness. In a way, he saved me, becoming the family I lost. It's strange comparing the two. Like night and day, death and life.
>
> I really did fall in love with Kamau. In fact, I would have fallen deeply in love with him if he had not told me the truth. And it

wasn't until much later that I realized how courageous he had been for expressing such a thing. How merciful he was for doing that. When I found out the truth, I hated myself for having fallen in love with him, but I couldn't help it. I fought with myself over the years, holding onto what he used to be, believing that a man like him could never change, but I saw it for myself the day I decided to leave you with him, Solomon.

Now, I'm choosing to let go and finally forgive him.

I hope you can forgive your father too one day, Solomon, as I have done.

Richard closed the journal. He sat quietly for a moment, bewildered, his gaze fixed straight ahead as the words sunk in.

He dissolved into helpless tears, happy for now being certain she had forgiven him.

"Papa, are you all right? You look funny."

Richard nodded, but no words left him. He rubbed his eyes as tears splattered onto the journal. Tiny fingers brushed across his cheek. Richard looked down to see Solomon outstretching his arms, reaching for him.

Then, Solomon placed both hands above his head, opening and closing them, attempting the bunny ears to cheer Richard up. Richard chuckled, seeing Margret in the action. How happy she had been when she was alive. And a part of him felt like he had her with him, still giggling at his funny faces. Richard smiled and kissed his son's hand.

Richard didn't know if he'd ever see Zora again or if she'd ever return for Solomon.

He thought of what he wished he could have told her, how he'd never received the chance to tell her how much he loved her. How he'd never said thank you for all the many things she had done to help him, comfort him, reassure him, and just be there in his worst hours.

Then again, maybe he'd said all that needed to be said.

ACKNOWLEDGMENTS

Thank you so much for taking a chance on my debut novel. It took a unique perspective on a fictional slave narrative, having a character viewpoint that might be considered controversial to some. Your interest and willingness to go on this journey with me, taking a peek into the wild stories that occupy my mind 24/7—it means the world to me.

Kiki, my second mother, thank you so much for welcoming me into your home right out of college. Your unwavering support, endless patience with my self-doubt, and endurance of my constant questions about whether I was a mooch or not mean the world to me. You always reassured me and made me feel not only welcomed but safe enough to share my thoughts. On top of giving me a place to stay, you let me use your home as my creative sanctuary, a place where I could share all of my problems, dreams, and story ideas. I would not have started this story when I did had it not been for you. I remember that day in your room when I told you the plot of *Firsthand*. Your eyes lit up, and you expressed genuine excitement, saying you'd love to read a unique story like this and could see it becoming a movie. That put a spark in me that night, so I set out to write a very detailed chapter outline just for you. You were the very first to read my initial draft. I'll never forget the night when you burst into my room at 2 a.m. to passionately rant about the book, telling me how you couldn't put it down. And when you did, you felt like a crack addict craving the next fix. I smiled so hard that night. That conversation fueled me to write even more. Who would have thought that a twenty-thousand-word outline would turn into this wonderful novel?! Your compassionate guidance is invaluable. I would not be where I am now if not for you. A simple "thank you" isn't a strong enough phrase to convey the sheer amount of love and gratitude I have for you. And, oh, by the way… *whispers* "Seven days."

Ma'Kayla, thank you for existing! Thank you so, so much for being there to listen to my stories and laugh with me, and thank you for just being you. You gave me so much support even in times you might not have realized—singing to me when I was having a mental breakdown, barging into my room to talk about your day or share crazy thoughts and stories, and performing your mini dance concerts. You're like a sister to me, and I will always, always love you. And just so you know, *I* am the first child.

Uncle Ronald, thank you for your marathon-long conversations, telling me that I was good enough just as I am to write and publish my book, even when I didn't believe it.

Uncle Gerard, thank you for showing interest in my story concept and promising to buy a copy—or maybe ten.

Ryley, thank you so, so much for helping me outline this story. You are the sole reason it had such a strong foundation. Collaborating with you was like having a best friend as a creative partner. It was easy bouncing ideas off you. You pulled the ideas from my head, easily mirroring my vision. And thank you for having the stomach to help me with all the nitty gritty bits. Your honest feedback, especially when pointing out parts of my plotting that felt wonky, has been instrumental in making the narrative better. Conversations with you felt like talking to an old friend, and I loved every moment of it. I have an idea in mind for a sequel, but I don't want to do it without you. Your input is indispensable, and I'd love to work with you again someday.

A big shout-out to Desty and Natasha, too, for being amazing collaborators in also shaping the storyline of this project. Their suggestions really helped add some flavor to the narrative. I'm truly grateful for their support.

David Heffernan, thank you so much for helping me with research for my novel and for patiently addressing all of my questions regarding slavery and the 1800s. If there was ever a moment that highlighted the immense importance of historians, it was definitely during this project.

Annie, thank you for being such a freakin' word wizard of an editor! You helped expand my passages and gave this story a true nineteenth-century feel. You made me love my story all over again!

Dad, thank you for your feedback on my story. I truly appreciate it, even if it sometimes felt more like an essay critique. I'm always grateful for your wisdom, intelligence, and the unique perspective you bring..

Abby, my dear, *highly* supportive friend, thank you so, so much for having an open mind and listening to me ramble about this book, and even going as far as to read and critique my first draft. You helped by pointing out inaccuracies so I could make this as authentic a story as possible. No matter what conversations we had, you'd always take the time to gush over how happy and proud you are of me and my journey as an author, and that always lifted my spirits. You're the best!

Kim, thank you for beta-reading my detailed chapter outline on CritiqueMatch. You offered amazing feedback in the early stages. You are so sweet, and I wish you lots of success in your own publishing endeavors.

Purity Jandi, thank you so freaking much for being my beta reader. You are one of the kindest people I've ever met, a truly pure gem. When reading your feedback, I only felt warmth, even for the hard-hitting critiques. They were funny and so incredibly insightful. Your knowledge and skill for storytelling are indispensable and enviable. Thank you so much for your insight and helping me make hard decisions regarding the direction of my story. You are truly a diamond in the rough, and I'd love to work with you on many projects to come.

Paula, thank you for the hilariously honest and entertaining beta-reading comments. I was cracking up all the way through.

B.M. Eldr, thank you so much for beta-reading my story and helping me with rewrites. I lacked a lot of descriptive details and had trouble with "telling" instead of "showing", and you pointed them out and helped me not only expand but add a lot more impacting emotion to my work. You even helped and encouraged me when I had imposter syndrome. You are extremely kind and patient. Always putting your best foot forward and delivering quality work.

Chey, thank you for reviewing my work. Your input on one of my character's backgrounds added depth to the narrative and really made a difference.

Paige, thank you so much for having such a strong eagle eye for details and errors. Even after this manuscript was passed through two editors, you still managed to spot things that were completely overlooked. You are very kind, reassuring me that this was a story worth telling. It was the confirmation I needed that motivated me to trust my gut and move forward with this story. So thank you so much for being a part of this journey with me and helping me along. I hope to work with you again someday.

Predrag, thank you so, so much for such an amazing cover design! I cannot express how overjoyed I was to finally find not only a traditional cover designer but an interior formatter as well. Your creative eye is beyond amazing, and you envisioned my vision and the tone of my story perfectly.

Special thanks to Abbie Emmons. Though I've never met you, you have been my guide on this publishing journey and have made it so much easier. Thank you.

Thank you to all of my family and friends for supporting my dream. There are so many of you; I'd need to write an entirely new novel just to list you all!

And finally, thank you to my wonderful readers! Whether you loved or hated this book, thank you immensely for taking the time to read it! Never stop dreaming. Never stop creating. And never stop reading.

Richard (Master)

Richard (Slave)

Nini

Milton Keynes UK
Ingram Content Group UK Ltd.
UKHW020216040724
444921UK00015B/153/J